THE BLADE KINGS SERIES

TOTAL SHUTDOWN

RUTH STILLING

TRIGGER/CONTENT WARNINGS

You should be aware that while this book is a work of fiction and is, of course, a happily ever after, *Total Shutdown* does contain themes of the following: discussion of the death of a spouse (which is off-page and took place years prior to the book), discussion of parental death (also off-page and took place years prior to the book), discussion of motorcycle accidents, sexually explicit content and strong language.

For those who like being edged to fuck.
This one's for you.

Want to stay in the loop on all things Ruth Stilling?

Join my **newsletter** for release updates, book news, and more.
Sign up using the QR code below.

For exclusive first looks, art reveals, and the only place to see NSFW art, come join me on **Patreon**.
Join Patreon by scanning the QR code below.

PLAYLIST

"She's Like the Wind" by Patrick Swayze and Wendy Fraser
"Revolving door" by Tate McRae
"Pour Some Sugar On Me" by Def Leppard
"Don't You (Forget About Me)" by Simple Minds
"God is a woman" by Ariana Grande
"Siren sounds" by Tate McRae
"Dreams" by Fleetwood Mac
"Nothing Else Matters" by Metallica
"Times Like These" by Foo Fighters

ONE

SAWYER

October

She's like a wild fucking animal.

"You gonna take this off or what?" she asks, although it's more a demand.

A tear rips through the room, and one of the buttons on my white shirt pops off as she forcefully tugs it from my dark blue dress pants.

"You just ruined my shirt."

She looks down between us, shrugging a nonchalant shoulder. "Eh, kind of makes this whole thing easier."

Curling her fingers around each side of the collar, she pulls my shirt apart in one motion. More buttons cascade across my bedroom floor, bouncing underneath my dresser and bed frame.

Initially, I'm pissed, but when I notice the way her eyes land on my tattooed chest, my shirt now hanging open at the front, annoyance rapidly gives way to satisfaction.

"Like what you see, Collins?" I lean in to capture her mouth with mine.

She pulls back. "Hard line—too personal."

Running a quick hand over my left pec, Collins stops when her fingernails brush the bar piercing my nipple. "Some of your ink could do with a retouch." Her brown eyes find mine. "I guess that's what happens when you get older. Everything kind of … fades."

She plucks lightly at my piercing, and the sensation tents my pants further.

"I like this though."

As I bring my hands to her black leather dress, I palm her ass —something I secretly did all night as we sat next to each other in the booth—and I squeeze it gently. "You'll let me touch your ass, but not kiss you. You make no sense to me."

Eyes sparkling, she wraps her arms around my neck, rising on her tiptoes since I have at least a foot on her. Her pretty heart-shaped face is so close that I can smell her peach-scented lip gloss.

"I don't kiss anyone."

This woman never ceases to amaze me. Since she's the best friend of my starting center's girl, Kendra, you'd think I'd know her a little better than I do. But countless postgame nights at our local hangout have left me with nothing more than what I can physically see with my eyes—wavy, shoulder-length light-pink hair; deep brown irises; sharp black eyeliner; and lashes that have to be fake because, fuck me, how can they not be? All her clothes are black; in fact, it's the only color I ever see her wear. And I'm one hundred percent fucking sure that what lies beneath this hot-as-fuck mid-thigh dress is the tightest body I will ever touch.

Despite her previous comment, I wet my lips, and she smirks up at me in question.

"So, we gonna fuck or not?"

I roll my damp lips together, equally amused and turned on by her brash attitude. "You just want to use me, don't you?"

She drops her hands from around my neck, settling them on

my belt buckle. As she begins unlooping, I watch the crimson flush descend her chest—her low-cut dress can't hide it or the delicious curve of her cleavage.

"What do you want, my life story? Last time I checked, it wasn't a prerequisite for sex." Her tone is a mixture of sultry and exasperated, and my cock twitches in response.

Jesus.

"I don't even know your last name—you realize that, right?" I reply.

Ignoring my comment, she finishes on my belt and moves to my pants, unzipping and leaving them hanging open at the front.

As she takes a small step back, she pulls her bottom lip between her teeth, studying me.

"What?"

She shakes her head and reaches to her side. "Nothing. Your body is just better than I thought it would be. That's all."

I roll my tongue across the roof of my mouth, ready to tell her that she's brattier than I expected, but stop short when I register what she's doing.

Collins pulls the side zip on her dress over her full hip and then reaches up to her shoulders, dragging each thin strap down in turn.

Time slows as the dress falls to my wooden floor, leaving her in only a strapless black bra and a matching thong that sits high on her hourglass figure.

She's tattooed. A mermaid with an elegant fishtail wraps around the right side of her rib cage. I can only see the back of the mermaid and her face is hidden beneath her long, dark hair, but it's exquisite and so fucking hot on her perfect skin.

Unlike mine, it's the only tattoo I can see on her body, and I wonder if it has meaning.

My eyes then drop to her navel piercing—a black stone set on a silver bar. Her body is all woman and curvy. Even better than I imagined.

There isn't a flicker of doubt or hesitancy when she brings her attention back to my face, looking me straight in the eye.

I can't deny this woman intimidates me, but I maintain eye contact, mainly because that was the first thing that drew me in —her eyes and the way they shone beneath the lighting at Lloyd's Bar. Like two mugs of black coffee. I still can't work out where her irises begin.

I take a determined step toward her, shrugging off my torn shirt.

Her pale complexion flushes further when I reach out and wrap my hand around the nape of her neck, toying with her hair.

"You don't need to pretend like you aren't attracted to me." I'm a second away from kissing her when I stop, remembering what she said. "You knew the first time we met, when I offered to drop you home, that I wanted you, and you knew it again tonight, when you let me touch you while no one was watching. Let's not play around."

I still cringe at the memory from last November—of what happened after she randomly met Kendra in the bar restroom. Turned out, Collins was there to meet a guy, but when he didn't show and her phone got drenched from a drink, she needed a spare to call a taxi home. As I sat in the booth, watching her call for a ride, I got this overwhelming urge to do something completely out of character—spend the night with a woman I barely knew. I don't know whether it was the immediate attraction, fascination, or the fact that I hadn't gotten laid in so long that made me ask the question. But when she shot me down in flames, I instantly regretted it.

Yet here I am. Eleven months later. Still into her. Still just as fascinated by her zero-fucks-given attitude.

Way to torture yourself.

"Oh, Sawyer." She pats me mockingly on the shoulder, eyes diverting—very briefly—from my face to the tattoos painting my chest. "If I didn't want to play, I wouldn't be here. It's been a while, and, well …" She moves one of her hands from my shoulder to my back, trailing her fingernails down my skin.

I shiver, fighting to hide its effects.

"I figured, what's just one night? I don't usually go for hockey boys, but some are cute to look at, I guess, and all of them have fine asses." She bites down on her bottom lip, slipping her pointer finger beneath the waistband of my pants and then boxers. "Even the older, more experienced captains."

I feel a pang of unease.

Can I sleep with this girl?

I haven't slept with anyone in fucking months—and definitely not under these kinds of circumstances. A few dates and maybe we go back to her place for vanilla sex, only for me to end it a couple of weeks later—that's my usual MO.

I can count the number of women since my late wife, Sophie, passed, on one hand.

Collins pauses her finger and narrows her eyes cautiously. "You're good with one night, right?"

My throat feels thick as I swallow casually. Truthfully, I don't know what I'm good with. Our brief interactions over the past several months should leave me in no doubt about what tonight is—working out the sexual tension that's been building between us for way too long.

I swallow again and bring my hand to her right hip, looping my finger around her thong.

"I'm good with it," I finally say, sliding the material down her smooth skin. "But I think it's best if we tell no one about tonight."

She tips her chin up, brown eyes fixed on mine as she guides my free hand to the other side of her underwear and hooks my fingers through it. "Works for me. I'm not in the business of publishing my sex life, and I like to control what people know about me. Including you."

She starts backing up toward my bed, and a few paces later,

she lowers herself on my duvet, her attention falling to my hands. "One other thing."

I drag the soaked thong down her legs, a stronger sense of unease settling over me. Not only am I going ahead with this, but I also suggested we do it in secret. I'm not especially bothered about my teammates or friends finding out since we're not doing anything wrong. My real concern is Ezra, my only son. Other than Sophie's parents—who he's with tonight—he's my one constant and main priority. He's the reason why I rarely date, and him finding out about a one-night stand through a leaked story to the press is not what I want. You could bet your ass his preteen friends would find it on social media.

"What's that?" I ask, dropping her panties to the floor and pushing my pants and boxers down until they pool around my ankles.

I step out of them and lift my gaze back to hers.

Lying back on her elbows, she's all confidence—spreading her knees and showing me her perfect pink pussy.

"I might not kiss, but I don't mind your mouth here."

Don't fucking come. Don't fucking come.

Her winged eyeliner is slightly smudged around the corner of her left eye, and when I drop to my knees in front of her, I'm certain it will be right across her face by the time I finish my meal.

She won't do dating, she won't do kissing, she won't give me more than tonight. So, I guess I'll just have to make these next few hours count.

I hook her right leg over my shoulder, and her breathing picks up, satisfying me briefly.

My hand moves to her soaked inner thighs, and she sucks in a sharp breath when I tease my fingertips along her damp skin.

"I'm on birth control, and I get checked after each time I'm with someone."

My eyes snap to hers, chest tightening. "I haven't been with anyone in … a long while."

Collins's usual hard expression softens a fraction. "Okay. Good. Other than kissing, I'm comfortable with most stuff."

My fingers find her center.

Jesus, she's dripping.

Yeah, she's hot for me.

"Just …"

I pause and wait for her to continue. She doesn't.

"Just what, Baby Girl?"

Her eyes flare wide, and I fight back a smirk. I knew she'd hate that, but I couldn't help myself. She doesn't get to have it all her way.

I see that she wants to scold me for calling her a cutesy nickname, but she doesn't. Instead, she opens her legs wider, digging her heel into my shoulder.

"At thirty-five, you have nine years on me, and that makes you the oldest guy I've ever slept with. I expect you to be the best yet." She presses her heel in a little more. "Just don't put it in my ass. That's not something I offer up to anyone."

TWO

COLLINS

*G*oddamn, Collins.

Why the fuck are you here?

It has to be the early hours of the morning as I lie flat on my back, staring up at Sawyer's blue ceiling.

Who paints their fucking ceiling?

Men I shouldn't sleep with—that's who.

Did he have some leftover paint when he finished the walls or something? Or was he just bored?

A bit like me last night, with all the vanilla sex taking place.

I had known it. I damn well knew it would be a disappointment. From the second he crawled over me and started with the missionary position, I had known I'd be counting down the minutes.

At least I came.

Plus, he has a big dick, so that's something.

I roll over, facing away from Sawyer as he breathes softly into the bedroom.

Blue ceiling.

Yeah, I'm outta here.

Gently, I pull the duvet back and swing a leg out to the side, my foot meeting his solid wood flooring.

Thankfully, Sawyer stays asleep as I creep to the en suite on the opposite side of his room, grabbing my bag, dress, and underwear from the trunk at the foot of the bed. I pull the door open, stepping onto the heated white tiles.

I look like a fucking shit show—eyeliner smeared across my face and bedhead for days.

Unzipping my black shoulder bag, I find a pack of tissues and hold one under the running faucet, waiting for the warm water to kick in.

My left eye is worse than the right, and slowly, I manage to clean up my face before throwing the tissue into the trash.

"You promised yourself you weren't going to do this," I whisper into the dimly lit room, the only light filtering in from the Brooklyn streets outside.

Motionless, I stare at the running faucet, the flow of water mesmerizing and comforting. Everything Sawyer said last night was the truth; he doesn't know me, and I hardly know him. He's thirty-five and the captain of the New York Blades with a twelve-year-old son, and his wife died over seven years ago. That's it. That's literally the extent of my knowledge about this man, the majority of which I learned from other people. Oh, and he likes IPA, but only has one pint after a game and then moves on to soda.

I'd say I know his dick better than the person it's attached to.

But I'd be lying if I claimed my closed-off nature wasn't by design. Not just with Sawyer or any other guy I sleep with, but when it comes to everyone. I move from place to place and take temporary jobs before I move on again. My New York era is the longest I've spent anywhere since my childhood, and I'd say that's, in part, thanks to my closest friend and the girl I randomly met at Lloyd's last November. Kendra Hart is the one person I've connected with the most since my grandparents died and the main reason I renewed the lease on my apartment for another six months, although that's now on a rolling contract.

I like her. She's cool. That said, she is one hundred percent to blame for tonight. Without Kendra, I wouldn't have seen Sawyer beyond that first night. And I wouldn't be standing here, confused as to how average sex could leave me feeling some kind of way the next morning.

I don't sleep with a lot of guys, and the ones I do, I carefully select them to be sure they have a shared interest in going no further than a cock-in-pussy situation.

Sawyer Bryce doesn't meet my stipulation of no-strings fun. I knew that from the second I set eyes on him last fall, and that reality has become painfully more obvious with every sideways glance and look we've shared since. He makes me ... nervous, eliciting tingles not even my ex-boyfriend, Mike, could achieve. Huh, and, boy, was he an asshole—two years of my early twenties I'll never get back.

So, I guess you could say I don't trust easily, but more importantly, I don't want to. The only love affair I'm interested in pursuing is the one I have with my Harley-Davidson motorcycle.

Turning off the faucet, I root around in my bag and find a tie, securing my shoulder-length hair into a loose knot, and then I twist a few strands around my fingers until they frame my face.

"Hey, you okay?" Sawyer's deep voice permeates the silence.

I spin around to face the closed door, hands already reaching for my dress.

Stepping into it, I quickly do up the zip, foregoing underwear completely as I shove my bra and panties into my bag and close it.

"Collins?" Sawyer speaks again, his voice sounding kind of concerned.

I grab my bag and reach for the handle, quickly pulling the door open.

"Whoa, Jesus, fuck!"

Sawyer practically lands on his face as he falls forward. He was clearly holding his weight against the door.

I bite my lip and fight back laughter as his right arm flies up and grips the doorjamb, steadying himself.

"You know, it's generally unwise to rely so heavily on something that could move at any time, with or without your knowledge."

He narrows his eyes at me. "Is that right?"

His gaze travels the length of my body, and I ignore the tingles that resurface.

"Why are you dressed?"

I reach into my bag and pull out my phone.

Four a.m. *Shit.*

"I'm heading home." I nod over his shoulder, indicating my wish to leave.

He drops his hand from the jamb, crossing his arms over his chest.

Don't look at his tattooed forearms or the fact that he's only in black boxer briefs.

"It's not even light out."

I guess I could make up some stupid excuse, explaining why I have to go. Like work just called me into the shop for an urgent bike repair or I forgot I'd left my curling iron on. But bullshitting has never been in my wheelhouse.

I loop my bag over my shoulder. "We both got what we'd wanted, no? Post-hookup talk really isn't my thing."

My gaze drops to his groin—*for fuck's sake*—and a rogue grin spreads across my face when I notice his reaction. His dick is definitely growing.

Sawyer clears his throat, shifting uncomfortably. "Why are you such a bitch to me?"

My attention rests on his cock. "And why am I thinking it turns you on?"

He scoffs. "It doesn't." He pauses briefly. "Thinking about what we did last night does, but you being a brat does nothing for my dick."

My phone is still in my hand when I unlock it and bring up the Uber app. "I can be out of here in five minutes." I click Request on the time slot and drop my cell into my bag. "We don't breathe a word about any of this, right? You gave me a ride home, and I accepted. Simple."

I step forward, and he moves aside, but as I notice my boots lying on his bedroom floor, a hand wraps around my wrist, spinning me to face him.

Those goddamn green eyes.

He pushes a hand through his messy, dark hair, clearing the loose strands from his eyes. "So, that's it? You aren't kidding, are you? You're just going to grab your things and go. You have zero intention of talking about last night ever again."

I shrug, averting my eyes from his. "It was a one-night stand. I came; you came. It was okay. Six out of ten."

Sawyer's jaw drops, his hand tightening around my wrist. I sense he wants to pull me closer to him, but he doesn't.

"You just rated my performance in bed and gave it a shitty one at that."

I pull away from him, taking the few steps toward my boots. I realize, at this point, I'm not wearing underwear and my dress hits mid-thigh. I'm not especially keen on flashing him despite his mouth being all over me last night.

I sit on the trunk and quickly pull on my long boots, I want out of here as soon as possible. Apparently, my theory of fucking him out of my system did nothing to ease the tension between us.

"That's a pretty decent score. I regularly struggle to climax, and you managed that, so all things considered, I can probably up it to a seven."

When I'm finished lacing my second boot, I expect to look up and find Sawyer right where I left him.

Instead, he's standing in front of me, and his breath fans my lips as he bends down to my height, eyes way darker than I've previously seen. "I don't like being compared to other men you've been with."

My mouth opens, but no words materialize. Sawyer pins me with a glare that makes it impossible for me to speak. Heat pools between my thighs, and I quickly stand.

I grab my jacket from beside me as I feel the familiar buzz in my bag, telling me my Uber driver is outside.

Sawyer's huge frame towers over me, and I grin up at him, patting him twice on the shoulder.

"Now, if you'd had those eyes last night, we'd definitely have been looking at an eight."

He bites his bottom lip, grinning. I can tell he's enjoying this back-and-forth between us. Even if he claims my brash attitude is infuriating, I know that's not strictly true.

"Stay," he says, wrapping his big palm around my hip.

My phone buzzes again.

"And do what exactly?"

He pulls me into him. He's hard. "Fuck. Seems only fair to give me another shot at a higher score."

It would be so easy—one palm pushing his bare, ripped chest, and he would be flat on his back in seconds. I could hitch up my dress and sink right down, showing him how I like to be in control.

I shake my head, thinking better of it. I don't need Sawyer Bryce inside me again. One and done, and that's what I'm sticking with.

"No," I answer abruptly.

His hand falls from my hip, eyes narrowing. "Do you plan on completely ignoring me after every game from now on?"

A car horn sounds outside, and I immediately turn to leave.

I twist the handle on his bedroom door, glancing back at him. An odd feeling of regret rises in my gut, but just like the tingles, I push that down too. "Mackenzie."

He scratches at the back of his neck, obviously confused. "Huh?"

"That's my last name. Last night, you said you didn't know it, so I'm telling you now. I don't plan on ignoring you, Sawyer. In fact, I don't plan on changing anything between us at all. You're the hockey player whose teammate just happens to be dating my friend. We were both horny, so we spent a night together, and you said it yourself that you hadn't hooked up in a while. That's literally the extent of it."

Sawyer shakes his head and tips it toward the ceiling. "Collins Mackenzie." In his delectable Southern accent, he rolls the name around his mouth like he's testing it out.

I drop an exasperated shoulder, so damn ready to get home.

Finally, he brings his attention back to my face, heated gaze still present. "Nice name. But I think I prefer Baby Girl."

THREE

SAWYER

Sophie's parents, Alyssa and Dom, live only a couple of blocks away from me in Cobble Hill. Their brownstone house is identical to mine and has three floors, plus a basement. Ezra spends fifty percent of his time staying with them and the other half with me. Truthfully, I don't know where I'd be without them. Immediately after Sophie's death, I lost all ability to function, and Alyssa and Dom stepped up to help care for and raise Ezra.

It wasn't only my sanity hanging by a thread, but also my hockey career—I was ready to quit and take a regular job that didn't involve days or weeks on the other side of the country. Alyssa and Dom saved that too.

I reach into my coat pocket and pull out their house keys, unlocking the door and stepping inside.

"Hey, where are you at?" I drop my keys into the designated dish set on the console table and take the stairs down to the eat-in kitchen, where they nearly always are.

"Up here!" I hear Alyssa's voice call from the living area on the floor above.

Retaking the stairs, I make my way to the back of the house and find my in-laws reading on the couch. Ezra's completely oblivious to my presence as he sits on a single armchair and shouts some kind of instruction at the TV mounted above the fireplace. His headphones cover his ears, and he grips his PlayStation controller tightly while he obsesses over his latest video game.

I approach him, lifting a headphone away from his ear. "Hi. My name's Dad, and I'm here to pick you up."

He pulls his body away, offering me a quick smirk before his eyes flick back to the screen. "Right after this last battle."

"He's been playing for the past two hours." Dom closes his book and sets it down on the coffee table in front of him. "It's getting harder to pull him away and back into real life."

Alyssa's face is all in agreement. I glance quickly at Ezra and bite the inside of my cheek. It was a mistake, suggesting they buy him a second PlayStation for when he stayed here. But they were stuck for birthday gift ideas since the kid didn't have many other interests, and all I've ever wanted is for him to be happy.

"At least when it was just the laptop, he wasn't taking over the house," Alyssa adds, standing from the couch and making her way toward the staircase.

I scratch at the back of my neck and follow her down to the kitchen, heading for the fridge and pulling out a water.

"Want to stay for lunch?" she asks, grabbing a cutting board as she waits for an answer.

Each time I look at my mother-in-law, I see Sophie. With her wavy red hair and green eyes, it's like a glimpse at what my late wife would have looked like if she were still here and twenty-five years older.

"Yeah, that would be great, thanks." I take a seat at the island and open my water, taking a gulp and setting it down in front of me.

She smiles and grabs a knife from the block next to her, pointing it at my head. "No hats in the house; you know how I feel about them."

I pull off my Blades cap and wince at the state of my dark hair. It's always been on the longer side since I like to style it when I can, but today, it looks especially bad.

Alyssa's eyes land on the mess. "Rough night?"

I clear my throat and pull the water bottle toward me. "Didn't sleep all that well."

She lifts a brow and slices into a tomato. "You secured the win and put in a good performance. What's the issue?"

My throat feels thick as I clear it again and shrug a shoulder, the action reminding me of the bratty girl in my bed last night.

If I wanted, I could talk to Alyssa about Collins. She wouldn't have an issue or shy away from a conversation about another woman. She's the mom I never had since my parents are assholes and estranged, a bit like my brother. In fact, if I told her I'd hooked up last night, she'd likely pause on lunch and ask me to give her all the details. She's repeatedly told me to get back out there and make the most of my dating years. I'm in my mid-thirties, so I guess she has a point.

When she starts on another tomato, I inhale a deep breath and consider telling her the truth, but back out at the final second.

We agreed to keep what happened a secret.

"You going to drink that water or continue making a mess on my counter?"

Alyssa snaps me back to reality, and I look down at the torn-up label in my hand.

"You know what they say about stripping labels off bottles, don't you?"

I roll my eyes and look at her. "Are we really having this conversation? I'm not about to divulge my sex life, or lack thereof, with my mother-in-law."

She shakes her head and chuckles, getting back to chopping. "How many nights do you need us to take Ezra next week?"

I slide off the stool and throw the torn-up label in the trash before making my way back to the island and retaking my seat. "Three nights. This series isn't as long."

"Wait, I thought you said we were leaving?" In his black Fortnite hoodie and jeans, Ezra waltzes into the kitchen, snatching up a piece of tomato on his way over to the fridge. His brown hair is a mess, like mine, and his green eyes look glazed from way too much screen time.

"We're staying for lunch, so no snacking."

He closes the fridge door, offering me a huff that's typical of his age group. "How long will it be? I'm starving."

Alyssa lifts her eyes to him. "A half hour."

"Ughhhh." He throws his head back like it's the worst news he's ever received. "I finished up early on a battle because you'd said we were going."

I raise an unimpressed brow. "Whether we eat here or at home, it won't get you in front of the TV any faster."

Ezra flops down next to me at the island, and I nudge my shoulder into him.

"You spend way too much time on that thing, and anyway, you used to shoot hoops with your friends on a Sunday."

He doesn't look at me. "It got boring."

My eyes flick to Alyssa. She appears as worried as I feel.

"Then find something else you can all do," I reply.

He rolls his eyes, gaze averted as he looks around the kitchen. "Who do you think I'm playing Fortnite with?"

I go to reply, but I'm cut off by my phone—Archer's name is written across the front when I pull it out of my pocket.

It's unusual for him to call me on our day off. Normally, we talk in the group chat.

I climb off the stool and rest a hand on Ezra's shoulder, letting him know we aren't done with this conversation.

When I push through the patio doors and out into the yard, I hit Accept on the call. "What's up?"

"Where are you? I've been at your door for ages."

My goalie is as relaxed as they come. He doesn't get worked up off the ice or even at the crease, making him one of the best in the league. Though, right now, he sounds borderline frantic.

"I'm at Alyssa and Dom's, and I won't be back for a while." I pause. "What happened?"

He releases a long breath. "I think I fucked up, man."

I stop walking. "Are we talking hockey or something else?"

"Technically both."

I swivel back around and watch as Alyssa talks with Ezra through the glass door.

"Go on."

Archer clears his throat, and his surroundings turn quiet, like he's moved somewhere more private than outside my front door. I hear a car door shut and another sigh.

"Want me to guess?" I say, figuring this is hard for him to admit.

He chuckles low. "Yeah. Why not?"

I smirk, thinking of all the possible ways the biggest NHL playboy could land himself in shit. "You got into it with a girl last night, and she turned out to be even kinkier than you. When she pulled out the strap-on, you winced but went along with being pegged anyway. Trouble is, now you can't sit down."

Expecting him to laugh, I'm surprised but even more concerned when he doesn't react.

"I fucked another dude's girl."

"What?"

His voice is hoarse, steeped in regret. "I didn't know until this morning. Last night, after you left with Collins, I stayed behind for a while and then went to a club with some of the other guys. They left around one a.m., and that's when this hot-as-fuck blonde started talking to me at the bar." He puffs out a despondent breath. "I was planning to leave alone for once, but she was too fine to turn down, and after a couple more beers, my inhibitions dropped. So, I took her back to my place and fucked her brains out."

I pinch the bridge of my nose. "And how do you know she's got a guy?"

"Well, that's where it gets really interesting. Honestly, she kind of looked familiar last night, but I chalked it up to the beer goggles and that she was your typical supermodel-type girl. She ended up staying over since we had gone at it all night, and in the morning, while she was taking a shower in my en suite, her phone lit up with an incoming call." He swallows audibly. "The contact picture was Shane Stevens—the defenseman who got dropped to the farm team three seasons back."

Fuck. I move my phone from one ear to the other. "And you're sure she's his girl and not, like, his sister or something?"

He chuckles, but there's zero humor behind it. "Unless she calls him Sweet Cheeks for a joke, then, no, I'm guessing they aren't related."

I switch the call to hands-free and pull up my browser. "What was her name?"

Silence.

"Archer, what was her name?" I repeat.

"I … think it was …"

My head lops between my shoulders, and I squeeze my eyes shut. "You don't remember, do you?"

"I think it began with a *K*."

I bring the phone back to my ear.

"What do you think I should do?" he asks with hope in his voice, like I somehow have all the answers.

I guess, given I'm his captain and eight years older than him, I should have some words of wisdom.

"Stop fucking everything that moves," I reply.

"Helpful," he says dryly.

I run a hand over my jaw. "The easy thing to do would be to keep quiet since I doubt she'll say anything."

Archer hums. "She begged me not to say anything when I confronted her this morning. They're getting married in three months, and this is her first indiscretion … apparently."

If he were standing in front of me right now, I'd likely have my hands around his throat. God love Archer Moore—he's one of the nicest guys I know—but he can be really fucking reckless sometimes, especially when it comes to women.

I think about reaming him out for yet another one-night stand with someone he barely knows, but I stop myself when the image of Collins—who I now know as Collins Mackenzie—lying beneath me as I rolled my hips into her, flashes through my head.

I take a breath just as Alyssa knocks on the window, and I raise a hand, acknowledging her.

"The right thing to do would be to say something to Shane. You played with him for a number of seasons, and he's a good guy. He deserves to know what happened. Wouldn't you want to be told before you got hitched?"

"I guess," he replies quietly.

I start back for the house. "And once you've cleaned that up, call the team doctor and bring your STI test forward. It's possible she lied when she said she hadn't played away before."

"I'm never hooking up again."

I smirk—that's something I've heard him say a million times before.

My hand is resting on the patio door when he speaks again.

"Anyway, you can't judge me. I'd bet money you got into it with Collins last night."

I bristle, tongue swiping across my lip. I swear I can still taste her. "Wrong on two counts. I'm not judging you, and I spent last night alone."

He sounds doubtful. "It's okay to admit you like someone, you know. Maybe even move on with another person."

I depress the patio door handle, ready to wrap up the call. "Just focus on getting your mess cleaned up. I'll see you at morning skate."

FOUR

COLLINS

"Did you manage to fix the transmission issue with the Twin Cam 88? The owner reported the gearshifts aren't as smooth as they should be." Cameron sits at his desk, forearms folded across his chest, waiting for my response as I stand in his office.

I got the job at Smooth Running almost a year ago after I was fired from my old place for invoicing *Asshole Tax* to a customer who totally deserved it. At that point, I was ready to leave New York and move on to somewhere else, but then I landed a job here—a garage specializing in Harley servicing and refurb—and it was an opportunity I couldn't turn down.

Only, in retrospect, I kind of wish I had backed out of taking the job so I wouldn't have hooked up with the guy sitting in front of me. Cameron is a grade-A asshole and, unfortunately for me, now my boss. Though he wasn't when we were messing around.

After a couple of times with him, I realized the error in my ways—he was definitely a selfish prick who didn't much care for my needs in bed.

And if I'm not getting off with a guy, what's the point?

So, I ended it, and shortly after, he was officially promoted to service manager—though, unofficially, I like to think of him as Head Dickface.

It's only a matter of time before I bill him with an Asshole Tax too.

I stand at the entrance of his office, smiling sweetly. There are two chairs in front of me, but I have zero intention of taking a seat. "Yeah, I finished up on that before I left yesterday. The customer plans to collect it in"—I check my watch—"a half hour."

Cameron leans back in his chair, eyes raking over me. I force back an eye roll. I mean, *seriously*? I'm wearing dark blue overalls, which are basically more black from oil streaks—a little like my hands right now.

"And what about the service that was pushed back to lunchtime?" He swivels to his computer, unlocking the screen.

I save him the job of looking up one of our best customers. "Mr. Moran?"

"Yes." His voice is clipped.

I thumb over my shoulder, entirely too satisfied with myself. "He's in the shop now. I was running through an oil change when you summoned me." I make to leave. "Is that all?"

His jaw tics—something I previously found sexy, but now it just annoys the shit out of me. His face kind of annoys me in general.

He waves a condescending hand, and all I want to do is shove it in a starter clutch.

"Just make sure you finish up on Moran's bike before you take a lunch."

"You got it," I reply in a faux bright tone.

Twenty minutes later, I'm handing the keys to Mr. Moran and considering if I have time to head back to my apartment for the lunch I prepped but left in my fridge when I overslept and tore out the door this morning.

"I'm looking for a pink-haired bombshell. Has anyone seen her?"

I look up from the form I'm filling out, my attention snapping to Kendra—pro soccer player and center back for the New York Storm.

I check over my shoulder. "No one fitting that description around here."

Wearing training gear and a Storm beanie, Kendra lifts one perfectly manicured brow. "So, the pitch was frozen, and afternoon practice was canceled. Jack's about to head on a three-day away series, and I'm feeling needy."

I'm grabbing my bag, jacket, and keys before she even asks.

"How about a coffee date at Rise Up? I have a half hour before Head Dickface reams me out for being a minute too late."

"Absolutely." Kendra spins on her heel and makes for the door, me closely behind.

You can really feel the chill settling over Brooklyn as we walk the few blocks to our favorite bakery—one Kendra and Jack practically live in.

"He's still being an ass to you then?" she asks as we wait to cross the street opposite the café.

"Yep," I reply, exasperated just thinking about my boss.

It's fair to assume this girl knows more about me than anyone, including my fling with Cameron earlier this year. Kendra is the only person I've spoken to about my past, although I've held back on a lot of information, specifically about my childhood and some of the painful memories that still eat away at me. It's safe to say my relationship with bikes has not always been positive; sometimes, the easiest way to bury the memories is to not talk about them and avoid uninvited questions, as well-meaning as they may be. I've told her about my grandparents, who raised me before they died eight years ago, although, to be honest, there isn't much to tell there. They were old, and both died from pneumonia in the same year. She knows I'm an only child, and I'm every bit true to the stereotype—I don't like to share my food, and I'm pretty selfish when it comes to the TV shows I want to watch.

She asked me a few weeks back how my parents had passed, but again, I don't like to talk about it, and, honestly, there's very little backstory, only a tragedy I can't change. A truck driver was more interested in switching the track on his Spotify playlist than he was on the road in front of him. My dad drove an F-250, but that was no match for the eight-wheeler that plowed into the back of them at sixty miles per hour. After my grandparents broke the news and my puking subsided, I had never been more grateful for my bratty self since, that day, I'd insisted I stay home with a sitter and watch movies rather than head to a family dinner.

I was a delightful child.

Five minutes later, I'm sitting beside my unusually silent best friend in a usually chaotic and jam-packed Rise Up. The owner, Ed, is hurrying around the place, trying to keep orders moving.

I drop sweetener into my black coffee and begin stirring, waiting for her to speak. "You're quiet today."

She takes a bite out of her British cheese scone, eyeing me carefully. "I'm waiting for you to go first." She motions with her hand. "Tell me all about your ride the other night."

Without warning or permission, a flashback of that night pushes to the front of my mind. I buried all memories of my time in Sawyer's bed in the depths of my brain—or at least, I thought I had.

"And I think the coffee is ready." Kendra points to where I'm absentmindedly stirring the sweetener that likely dissolved a good while ago.

Reaching across the table, I grab some more and continue stirring it into my coffee. I don't look at her when I respond, figuring I can hide the lie more easily sans eye contact. "Nothing to report. He took me back to my place and went back to his." I add a casual shrug to help sell the ruse. "I'd guess he was reading a bedtime story to his son fifteen minutes later."

She tips her head to the side. "He's twelve. I doubt Sawyer is putting him to bed with *Charlotte's Web*." She takes another bite of her scone, swallowing quickly. "Besides, you can't even look at me. That tells me everything I need to know."

The flush rises on my cheeks, followed by a wave of heat.

Kendra finishes her scone and leans toward me, arms resting on the table, blonde hair framing her doubtful face. There's a mischievous glint in her brown eyes—one that dares me to deny it again. "You slept with Sawyer Bryce, didn't you?"

I shift in my chair, confused at my reaction. Why is admitting I had sex with a guy so damn difficult? I told Kendra about Cameron the day after it happened. I know whatever I tell her goes no further, but somehow, saying that I slept with Sawyer out loud would make the whole thing feel more real.

I lift my eyes to hers, and she sits back in her chair, satisfied that the look on my face is the answer she suspected.

She flicks her hair. "See, that wasn't so hard, was it?"

"It was a one-time thing." My throat feels tight, voice muted.

Ed sets a chopped cheese sandwich down in front of me, and I hurry out a, "Thanks," before I take the biggest bite I can manage.

As I chew around a chunk entirely too big for my mouth, Kendra studies me, that fucking glint back in her eyes.

"You like him, don't you?"

I swallow and shake my head. "No. He's not my type—I swear I've told you that before."

Her eyes narrow. "Based on what evidence? The fact that he's a nice guy with a cute kid, a successful and driven athlete, or a drop-dead gorgeous guy most women are desperate to date?"

Despite the accuracy of her observations, I scramble for an excuse. The truth is, he is a good-looking guy. Older than what I typically like, but handsome and was at least keen on looking after my needs in bed. Even if he was a six out of ten. I internally snicker at the memory of his reaction to that rating, taking another bite of my sandwich.

"Like I said months ago"—I break from my thoughts—"he has baggage, and I don't do any kind of relationship."

I drop a pickle onto her plate since I can't stand them and she's a total weirdo who can.

I live by a few rules, and getting into anything that could be perceived as serious with a guy with kids is one of them. I'm not okay with crossing a line where children can potentially get hurt or be dragged into a messy situation. I lost my parents, just like Ezra lost his mom, and he doesn't need any more potential complications. My gut feeling about Sawyer hasn't changed—I can tell he's a guy who doesn't do no-strings easily, and that's the exact opposite of my type. Even if, physically, he pushes all my buttons. And that's why I can never go back there—or more specifically, to his bed—again.

Kendra bites the end of the pickle, waving it around like it's some kind of prop supporting her argument. "Who's to say he wants anything serious anyway? I know when Jack and I started fooling around, it was initially for fun. Jenna kept saying it would be a good friends-with-benefits type of arrangement."

Jenna is the goalkeeper for the New York Storm and one of Kendra's closest friends. I like her. She occasionally comes to hockey games, and the times I've gone, she's been there.

"The only reason why your situation worked out with Jack was because, deep down, you both wanted more. In this instance, I do not." I take a sip of barely warm coffee. "I can just about hold down a job—never mind a relationship or a fuck-buddy arrangement." I scrunch up my nose. *"Plus ..."* I stress the word and bite my bottom lip. "I didn't feel a spark," I lie, knowing I definitely felt something unique between us. I lower my voice and lean forward. "Like, I came and everything, and he was well equipped, but it was kind of boring." The second part of my statement is more truthful, but I still feel shitty for saying it.

Kendra fights to keep the coffee she just sipped from spraying. She coughs down the last of her mouthful. "And what is it you want exactly? Chains and whips?"

I flush. *Again.*

"*Oh my God,*" she half gasps. "You do, don't you?! How did I not know you were into kinky shit?"

I gaze around the packed café. "Speak up a little, Babe. I don't think Dave at table four quite heard you."

She drops her shoulders. "Tell me. I need to know."

There are only two people who know my taste when it comes to the bedroom: Mike, my douchebag ex, and a guy I had a drunken fling with one weekend in Las Vegas—and I doubt he even remembers my name since I can't recall his, but he was hot. Every part of my life I keep private, and my sensory-play kink is definitely one of them.

I flick my eyes up to Kendra as she watches me intently.

I take a deep breath. This is *not* how I imagined my lunch break going down. "I guess you could describe me as a sensory seeker in bed."

Kendra quirks an interested brow.

"Orgasms are so much better when all five of our senses are heightened. Well, they are for me anyway." I bite on the pad of my thumb. "I've been known to come from just a guy's tongue teasing my neck. Then there's ice and hot wax play." I take a sip of now-cold coffee.

"So, like, running ice over your body?" Kendra asks.

I nod once. "Yeah, and then you can get into the harder stuff, like spanking, et cetera."

She runs her tongue across her bottom lip. "And that's not something you got with Sawyer?"

I balk. "Are you kidding me? He's not interested in that kind of thing. The second he switched to missionary, I knew I was just seeing it through to the end."

She shakes her head on a giggle.

"Plus, I like to do a lot of that stuff to the guy as well, and, yeah, they're not always that hot on it." I push my half-empty coffee mug away from me. "I mean, can you imagine me pulling out the whip and feathers and asking him to lie there while I had my fill?"

Kendra's giggle morphs into a belly laugh. "No, I guess not. But I will say this: I think you were his first time in a while. Jack told me he doesn't get with women often."

I run a hand through my hair. "Yeah, he told me. We also agreed it was a night to release some sexual tension for the both of us and never to speak about it again." I pin her with a look. "Which is why you can't say anything to anyone."

Kendra zips her lips shut. "I am a locked vault, Babe."

I nod once, deciding it's best to change course. "So, what are you doing after this?"

She pulls out her cell and checks the screen. "Actually heading back to the ground. They managed to get the pitch playable, so I have an hour of practice, and then I'm running a coaching session with Jenna straight afterward."

"The one for your new Girls in Sports Foundation?" I ask.

She hums and repockets her phone, looking kind of sheepish.

"What?" I press.

She just smiles, her usually rosy cheeks turning pinker.

"Well, this particular coaching session isn't exclusively for girls; we had a few boys show interest too …" She trails off, a smile still plastered on her face. "Ezra will be there."

It takes me a second to connect the dots, but then it hits me. "Wait. As in Sawyer's son?"

She nods tentatively.

"Yep. Apparently, he's really withdrawn around people, so

Sawyer is trying to get him into sports. He figured soccer might be something new for him. Sawyer told me he likes it in PE."

I drop my face into my hands, groaning. I can't say I'm embarrassed about anything; I'm just not used to sharing these parts of myself with anyone.

"You have to bring your best poker face."

She stands from her chair and rounds the table, wrapping an arm around my shoulders.

"Don't worry, Babe; this girl won't say a thing about what she knows … or that you wanted to spank his ass hard right after tickling it with a feather."

FIVE

———

SAWYER

I fucking hate Colorado.

I hate even more that we lost by the smallest margin and the winning goal was down to me. This place makes me lose my damn mind every time we travel here, but tonight, I was barely present on the ice.

"I need to get out of this arena and back to the hotel."

Jack pulls up alongside me, removing his mouthguard, looking kind of doubtful. "I mean, we can definitely head back to the hotel and hide and order room service." He tips his head over his shoulder. "But first, they need you in the mixed zone."

Fuck.

At my expression, he taps a gloved hand against my helmet. "Just play nice with the reporters. We don't need a repeat of last time."

The dynamics between me and my center would lead anyone to conclude that I was the rookie and he was the captain. But I have an excuse for my bad mood and disdain for this place each season—this is where I was when Sophie passed away. The pulmonary embolism in her lung had taken her quickly while I was deep into the second period in this very arena. Playing here fills me with a sense of unease and anxiety as I wait for the next thing to go wrong.

"I need to get out of my gear and into the weight room ASAP," I tell him.

I'm off the ice and heading for the locker room in seconds, Jack following close behind.

Most of the guys are silent as we change, and some head for the showers or straight for a cooldown.

I'm pulling on my sneakers when Archer flops down on the bench next to me, Jack on my other side.

"I don't need you to tell me that final goal wasn't my mistake. Because it was. I took my eye off their winger and should've anticipated the assist."

"Yeah, true," Archer says.

I turn my head to face him, finishing up on my lace. "Don't hold back with the honesty, Moore."

He just smiles at me.

I take a look around and see most of the guys have now filtered out of the locker room. "Anyway, you got an update for me on the …" I trail off on adding more detail since Jack's sitting on the other side.

"He hasn't told him yet," my center confirms, he must've been clued in on what went down last week with Shane's girl.

I stand, hands propped on my hips. "And do you plan on taking my advice or letting the guy marry a cheater?"

Archer throws an exasperated hand out in front of him. "I'll tell him. I'm just not that hot on the idea."

I know my mood has everything to do with how I feel about this series and nothing to do with my goalie, but I can't shake my irritation.

"You were hot on her when you took her home, though, weren't you? Playing around means, sometimes, you have messes to clean up. This is undoubtedly one of those times."

Archer grumbles, picking up his towel and heading for the locker room door. "Always so fucking judgy."

When the door slams behind him, I turn to Jack.

"I don't need any kind of smart-ass comment right now …" I blow out. "Especially not one about how I'm a grumpy old man."

I love this kid, truly. But the incessant smile he wears makes me want to wipe it straight from his face. And he knows it.

Jack's smile fades, replaced with an empathetic look. He knows I'm struggling right now, and he's all too aware that I'm reaching the limitations of my patience. He opens his mouth to say something when the door swings open and our coach, Jon Morgan, strides in.

"Bryce, why aren't you in the mixed zone, giving the scheduled interview?"

I look down at my training gear. "I was headed for the weights room and then for a shower. I need to cool off first."

He pushes a frustrated hand through his hair. Jon is a former NHL star, and several seasons back, he was the captain for our rivals, the Seattle Scorpions. He's also Jack's stepdad.

"The interview is due to take place in five minutes. They want to run this one earlier, so you'll have to cool down and shower later."

He braces the locker room door open, asking me to follow him.

I drop my head between my shoulders. I've been captain of the Blades for a long while, and most of the responsibilities I enjoy, though talking with the media is not one of them.

"I'll be right out."

Five minutes later, I'm in front of a multitude of cameras and reporters, waiting for their usual quick-fire session.

I look around the room and pick up a bottle of BodyArmor, taking a pull when the first reporter speaks.

"Disappointing result for you tonight. Walk us through it and what went wrong."

I smirk and pull at the back of my neck.

Isn't it fucking obvious? Jesus, who pays these people to ask such moronic questions?

Linking my fingers, I rest them under my chin, shouldering a professional demeanor. "The team put in a great performance, and the game was hard-fought and as intense as we've come to expect when we travel to Colorado. I take responsibility for the final goal; I was a second behind the play and didn't anticipate the forehand pass Reid made. I should've cut it out, but I didn't."

I lean back in my chair and take a sip of my drink as Coach answers a question from a female reporter.

Despite the room being packed with people and cameras, my attention drifts momentarily to Collins. I can't lie and say she hasn't been on my mind since that night a week ago, and the regret of only getting her last name and not her number has settled in my gut. That said, who am I kidding? I had to practically pry her identity from her, never mind getting her digits.

And what exactly would I message?

Hi there. Thanks for the one-time sex we shouldn't be acknowledging. You told me it was adequate at best, but I can't stop thinking about the way your mouth fell open when you came. I want to fuck you again sometime if that's okay?

"Do you believe it's achievable?"

I snap back to reality, registering only the last part of the reporter's question.

"Sorry. Can you repeat that?" I ask with a headshake.

The reporter pauses and checks his notepad. "The playoffs—do you believe this loss will set you back in your pursuit to qualify, or do you believe it's achievable?"

I fold my arms across my chest, throwing Coach a look.

"It's not even November; we're barely a month into the

regular season. I'd argue it's way too soon to start making calls on the playoffs."

The reporter looks like he's about to disagree, and I cut him off with a raised hand.

"There isn't anything more to say. It was a ridiculous question thirty seconds ago, and it still is." I run my gaze across the room. "Next question."

All conversations fall silent as the reporters look between each other.

I take another sip of my drink, already done with this interview.

From the back, a red-haired male reporter raises his arm. I don't recognize him as a regular in the mixed zone, and he looks kind of hesitant.

"My question is for Bryce."

He clears his throat. I do not like the look on his face or where this is going.

"An hour ago, some photos surfaced on social media. You were pictured with a pink-haired woman we hadn't seen before. You looked pretty cozy as you walked through Cobble Hill. Can you comment on these images, and is this woman a new love interest? I know you lost your wi—"

"Are you being for real right now?" I growl.

I sense Coach shift in his seat next to me, but I couldn't care less.

The reporter stares straight ahead, waiting for me to speak again.

"Why are you bringing personal questions into a professional interview?"

It's a rhetorical question, and he knows it. But regardless of my rage, panic swells in my gut.

Where did those photos come from, and why are they only appearing now?

What happened was supposed to be private. We agreed to keep it between ourselves.

I bring my attention back to the room. Whatever it is that's circulating, no doubt posted by some random person after their five minutes of fame, it needs to be squashed.

"I was making sure a woman got back to her place safely that night. We don't know each other, and I don't expect to see her again." I push back my chair and stand, grabbing my drink bottle and hating the way it feels to deny any knowledge of Collins in my life.

Leaning down to the microphone set on the table, I add, "If you want to engage in press conferences with me in the future, I suggest you refrain from speculating on my personal life. That includes anything related to my late wife or other women you know fuck all about."

SIX

COLLINS

The only reason I'm here, in Lloyd's Bar, right now is for my girls. Kendra and Jenna just got named in the national squad, and I know how much this means to Kendra. She'd been trying to break into Team USA for a while, and injuries held her back. Understandably, they want to celebrate, and I'm not about to bail on them after the game because I'm avoiding Sawyer Bryce.

He denied even knowing me.

I don't know who snapped the photo or why they waited a week to post it—maybe because they knew it was a dickhead thing to do, but couldn't resist in the end. Regardless of how the images got out, I'm pissed.

The look on Sawyer's face when he casually brushed me aside a few days ago was beyond cold.

I get it; we agreed to keep it just between us—it's what I wanted.

That's what he needs to do, not just for him, but for Ezra too.

Not acknowledging that night was what I'd told him I wanted.

Right?

Ugh, why is life so fucking confusing? And why am I even bothered at all? I figured I'd meant more to him than a complete denial of my existence—or at least, I thought his face would portray some kind of emotion when he thought about me.

Maybe that night was forgettable. Maybe I was a six out of ten too?

Maybe I need to get a goddamn grip on myself and stop being emotional over something that isn't all that important.

When Jack slides into the booth next to Kendra and holds her face between his hands, the knot that was forming in my stomach tightens just a little more.

I drop my gaze right as Archer sits down, wrapping his big arm around my shoulders.

"Has anyone seen this pink-haired girl before? Evidently, she doesn't exist."

"Has anyone seen Archer's sense of humor?" I pick up my cocktail and take a sip. "He seems to have misplaced it."

Opposite me, Jenna snorts softly. "I don't think I can imagine my life without you in it, Collins. You have to stay in New York forever."

I'm ready to tell her I'll be here for as long as I have a job when Sawyer joins us at the end of the booth. I promised myself I wouldn't look at him tonight, but my eyes betray me for the briefest second as we lock on each other.

He's wearing the same dark blue suit he wore the last time we were here—the one I tossed on his bedroom floor.

I shift my attention back to Jenna and Kendra. "I'll be the first to congratulate you both on making the squad. It's absolutely deserved." My attention lands on everyone but the broody captain I can feel watching me. "Great win tonight against the league leaders too."

I feel awkward—the whole atmosphere does tonight—and I know it has everything to do with my mood. I should be grateful Sawyer denied knowing me and had his agent pull the images.

"Actually, while I have you all together"—Jack's British accent cuts through the tension—"Darcy is visiting next week, and we wanted to invite you guys over to our place for dinner. She has some kind of announcement she won't tell me over the phone."

Ten seconds ago, I'd have said I was easily the most uncomfortable person sitting at this table, but from the way Archer's arm tenses at the mention of Jack's baby sister, I'd hazard that award might go to him.

"What day next week? I'll need to check if Dom and Alyssa can have Ezra," Sawyer asks.

It's the first time I've heard him speak since he stormed out of the interview in Colorado, and I can't help but glance at him again.

He keeps his focus on Jack.

"On Saturday night. She's staying at our place for five nights and then heading back to Oxford," Jack confirms.

"And it's a British-themed night with shepherd's pie and trifle for dessert." Kendra sits back in the booth, gazing off into a food-induced fantasy.

"I can't make it," I blurt out, all eyes darting to me. I guess that did come out kind of weird. "I have a thing on that night."

Even weirder.

"What thing?" On a frown, Kendra sits forward, looking kind of hurt that I don't share the same enthusiasm for what is essentially minced meat, potatoes, and a few scattered peas.

But it's not what's on the menu that's driving my reluctance. I like spending time with the kind of friends I've never had before. I just don't want to be around *him* for a moment longer than necessary. What doesn't make me feel good, I cut out immediately. And Sawyer Bryce does not make me feel great about myself right now. Since the interview, the tingles he induced have gone, leaving irritation and borderline resentment in their wake.

I clear my throat, scrambling for a plausible excuse. "I'm heading to a Harley Rendezvous event that day; it's been a while since I could make one, and I prebooked the tickets."

Kendra slowly nods, like she's not buying it. "That's a shame. I know Darcy was looking forward to seeing you."

"Did she … happen to hint at what the announcement is about?" I hear Archer ask, but my attention is no longer in the booth as Sawyer gets up and walks over to the bar, scrolling on his cell before putting it to his ear.

In a separate conversation and a quiet voice, Jenna leans toward me, her soft face shining in the glow of the dim bar lighting. "Does your absence have to do with the images posted online of you and Sawyer? I know how you like to keep your privacy and everything." She quickly checks over her shoulder. "Or is it awkward since you two …" She trails off. "You know …"

Bracing my elbows on the table, I drop my face into a hand, not even bothering to deny that we hooked-up. I know she isn't about to tell anyone. "It's neither of those things. I genuinely can't go on Saturday, and to be honest, I'm kind of tired from working long hours at the shop."

Before Jenna can respond, my jacket's in my hand as I stand from the booth. "I don't want to come off as rude, but I think I'm going to head out."

On my final words, Jack, Archer and Kendra pause on their conversation.

"Want me to give you a ride home?" Jack asks.

I shake my head. "No, I'm going to get the bus. There's one in, like, two minutes."

With Sawyer's back still to the group, I seize the opportunity and squeeze past Archer and his teammate, making for the door and not stopping to look back.

The second I'm hit with the freezing fall breeze, I draw a

gulp of air into my lungs, letting it rest there before I swallow it down.

Come on, Collins. Get it to-fucking-gether.

"There aren't any Harley Rendezvous events in late October."

I spin around on the frozen sidewalk and come face-to-face with Sawyer. He's standing with his phone still pressed to his ear and a rogue grin on his face.

"The recorded message I'm listening to just confirmed it. Well, unless you're heading to Red Rock in Vegas."

I turn back toward the bus stop, not saying a word, but I can feel his eyes as they bore into my head.

He releases a long sigh that shifts a few strands of my hair, and I reach behind myself, pulling my collar up so I can't feel it.

"I thought you said nothing would change?" he asks quickly.

"Changed my mind," I clip back.

He moves to stand beside me, and I continue facing forward. I know I'm being bratty, but I don't have it in me to care.

"What's going on, Collins?" he presses, his voice a touch agitated.

My bus sails past the stop, and I close my eyes, irritation growing.

"It's probably best if you head back inside. You never know who could be around to take more photos. You don't know me, remember?"

When I look up at him, he's already staring down at me, his green gaze showing he's confused by my behavior.

"You would've preferred I told the world your name and that the images were taken right before we got naked together?"

My eyes flare wide, and I quickly check that no one heard that.

I remain quiet since I don't have a decent response to his logic. No, I don't want the world to know who I am, and I *defi-nitely* don't want them to find out about our hookup.

"You're really starting to piss me off—you know that?" I push out, pulling out my phone to check on bus times.

He rocks back on his heels, and I swear he chuckles low. "Tell me a time when I'm not antagonizing you. All I need to do is breathe, and you're aggravated by me."

"You made out like I was nothing to you."

He looks at me then, and I do him.

"It wasn't so much what you said, but *how* you said it. That night really must've been forgettable." My warm breath forms clouds in the freezing space between us.

Sawyer's full lips twist. "Let's not forget you were the one who graded me as average. But for what it's worth, 'forgettable' is the opposite of how I'd describe what we shared."

I pocket my phone, another bus due at any second. "Anyway, whatever. It was a mistake we won't be repeating."

Despite our noisy surroundings, I don't miss the rumble from his chest.

"Is this where you back off from the group and then leave town?"

I reach into my bag for my bus pass. "I have a couple of things keeping me here, but, yeah, maybe. Work kind of sucks right now, and my place is on a rolling lease."

He doesn't respond to that, and silence stretches between us.

"I guess if I offered you a ride home, you'd tell me to shove it up my ass, right?"

A playful smile tugs at his lips, and I tear my eyes away from it.

"I really think it's best if we reduce our contact to the absolute minimum. I'll see Kendra and Jenna outside of game days. That way, you won't be called out when the press inevitably catches on that I do, in fact, exist."

He runs a hand through his hair, and I step toward a second bus as it pulls up alongside the sidewalk.

"Enjoy the event on Saturday," he calls after me.

I pause and turn over my shoulder, eyes narrowing as contrasting emotions swirl in my stomach—amusement, annoyance, and downright frustration at the way this guy creeps under my skin with such ease.

"Yeah." I grin at him. "Fingers crossed I'll rate it more than a six."

SEVEN

COLLINS

It's two days later when I pull my bike up outside Rise Up and push through the door in full leathers. The one good thing about this kind of weather? I'm not sweating my tits off when dressed like this.

Since I'm five minutes early for meeting Kendra, I join the line and put in my regular black coffee and sandwich order with Ed.

The last forty-eight hours has seen my mood improve, thanks to two much-needed days off and binge-watching multiple '80s movies. With a few exceptions, I've concluded that I was born in the wrong decade—'80s music, bikes, movies, and the vibes in general were far superior to anything this century has to offer.

Ed hands me my coffee and nods toward the back of the café. "Kendra called ahead of time and asked if I could save three window seats, so you're right over there."

I frown as he sets the chopped cheese sandwich on my tray. "Three?"

He nods. "Yeah, I thought maybe you were meeting her and Jack?"

"Not that I'm aware of."

Ed's attention snags on my bike parked outside. "Nice wheels. Is it a Glide Ultra Limited?"

"You know your bikes?"

I'd pin Ed as in his forties, so it's not surprising that he'd recognize my black 1981 model.

"Yeah, I refurbed her a year back. She was in a bad state when I picked her up. The owners were ready to scrap her for parts, but all she needed was some TLC."

"Wait. You're the pink-haired girl from the photos."

At the sound of a young male voice, I turn with my tray. Initially, I only see Kendra, her black Storm beanie pulled low over her blonde hair. Then I set eyes on a much smaller, younger version of a guy I essentially told to fuck off two days ago. Same dark hair, same green eyes. Same everything.

Ezra.

Kendra doesn't say anything, eyes scanning my leathers.

I take the opportunity to throw my friend a *what the fuck* glare. She could've told me she was bringing him here after soccer practice.

She smiles sweetly, and I pull my attention back to the twelve-year-old giving me a once-over.

He cocks his head to the side and smiles. *Jesus*, even their facial expressions are identical.

"You *are* the pink-haired girl." He adjusts the training bag thrown over his left shoulder. "Do you only wear black?"

Kendra rolls her lips together, fighting back laughter. "That's the exact same thing I thought when I first met you," she giggles.

I'm not good with kids. I'm terrible with people in general, but kids? Yeah, I'm at a whole new level of ineptness. They're a bit like bear cubs—unpredictable, but kind of cute. And I don't know what to do with that. Other than when I was one myself, I've never been around them, and with no experience to guide me, interacting with or knowing what to say to them doesn't come easily to me.

"I like black." I lift a shoulder and start for the reserved bench at the window.

"Ezra, why don't you go ahead and follow Collins? I'll get our order in."

"You are the pink-haired girl in the pictures with my dad, right?" He repeats his question as we reach our seats.

The last time I was in this café, Kendra told me Ezra was withdrawn and not very sociable.

Unlikely.

"You ask a lot of questions, don't you?" I bite down on my sandwich as he takes the stool next to me.

While he plays with the toggles on his dark blue hoodie, I take in his profile. He has a smattering of freckles across the bridge of his nose, and I wonder if they're also from his dad or if his mom had them too.

"The other kids at school, they said Dad definitely had a girl-friend, and he was lying when he denied he knew you. They said he was dating a 'college girl.' " He studies me for a couple of beats. "How old are you?"

I am so out of my depth right now.

I stir my coffee profusely. "How old do you think I am?"

He twists his lips to the side, deep in thought. "Twenty?"

I scoff. "I wish. I'm twenty-six, meaning your friends are doubly wrong. I'm not a college girl, and I'm also not your dad's girlfriend."

His shoulders drop an inch, and I don't like that they do.

"They aren't my friends."

"Okay, I ordered you a grilled cheese." Kendra sets a straw-berry shake down in front of Ezra, and he immediately starts playing with the straw. "I'm going to use the restroom." She flashes me another smile and heads off quickly.

I turn back to Ezra, uneasy over his last comment. "But you have friends, right?"

He puffs out a breath. "Some, I guess, mainly on Fortnite."

"As in the video game?"

He takes a pull from his shake. "I'm good at it, so that makes me popular with them."

I sip my coffee, searching for a way to brighten the dejected look on his face. "I get that. I'm good with bikes and refurbishing them. I have an Instagram page dedicated to my girl outside." I tap the glass in front of us. "I documented her overhaul from start to finish, and my page got popular really fast."

"Wait." Ezra leans toward the window, craning his neck to look down the sidewalk. "That black motorcycle is yours?"

I glance down at my leathers. "Who else would it belong to?"

His eyes widen a touch. "That's so cool. How many followers do you have?"

"Ummm … maybe ten thousand?"

His jaw pops open. "That's so many. Dad has, like, a million, but he never posts on there. When he does, it's all boring gameplay and sponsor crap."

I fight back a snort. The potential for banter with Ezra at his dad's expense is real, but I resist the urge to keep down this route and change course.

"So, you were at soccer practice with Kendra?" I ask.

He scrunches his face up, pushing away his milkshake. "Dad thinks I need to find a sport to play. He keeps going on about 'too much screen time.' Blah, blah. Thing is, I don't like sports— never have, never will. I'm not that big on going to hockey games either."

This lunch date has somehow gone from wanting to ream my friend out for turning up with a kid I never thought I would meet to immediately enjoying his company.

Ezra's grilled cheese is set down in front of him right as Kendra joins us.

"Okay, so your dad will be here in a few minutes. He just finished practice."

I choke on my coffee. "Like, coming here?"

I didn't share my and Sawyer's exchange at the bus stop with Kendra or my feelings about the way he answered the media in Colorado. She wouldn't get it. She'd just see a guy trying to protect my privacy, along with his own, and doing what we'd agreed. But finding reasons to be pissed at someone is an easy way to keep your distance.

"Jesus." Kendra stares down at Ezra's plate, pulling her coffee mug toward her. "You eat faster than Jack."

His head darts to me, eyes wide. "Can I see your bike before I go?"

A tiny smile traces Kendra's lips.

"You can look. But I can't take you out on it or anything," I say, unsure if I should allow even that.

"Awesome." Ezra's already off the stool and heading for the door.

I take a second to look at Kendra. "Did you deliberately set this up?"

She shakes her head, taking a large sip of coffee. "Seriously, Sawyer was supposed to get him straight from practice, but it got delayed, so I offered to bring him here for something to eat."

I slide off my stool and raise a brow. "Are you staying here or coming out with us?"

She peers down at her almost-empty—and probably cold—coffee. "I need to stay and finish this."

"Huh, yeah, okay," I reply, taking off out of the café and after Ezra.

"This bike looks kind of old," Ezra says as we stand next to each other on the sidewalk, his hands in the front pocket of his hoodie. "But old in a cool way."

"It was built in the '80s."

His jaw drops open. "Wow, that was a really long time ago."

I nod and suppress a laugh. "Similar time to when your dad was born."

"Really?" he asks, doubt across his face.

"No lie." I nod, knowing technically Sawyer was born in the nineties, but he's old all the same. "She has all her original parts, bar a few pieces that were broken when I got her."

Ezra just stands, staring at the bike.

I know I shouldn't, but the passion I see in his eyes overrides all common sense, and I'm speaking before I can stop myself. "Do you want to sit on her?"

His attention whips to me. His pure excitement makes me feel only good things. "For real?!"

It isn't so busy today, and I guess thirty seconds wouldn't hurt.

I pinch my thumb and forefinger at him. "I'm talking seconds. That's it."

Standing at the front of my bike, I hold the handlebars to keep it steady as Ezra climbs on. Unlike a Low Rider—which I would struggle to ride, given my petite frame—this model sits slightly higher, and since Ezra is tall, like his dad, he doesn't struggle to get into a comfortable position.

He wraps his hands around the rubber grips, checking out the analog speedometer. "Does it go really fast?"

"Top speed is a hundred and ten miles per hour."

He drops his shoulders. "That's kind of slow. Dad's Lamborghini goes way faster."

I'm aware from when I last rode in it.

"It's more built for comfort and cruising, not to race."

He nods his head, turning over his shoulder at the empty seat behind him. "Is this for another per—"

"Ezra, what are you doing?" interrupts an unimpressed male voice, and we both turn toward it.

EIGHT

SAWYER

"What does it look like, Dad?"

I don't know who to look at first: my son, straddling a retro Harley on the side of the road, or the woman I can't get out of my mind—and likely never will now that I've seen her in full leathers.

Jesus.

As I draw nearer, Collins adopts a confident stance, hands propped on her hips. "It's all good, *Dad.* Ezra here wanted to have a look at my bike. He's really into it." She throws me a look that's impossible to misinterpret—*let the boy do his thing.*

Ezra drops his attention from me back to the bike as he studies it carefully, and I take the opportunity to edge a little closer. Her eyeliner is bolder than usual, and her hair blows in the chilling wind.

"You know he's twelve, right? Way too young for motorcycles."

She lifts a shoulder. "Obviously, I wasn't going to let him ride it, and I was a similar age when I discovered bikes."

I study her for a beat, feeling like she just told me something she hasn't shared before. I want to know more about her past but pause on an inquisition since I know it won't get me anywhere with her. "Did I just learn something about you?"

She scoffs lightly and flips her hand at Ezra, asking him to climb off. He does and steps onto the sidewalk, pulling out his cell to take pictures.

"In fact," I muse, "I knew you were into bikes. I just didn't know you had one of your own."

"Two," she replies quickly. "Technically, I have two bikes. The other one is in the garage where I work. In my spare time, I restore it. I'll probably sell her when I'm done." She reaches out and runs a hand over the pristine black leather seat. "Would be hard to part with this old girl though."

So much of me wants to ask what's so special about this bike that makes it indispensable to Collins. From reading between the lines and based on what she's told me, I know she doesn't see much as permanent—not where she lives or where she works, and maybe not even the company she keeps.

For the first time, as I watch her inspect the Harley-Davidson that looks like it was manufactured in the '80s, I see something that resembles emotion. Like this is a part of her she can't let go.

"Does she have a name?" I ask, crossing my arms over my chest. I probably shouldn't push, but I can't help it.

She tips her head to look at me, her expression reverting back to the familiar hard one I'm used to. "No."

I don't believe her.

"You could never part with something you haven't even named?" I challenge.

Collins climbs onto the bike and reaches behind her, unlocking a box fixed to the back. She pulls out her helmet and smooths a hand down her hair.

"I said it would be hard to part with her, not that it would never happen. Giving anything a name makes saying goodbye all the more difficult."

She turns to my son, who's still busy taking photos, a warmth in her eyes. "It was nice to meet you, Ezra. Maybe I'll see you around again sometime."

With one motion, she starts the bike, and the engine roars to life.

I scrub a hand over my jaw and summon all the gross thoughts I can conjure. Anything to counter the visual of her kick-starting that bike.

"I guess I won't see you on Saturday since you'll be heading to the event in Vegas, right?"

She pulls her helmet on, wavy pink strands falling below it and resting on her shoulders.

Collins shifts into gear, glancing at me briefly. "Correct." She's grinning—I can tell by the creases forming around her eyes. "I guess I'll see you when I see you. Or not."

"ALL RIGHT, THAT'S ENOUGH SCREEN TIME FOR TONIGHT. GO brush your teeth and head up to bed." I thumb over my shoulder toward the stairs.

Without any kind of protest, Ezra slides off the barstool, where he sat for the past half hour, staring at his laptop, and heads straight upstairs.

As his foot lands on the first step, I set the plate I wiped on the kitchen counter.

"You didn't tell me how soccer practice was," I quickly say before he's out of earshot.

He pauses, looking uninspired, and my heart sinks a little further. There has to be at least one sport he enjoys. I can barely get him to my own hockey games.

"It was fine," he replies unenthusiastically.

I flip the towel I was using over my shoulder and walk toward him. "Kendra told me you're a natural. Especially in goal." Which I guess is unsurprising, given he's way taller than average height for his age.

Ezra knocks his knuckles against the wooden handrail. "Why did you lie?"

Not where I thought this conversation was heading.

"What do you mean?"

He drops his shoulders, frustrated with my denial. But I honestly have no idea what he's talking about.

"About Collins. I saw the pictures that were posted online, but you never once said anything to me. You just denied even knowing her on TV."

I hoped my agent had gotten to the pictures before Ezra or his friends noticed them. He rarely watches my games, let alone post-match interviews, so I figured I could let this one slide.

Obviously not.

"Is she your girlfriend?" he asks before I get a chance to respond.

The word hits me like a ten-ton truck, knocking me right off guard. He's been quiet since the second we said bye to Collins, but I chalked it up to him being tired from practice. Clearly, his mind was on something else.

It's the first time he's asked me about another woman. We've talked about his mom, but not in too much detail. When he asks questions, I give him answers and show him the photos I have of her, including the ones of Sophie holding him as a baby. I just never anticipated a time when he would ask me about anyone else. I guess because I never thought that time would come.

"Collins is Kendra's friend; she's been to a few of our games, and that night, I was walking her back home since she lives in the same area as us," I answer the question, praying he doesn't interrogate me further.

I hate lying to him, but I really don't want him to know about our hookup. It's not information a twelve-year-old needs to know. The pictures must've been taken in the dark and without a flash; otherwise, I'd have noticed it at the time and asked the asshole to respect our privacy.

Ezra rolls his lips together, deep in thought. "If you knew her and she's a friend, then why did you lie and act like she was nothing?"

The pissed look on Collins's face that night outside the bus stop is right in front of me as I take questions from my son. I didn't want to deny her existence like she was some kind of stranger; it felt wrong to me, too, but seriously, what choice did I have?

I blow out a long breath. "Because she's a very private person, and I didn't want her to be identified. Besides, I don't know if you would describe us as friends. She's someone I know."

Ezra's brows pull together. "But you like hanging out with her, right?"

I prop my hands on my hips and shake my head slowly. "I wouldn't even say that we've hung out togeth—"

"Because I do," he rushes out, cutting me off. "I like hanging out with her. She's cool, and she likes bikes, which are way more interesting than goddamn sports."

"Language," I scold.

He rolls his eyes and starts up the stairs. "Whatever," he huffs out as I track his movements until he disappears out of sight.

I stand there, rooted to the spot, wondering what the fuck just happened when my cell starts vibrating on the kitchen island.

I skid to a halt having raced over to grab it from next to Ezra's laptop before it goes to voicemail.

"Hey," I say, not even bothering to check the contact.

"Worst. Advice. Ever." Archer's unimpressed tone is unmistakable.

"What was?" I ask, my brain still catching up with the

conversation I just had with Ezra, never mind processing what my goalie has to say.

"After practice today, I found out Shane was in town, seeing some of the guys for a few beers. With your *advice* still ringing in my ears, I thought it might be a good opportunity to tell him face-to-face—you know, man-to-man."

I close my eyes and take the stool Ezra was previously using. "And?"

"And I'm calling you ahead of morning skate to give the heads-up on the bruised jaw I now have."

"Fuck."

He huffs out a humorless breath. "I can confidently confirm that my playing-around days are over, as is the era of me listening to you."

"Other than landing one on you, what did he say?"

This time, he does laugh, but it's dark. "He told me if he ever saw me again, he'd break my legs."

"Did you hit him back?"

A couple of seconds of silence pass before he speaks.

"No. I didn't particularly want the title of Bar Fighter to go with Resident Playboy." He pauses again. "My agent is telling me some photos of the hit made it on the internet. I can't look at them."

"Hang on," I say, grabbing my reading glasses from the counter opposite the island and waking Ezra's laptop before punching in the password. "I'll take a look for you. They're probably already down though."

Archer shares the same agent as me, and he's known for being fast at getting shit like this taken down, although seemingly, he's not as fast as Ezra's peers.

As soon as I hit the last digit of his password, I pause, staring at the screen.

"Oh fuck, they're really bad, aren't they? Coach is going to ream my ass out tomorrow morning." Archer groans, assuming my silence is in response to what I'm seeing.

I still don't say anything.

BikerCollins.

An Instagram profile with over ten thousand followers and a hundred different posts—some Reels and other static images—lights up the screen in front of me.

I click on her latest upload—a Reel of her refurbing the Harley she was talking about. She's dressed in ripped denim shorts, black Doc Martens boots, and a worn gray Def Leppard T-shirt. Her hair is thrown up in a bun with pieces framing her face as she talks to the camera, walking her followers through some kind of step-by-step instructions. Thankfully all in silence since Ezra has the volume on mute.

How did he find out she had this profile? Did she tell him? Did his friends find it? Or did he perform a random Google search on her first name?

Regardless, *nothing* gets past this kid.

"Sawyer, talk to me."

"Huh?" I blink multiple times and come to.

"The images—are there any on the internet?" Archer asks.

I close the window and run a quick search—no hits. "Nothing. Already taken down, I guess."

Archer breathes an audible sigh of relief and then starts talking, but like the bad captain and friend I am, I zone out again.

Ezra was viewing her Instagram profile.

I click a couple more buttons.

And by the looks of his search history, he's watched multiple Reels and viewed nearly all her other posts.

I scroll further into his history; he's been searching for images of us together—obviously showing no hits—and random questions about Harley-Davidson motorcycles.

Fuck me.

Did I just find my son's new interest?

NINE

SAWYER

"You plan on removing your helmet at all today?" Jack tips his head at Archer as we stop mid-practice to take in fluids.

"True. By the time we got to the rink, you were already on the ice, padded up and stretching," Emmett Richards, one of the team's longer-standing defensemen, replies.

Archer throws me a look and takes a pull of his drink. I haven't seen the extent of Shane's hit, but I'm guessing he landed a good one on him.

With a deep sigh, Archer pulls his helmet off, and Jack's eyes bug out. Since he didn't leave practice yesterday with any injuries, it's obvious he sustained the massive purple bruise along the underside of his jaw overnight.

"The fuck happened? Wait, did you meet up with Shane and some of the other guys last night?" Jack asks.

Nodding, Archer lightly runs a gloved hand across his face. "He was out with a few of the other guys on the farm team. I'd heard they had a few days off in between games and Shane and a couple of others were going out in Williamsburg. I turned up at one of the bars I knew they were hitting and pulled Shane aside." He clears his throat and winces. "Told him what we'd discussed." He rolls his eyes at me, still convinced it was bad advice. "And next thing I knew, his fist was in my face."

Jack reaches across, patting Archer on the shoulder. "I think this season might be your turn taking home the prize for pissing off teammates."

Archer raises a single brow in response. I mean, Jack isn't wrong; fucking another dude's girl isn't a great move.

"One, he isn't my teammate, and two, I had no idea it was his girl—"

Emmett chokes on his water, interrupting Archer mid-flow. "Wait, you slept with Kassie?!"

"See!" Archer points my way. "I was at least right when I said her name began with a *K*."

I clap sarcastically, and Emmett shakes his head.

"Damn, man. Boning another guy's girl. I heard they're engaged too."

Archer tips his head back and groans, his dark hair dripping with sweat. "As I was saying, one, he isn't my teammate, and two, I didn't know she was with anyone."

Archer resets his focus on Jack. "Tyler was one of the guys out with them. He said I'd been hanging out with you too long if I was now stealing another guy's woman."

On a headshake, Jack squirts his drink into his mouth. "A year on, and Tyler still can't accept that Kendra not only got an upgrade, but he was never part of the race to begin with."

"Yeah, well, unlike you and Kendra, I was never interested in getting with *Kassie*." Archer accentuates her name for effect. "It was a fuck back at my place, and that was it. You and Kendra were always meant to be."

I hum in agreement. I can't argue with that logic. I wouldn't be shocked if, in the next six months, Jack isn't down on one knee. The way he looks at Kendra—and she, at him—reminds me a lot of the love I shared with Sophie, something I've not experienced since. It's a once-in-a-lifetime kind of feeling.

"All right, Friday's game against the Destroyers is going to be hard as fuck—I think we all know that."

Coach Morgan skates over to where the three of us are standing by the boards.

"Is that your technical analysis?" Jack asks his stepdad, earning a narrowed gaze from Coach.

"It's exactly as I described it," he replies, his attention snagging on Archer's face. "And do I dare ask how you got that?" Coach tips his chin at our goalie, circling the area where Archer's jaw is bruised.

Archer shakes his head and drinks, probably with a sense of relief that the pictures from the bar fight didn't get far and that, evidently, Shane and his teammates opted not to report anything either.

Coach clears his throat and pulls a clipboard from under his arm. "In preparation for this Friday's game, there are some plays I want to work on for the second half of practice. Take a minute to reboot, and then I want you all at center ice, ready to leave it all out there. Richards, I could use you right now though, if you have a second?"

Our defenseman nods quickly.

Coach gives Archer's face one last look and skates off, Emmett hot on his heels.

Jack turns to me and Archer, setting his bottle rink side. "That reminds me about this Saturday night. Darcy's flight lands at five p.m., so shall we say seven thirty to give her a chance to make it to ours and get changed?"

"Does she need a ride?" Archer perks up, and I know it's at the mention of Jack's sibling.

Jesus, this guy never changes.

Last season was Jack's first in the NHL, and Darcy traveled to New York to watch on a couple of occasions. It was as obvious back then as it is now that Archer digs Jack's younger sister.

"No," Jack drawls, his posh British accent really showing. "She doesn't need a lift because her brother will be at the airport, waiting for her."

Archer smiles around the spout on his drink bottle but quickly straightens when he sees the look I'm giving him.

Though his playful grin fades for only a second, and I know exactly what's coming …

"Talking of rides, are you still going, Sawyer? You know, since Collins can't make it," he asks innocently.

I deadpan, "Why would Collins being there or not have any effect on my attendance?"

His playful grin turns devilish. "Oh, you know, just thinking she might need some kind of help getting home." He pauses and takes another sip of his drink, setting the bottle down. "Or back into your bed," he says, pushing off the boards to join Coach and the team as they gather at center ice.

"Last week, I asked on my Stories if you guys had any particular issues with the Road Glide model. The response was overwhelming with a ton of you reporting the cam chain tensioner, especially in older models, such as the one I have here. This is my own bike I refurbed a year ago, and the cam chain needed a full replacement. If your bike isn't running as smoothly, if it rattles, or if the performance is hindered, I would advise this to be one of the first things you look at since leaving this issue for a long period can lead to severe engine damage."

"Wait up."

Jack's muted voice—along with his knock on my driver's window—has my head darting in his direction.

Since I don't have blacked-out windows—un-fucking-fortu-nately—his attention immediately drops to the cell phone in my hand, the screen lit with Collins, wearing her usual ripped black denim shorts and a rock-themed T-shirt, as she stands from a crouched position next to her bike and looks at the camera.

I'm scrambling to lock the screen when it flies from my hand and across the center console, dropping between the seats in my truck.

Fuck.

I knock my head against the steering wheel and blow out a defeated breath.

He taps again, and without lifting my head, I lower the window for him.

When he remains silent, I turn my head slowly and see his blue eyes sparkling with the kind of mischief I've come to expect from this guy.

Obviously fighting back laughter, he clears his throat. "I stayed behind for some extra gym work and saw you still parked up. I was wondering why you were still here …" He rolls his lips together and finally loses it, full-on buckling over in the middle of the players' parking lot.

He rests a hand on the windowsill, and I'm half tempted to close the window on it.

"Oof …" He pants hard. "Hang on. I need a second."

I sit back in my seat, folding my arms across my chest as I wait for my—now-former—closest friend to get his shit together.

"Okay, okay. I'm good," he breathes out. "I was going to ask if you wanted to bring Ezra on Saturday."

He's still smirking when he delivers the question, but I choose to ignore it. Maybe Alyssa and Dom would like the night off since they'll have Ezra over for the game on Friday night.

"Yeah, sure, that sounds good."

Jack nods, his eyes falling to where my cell disappeared a

few seconds earlier. "Okay, Kendra wants to know if he's picky over food?"

I shake my head, grateful that, as a single dad, I've never had to deal with that. "No, he'll be good."

He nods, tucking his hands into his pockets. "We, errr … ever going to talk about Collins, or do you plan on secretly watching her content for the rest of time?"

I push my head further into the rest, closing my eyes. "There's nothing to talk about."

He makes a doubtful sound, raising a hand to scratch his neck. "My best guess is you left the locker room around a half hour ago—at least." He motions to the seat where my phone is buried. "If you've been scrolling through her motorcycle page for at least half that time, I'd say there's everything to discuss."

Try forty-five minutes and all that time.

"Like I said, there's nothing to talk about."

He shakes his head and looks off down the empty lot. "What have you got against following what you want? You've been obsessed with her since last Novem—"

"I'm not obsessed with her," I snap, shifting my truck into gear since the engine is already running.

Jack runs his tongue across his bottom lip and steps back from my truck, granting me access to drive away.

I don't move forward, instead gripping the top of the steering wheel with white knuckles. "Listen, I like her, yeah. But I can't let myself think any further than that. Especially when she isn't into me."

TEN

COLLINS

Technically, I should be in Las Vegas. In reality, I'm standing outside Jack and Kendra's apartment with a bottle of Chardonnay in one hand, my other one hovering over the door.

Up until a few hours ago, I talked myself out of showing up tonight. Fake Harley Rendezvous event or not, the best place for me was sitting on my couch, on my own, watching movies. I'm still not convinced this is a good idea, like being around Sawyer Bryce.

Still, I'm here. When I pulled on my boots and raced to the store for the wine I'm holding, I told myself this was about my friends and not letting them down. And it is.

The door swings open before I've had a chance to knock, and Kendra throws her arms around me.

"Oh my God, you came!" She immediately pulls back, a slight wince on her face. "Sorry, was that too much? I know how you feel about the invasion of personal space."

With my free hand, I pull her back into me. "I can make exceptions for certain people."

We break apart, and I hold up the wine—my turn to wince. "I

figured it was polite to bring a bottle, but this also doubles as an apology. I know I said I wasn't coming, but … yeah …" I trail off since I don't have a valid explanation for turning down the meal—other than to avoid Sawyer.

Kendra takes the wine and moves aside for me to enter the apartment. I step in, and she sets the bottle on a table just inside the door.

"You know he's here tonight, right?"

I nod and pull off my jacket. "I know. But just because we slept together doesn't mean we should avoid each other for the rest of time." I blow out a breath, and Kendra takes my jacket, hanging it up on the coat stand next to her. "Besides, I'm here for my friends."

Warmth illuminates her face, right before she purses her lips. "Ezra's here too."

My eyes dart to hers, and Kendra smiles knowingly, probably thinking back to the way we interacted at Rise Up.

"He is? I figured he'd be with a sitter or something."

Shaking her head, she takes my hand, leading me toward their dining room. Since the kitchen and living area are empty but I can hear voices, I assume everyone is gathered in there.

She stops just outside the closed door. "For what it's worth—and I know I wasn't there—I don't think that night was a mistake. I've seen the way you look at each other." She bites her bottom lip and smirks. "Or more the way Sawyer looks at you. Don't shut something down that might be good before it's even had a chance to grow."

I lift a brow. "How much have you had to drink?"

"Not a drop." She chuckles softly and opens the door. "Guess who decided to show."

"Collins! Oh my God!"

Darcy flies from her chair at the head of the table and makes a beeline for me, wrapping her arms around me and giggling.

Jack's sister is pure sunshine—the complete opposite of me

in every way. With her long honey-colored hair, taste in bright clothes, sparkling blue eyes, and extrovert nature, she makes my black jeans and lace cami top appear even darker. She reminds me so much of her mom, Felicity—who I've met at games a few times since her husband, Jon, is the Blades coach. Darcy is genuinely one of the kindest souls on earth, and I've managed to decipher all of that just from the handful of occasions I've met her.

I guess you could say she's an open book.

"I didn't think you were coming. Jack said you were going to some kind of motorcycle event in Vegas."

Up until I met Darcy, I always considered Jack to have a strong British accent, but it's clear it's lost some strength after years of him living stateside. Darcy's accent is like stepping onto the set of *Bridgerton*.

She releases me from a vise grip, and I scan the room, my eyes landing on Sawyer and Ezra sitting on the opposite side of the table. The last available seat is next to the twelve-year-old boy with eyes like saucers.

My body flushes warm, and I refocus on Darcy. "Couldn't miss your announcement."

"Well, good thing I haven't said anything yet," Darcy replies.

"Can't imagine you got a refund on your tickets or travel costs this late notice."

I follow the voice, my gaze landing back on Sawyer. With his fingers laced under his chin, he pins me with a challenging look. If I allowed my brain to go there, I might think he doesn't mind me showing up; perhaps he's even happy about it. Which surprises me since the last time we spoke, I was a brat.

Jack stands from his place next to Archer. "Okay, if you take a seat next to Ezra, I'll fetch the food."

"HOW MANY BIKES HAVE YOU FIXED?" EZRA FIRES HIS TENTH question in as many minutes. He takes a huge mouthful of food, washing it down with a Diet Coke.

"When you say fixed, do you mean as in refurbished or actually got it working again?"

He shrugs and reaches into his pocket, pulling out his cell. "On Insta, you mainly talk about mechanical faults."

"Not while we're eating." Sawyer points at Ezra's cell, and he quickly repockets it.

I take a bite of the shepherd's pie Jack made—which is surprisingly really fucking nice—and smile around the fork.

"You found my Instagram page then. I guess it wasn't that hard since my handle is my first name."

Ezra nods, but I don't miss the way his dad flushes before he picks up his water glass and takes two big pulls.

"If we're talking bikes mended, then I've lost count. I do it every day for a living. Plus, my followers generally find more value in problem-solving their mechanical issues. Although I prefer to create content on restoring older bikes back to their former glory."

"Can I come see your bike downstairs?" Ezra asks.

I shake my head once, eyes briefly lifting to Sawyer. "I'm sorry. I took the bus here tonight."

Ezra's face drops, and something unfamiliar tugs in my chest.

"Can I come see it another time? Maybe at your place?"

"Ezra," Sawyer immediately interjects, "you can't just go around inviting yourself to people's homes." He shakes his head.

"I'm home tomorrow, if that works for you?" I look at Ezra, the invite leaving my mouth before I can process what I said.

His excited eyes flare wide, and I peek up at Sawyer.

"If that's okay with you?"

"Can I? Please?!" Ezra practically begs his dad, garnering attention from the rest of the table.

Sawyer takes another sip of water, setting the glass back down and running a palm across his mouth. I can see the conflict on his face, and I'm about to offer him a way out when he nods once.

"All right."

"Awesome!"

Ezra holds his fist out for me to bump, and I reciprocate. The second his smaller knuckles meet mine, I'm thinking through all the parts and tools I can show him. I just cleaned and waxed my bike yesterday, but I guess there's no harm in going over it again.

"Call me impatient, but at what point do we get to know your secret?" Archer announces from the other end of the table, looking kind of stressed.

"It has to be an engagement," Sawyer offers. "Or maybe a pregnancy."

Darcy holds up her left hand. "If I were engaged, would it not be pretty obvious?" Her face then scrunches. "And I'm twenty-three and finishing my post-grad; babies are not on the agenda right now." Her face drops slightly but then resets to her usual bright self.

"Spit it out, woman," Jack says.

She glances around at us all. "I'm moving to New York!"

With one slap across the back, Jack dislodges the food caught in Archer's esophagus.

"With Liam?" he asks, adding another thump between Archer's shoulder blades as he inhales a deep breath and recovers.

"Yeah, well ... me moving isn't the only thing that's changed." Her voice is lower, a touch of sadness to it. "I broke up with Liam."

I can't be sure if it's to curb the coughing fit or buy himself a second, but Archer reaches for his beer and chugs half of it down.

"Wait, I have so many questions." Jack holds up a hand. "You were living with Liam. Where are you now?"

Darcy lifts a shoulder. "At a friend's. We broke up, like, two weeks ago, and I moved out. It just wasn't working anymore. Maybe we'd drifted apart. I don't know. I guess the final nail in the coffin was when I got offered an associate editor position in Manhattan. Starts in a few months, and I couldn't turn it down. Oh, that, and I caught him cheating," she tags on casually, like she's determined not to let a man get to her.

My kind of girl.

I don't know whose face looks redder—Jack's or Archer's. But I'm guessing they're both pissed at what her long-term boyfriend, Liam, did.

Darcy's eyes glaze, and I push back my chair, picking up my plate. I'm not good with emotions since I never know what to say. I take the change in atmosphere as my cue to leave and make myself useful.

"Okay, let me gather up all of these." I pick up Ezra's empty plate just as Kendra collects a couple more. "I got it," I say to her, tipping my head at Darcy. "You stay."

She smiles and rounds the table, heading straight for Jack's sister as I make for the kitchen, balancing five plates and two serving bowls in my arms.

I make it to the counter just in time and set the whole lot down, shaking out my aching arms before filling the sink to rinse the plates off.

"You didn't have to invite Ezra over, you know. I could've taken him to a motorcycle event."

I spin around and find Sawyer standing a couple of feet away from me.

He grins down at me, hands tucked into his dark blue dress

pants, strong, tattooed forearms on display with white shirt-sleeves rolled to his elbows. "I heard they have great events in Vegas."

My hands grip the marble counter behind me, and after a short stretch of silence, Sawyer reaches around me and turns off the faucet.

His fresh cologne—the same scent he was wearing the night we hooked up—wafts over me, and the tingles I convinced myself were long gone tickle my body, down to my toes.

He lets out a long exhale as his eyes drop down my body. It's subtle enough that he can convince himself I didn't notice, but I did.

"I didn't want him to be disappointed." I don't recognize my own voice; it sounds thick and tense. I quickly clear my throat. "I have a day off, and I really don't mind. Sharing my passion makes me happy."

Sawyer smiles at that, his tongue peeking out to run across his bottom lip. "I've finally found something that makes you smile, huh?"

I fight back the urge to do just that and he steps a little closer.

"Is there anything else that makes you happy, Collins?"

The tingles intensify, and I bite the inside of my cheek, attempting to suppress them. "Personal space is always a winner."

He throws his head back and chuckles low toward the ceiling. "You know what I think?"

I grip the marble harder. "Enlighten me."

In a fast move I don't expect, Sawyer tips my chin up with his finger, pinning his green eyes on mine. "I think giving me shit makes you happy."

He's not wrong; I can't deny that a guy who can banter turns me on.

"Shame your comebacks are crap though," I reply, swiping his finger away.

He maintains eye contact, and I could kick myself when my eyes fall to his full lips. I remember a lot about that night—probably more than I should for a one-night stand. But one thing we've never shared was a kiss.

I shake away the urge.

"Am I invited to your playdate tomorrow?" he asks, tone subtly flirtatious.

I reach to the side and grab a cloth, ready to start working on the dishes. "Depends. If talking about bikes will bore you to death, you can just drop off and go find something sporty to do."

Laughter filters from the dining room, and Sawyer releases me from his penetrative gaze, looking over his shoulder.

"I think I can stand your company for an hour." He turns back to me, challenge all over his face. "How about one p.m.?"

He reaches into his pocket and hands me his phone.

"What do you want me to do with this?" I ask.

He tips his chin at it. "Your address would help since I never dropped you home that night."

I drop my head, trying to hide the flush that warms my cheeks.

Get a grip, Collins. He's just a man.

"Oh yeah. Duh," I quickly reply, my head spinning with his proximity.

Opening a new contact, I enter my address, offering the phone to him when I finish the zip code.

Sawyer doesn't take it back. All he does is smile at me. I want to look away and break whatever trance he has me in. I also don't. The tension between us is addictive, and the more we interact, the more it builds.

Dangerous. This boy is dangerous for you, Collins. Especially now that you're spending time with his son.

Catching feelings is not an option for anyone in this scenario.

"Add your cell number too," he requests. "You know, just in case we get lost and need directions."

ELEVEN

SAWYER

The following afternoon, I pull my truck up alongside an industrial-style building.

Ezra looks across at me, kind of shocked. Despite it being only a ten-minute drive from my place, the area is different, and the streets are pretty intimidating, even in broad daylight.

"Is this where Collins lives? You told me she lived in a house like ours," he asks, one brow lifted.

"Ah, yeah, 'bout that …" I pull off my sunglasses and rest a forearm over the steering wheel, preparing for a dressing-down from my son, but also smiling because this place is *so* Collins.

Across the street, a red overhead garage door starts moving, and slowly, Collins comes into view, distracting Ezra's attention and saving me from another awkward explanation. Wearing tight black leather pants, her usual black boots, and a different rock T-shirt from the ones I've seen on her Instagram profile, I silently remind my dick that getting a hard-on right now—in front of my son and the girl who evidently finds me borderline insufferable —is not the best idea.

Since she's barely five-four—my best guess—she clings on

to a black cord above her head, her shoulder-length pink hair blowing in the fall breeze.

She motions with her other hand for us to join her, and Ezra is out of his seat belt and the truck in a split second, racing across the road in the process.

I seize the opportunity and give myself a second to gain some control.

"She isn't interested in you." At this point, I don't know if I'm talking to the guy downstairs or myself. "She's passionate about motorcycles and not the thought of another night with you. You're here for Ezra, and that's it. No funny business and *definitely* do not check her ass out in those pants."

On a final exhale, I swing my truck door open and head across the street to join them.

"We get to wax it?! All right!" Ezra sounds like a kid on Christmas morning when he catches a yellow microfiber cloth midair.

I fight to look anywhere but at Collins as she bends down to grab something from one of the tool chests stored at the back of the garage.

This isn't the place she films in—which looks more like a professional garage with a painted gray floor and bright lighting. This garage has exposed brick walls with motorcycle wheels hanging from them. The lighting is softer with industrial-style bulbs and a smooth, unpainted concrete floor sporadically stained with oil. A red neon sign, lit on the back wall, reads *BikerCollins*.

"Waxing helps to preserve the paintwork." Collins's voice draws me back to reality. "Once it dries with a hazy appearance, we can remove the wax with a detailer."

She tosses me another microfiber cloth, and I catch it with my left hand.

"You can start on the saddlebag, and we'll work on the wheel arch."

Just as Collins is showing Ezra what to do, I apply some of the wax and move the cloth in rhythmic circles, reminding me of the way I worked her clit until she came in my mouth.

Your son is here.

I clear my throat, desperate to distract my mind. "Do you live in this building?"

Crouching next to Ezra, Collins shakes her head, her eyes briefly finding mine before falling back to the bike. "The apartments above this garage are all rented out. I live across the street in a one-bedroom place. Originally, I had a garage on the other side of town—which was a pain in the ass to get to. Then, when I was about to relinquish the lease on my apartment, this garage came up. It's not cheap, but it's way better than what I had."

I circle my cloth a couple more times, something in what she just said making me feel uneasy. "I remember you saying you're on a rolling lease now."

Her brown eyes flick to me again, surprise in them. Perhaps she didn't expect me to remember details from the night we spent together. Truthfully, I remember it all. "Yes, that's right. I prefer it this way since it gives me flexibility to leave when I want."

She falls quiet for a brief second.

"Do you plan on leaving New York?" Ezra asks, sounding kind of worried—and a similar feeling constricts my chest.

There is absolutely no logical reason why I should feel any kind of way over the thought of Collins leaving town. But I do. And it's getting harder to ignore. It's frustrating and building all the time.

When she got in my Lamborghini that night, we both knew that I wasn't driving her home. I didn't even ask for an address as I pulled out of the parking lot and drove back to my place in virtual silence. For her, I knew it was about sex, scratching an itch that had been intensifying since we'd met that first night. For me, I was horny and wanted her so damn badly, but I can't deny that when I put my hands on her, there was more at stake than just a fuck.

Maybe she worked that out; maybe she saw it in my eyes when she told me she didn't kiss. Maybe she had considered more than a one-time thing when I palmed her ass at Lloyd's.

Whatever she thought back then, clearly, nothing has changed since she walked out of my place at the ass crack of dawn. If anything, her determination to keep me at arm's length has only gotten stronger.

Conversely, I feel like I'm moving in the opposite direction. Talk of her moving out of town, maybe to a different state, pulls at me in ways I shouldn't let it.

This girl is a free bird, a whirlwind, a fucking tornado—knocking people off their feet as she passes through for a brief time—and her effect is so damn difficult to forget long after she's gone.

Joanne, my housekeeper, has washed my sheets every week since Collins slept in my bed, but somehow, I can still smell her on my pillows—a rich amber scent that drives me to the point of insanity.

Collins thinks I ignored her existence when the press asked me about her, and that pissed her off. The fact is, her response satisfied me in some way; it encouraged me to think she was bothered about us on some kind of level.

But the thing is, I think if she knew the real truth about how I feel, she'd be way more pissed, maybe even freaked out.

I'm growing obsessed with her. She's given me nothing to go on, only tiny crumbs, partial smiles, fleeting looks. And despite my best efforts to keep a lid on my feelings, I'm failing.

And now, as I watch the way she lights up my boy, there's a real part of me that worries if she does leave—unlike a tornado, where you can rebuild and recover from its destruction—moving on from her impact might not be as easy, and perhaps not just for me, but for Ezra too.

"OKAY, WE SHOULDN'T BE MORE THAN FIVE MINUTES," COLLINS says, finding a spare helmet and trying it on Ezra for size. She watches me closely as she secures the strap under his chin. "This was one I had a few years back; it's older, but still good."

Collins looks at Ezra, who climbs on the back, following instructions as she talks him through how to sit correctly on a bike. Dressed in full black leathers that unsurprisingly fit my son since he's around the same height as her, he listens intently.

Finishing up, she knocks his helmet with a glove-covered fist. "I was worried we might have to go a size down with this but you have a big head, so it fits perfectly."

His shoulders drop in jest. "Ha-ha, hilarious."

Pulling on her helmet, she checks Ezra's all good and cranks the engine, filling the garage with a roar and pulling a shriek of delight from him.

Thump, thump goes my heart.

When she shifts into gear and flicks back the kickstand, her usual defensive gaze mellows a fraction, letting me know she'll take good care of him.

I nod once as she carefully pulls out onto the street and increases speed slowly. Ezra's elated screams are unmistakable and fade the farther away they get.

It's just me and the garage for the next few minutes, and I find myself heading toward the row of drawers set across the back wall.

I always considered myself a closed book, especially after Sophie died. Getting close to people was a surefire way to get hurt, purely because their fate—and my own—was uncontrol-lable. If someone had told me how our marriage was going to end and how soon, I wouldn't have believed them. The Sawyer from years ago had faith in fate, faith that really bad things didn't happen to good people.

The Sawyer back then was fucking naive.

Pulling open the top drawer in the red metal cabinet, I'm not shocked to discover tools, but I am surprised by how neatly ordered they are. Each having their own place and sectioned out. Perhaps it's the way Collins lives her life—by the seat of her pants—that made me assume her workstation would be similar. Yet it's the total opposite.

The second drawer is the same, but this time, screws and bolts are categorized by size and dimension, labeled carefully and organized into containers.

Next to the industrial-style metal cabinet sits a mahogany French dresser—the kind of thing you'd expect to see in a country kitchen and not a garage like this.

My interest piqued, I pull the first drawer open and immediately pause when I see a black photo album sitting at the top.

This feels like an invasion of privacy, but equally, I know the chances of Collins ever telling me more about her life is slim to fucking zero.

I know because, in many ways, we're the same.

And I want to know more about her, even if they're just pictures of the family dog. Every part of her fascinates me, to the point where I'm picking up the album and closing the drawer with my hip.

Though this is no family album, no images of dogs or Collins as a baby.

These are all from motocross competitions—and top-level ones at that. I know fuck all about the sport, but I'd recognize the SuperMotocross logo anywhere.

"Jesus," I say out loud, turning to the next page.

The next photo is Collins, same pink-colored hair, same everything, just around ten years younger and with a bronze medal hanging around her neck and no makeup. She smiles at the camera, posing with the silver and gold medalists as they stand on the podium together.

I begin flicking through pages faster, each image revealing more about her life, telling me more than I know she ever would herself. Before, I'd never have described Collins as unhappy—more content with what she had in life. But after seeing these images and catching a glimpse of a smile I've never seen, I realize my girl has layers for days.

A roar filters down the street, and I quickly turn and shove the album back into the dresser, pushing on the drawer just as Collins pulls back into the garage.

When she lifts the visor on her helmet, her gaze is suspicious —or maybe it's just my guilty brain playing tricks on me. Her attention rests on the drawer where the album's kept, and I follow her eyes.

Shit. It's not fully closed.

"Dad, you *have* to buy me a bike like this one. Cars suck." Ezra croons as Collins releases the kickstand and helps him off the Harley.

"Is that right?" I reply, leaning against the dresser and crossing my ankles, trying to emulate a casual pose in a bid to counter her suspicions.

Collins still hasn't said anything as she pulls her helmet off and shakes out her hair.

Holy shit.

"Did he do good?" I ask her.

She hooks her helmet over the handlebar and unzips her leather jacket, Ezra doing the same with his.

"He did." Collins's face is full of mischief, but the kind that makes you feel uneasy, like you've been caught in the act and she fucking knows it.

She walks toward me, stopping only a foot away. When she reaches down to my side, shutting the drawer fully, her perfume hits me. Her eyes never leave mine, long black lashes framing deep brown pools that pull me in and make it hard to look away, even if I wanted to.

In this proximity, I can see—and appreciate—how skilled she is at applying eyeliner, the wings at the corners of her eyes sharp and identical to each other.

I wonder how long she's been wearing her makeup like this since I couldn't see any evidence in the photos.

"I need to get to an appointment," she says, voice low and laced with an emotion I can't decipher.

Anger, hurt, skepticism?

I can't be sure what it is, but my level of discomfort kicks up another notch.

I nod once and push off the dresser, rounding Collins and making my way over to Ezra and the door.

"That was so cool, Collins. Thank you," he says.

I ruffle my hand through Ezra's floppy, dark hair as she turns to face us, her eyes immediately softening for my son.

"You're welcome."

"Maybe we can do it aga—"

"I think once is enough," I cut him off and place a hand on his shoulder, which is immediately shrugged away.

Despite knowing I just landed myself in the hottest water possible with the one woman I have ever known to simultaneously intimidate and intrigue me in equal parts, I regret absolutely nothing about this afternoon.

He has no recollection of his mom, but I remember the way Ezra gradually closed off the longer he went without Sophie in his life. The past six months have been the worst I've seen him, and it's broken my damn heart to witness and be powerless to change things around.

That is, until today and the past hour we've spent in this old, borderline run-down garage.

Collins picks up a microfiber cloth and the pot of wax they were using earlier, handing them to Ezra when she reaches us.

She doesn't look at me, her attention solely on him. "I had a lot of fun today. You can come around and help me anytime you want."

His face illuminates like the goddamn Fourth of July.

Like I was saying, tornado.

TWELVE

COLLINS

An hour ago, I was sprawled across my couch, dressed in my favorite sleepwear and fluffy socks, with a bucket of sweet and salty popcorn and the original *Terminator* movie set to keep me company all night. But then Kendra called and asked what my Wednesday night plans were.

They were exactly as I just described them, but my closest friend had other ideas—along with a convincing plea—when she ordered me to "get dressed up" and come to a cozy cocktail bar on Smith Street because we were having an impromptu celebration for Darcy, her new job, and her newfound freedom from "Fuckface Liam."

At that point, I was in. Drinking to the demise of asshole men is one of my favorite pastimes. If anyone can relate to new starts and breaking up with cheating boyfriends, then it's me. Like I said, my Mike era was a waste of my early twenties and a mistake I've learned from when it comes to trusting guys.

Naturally, the boys are here, too, and the second I push through the door, my eyes instantly find the back of Archer's head. He tips his face toward the ceiling, laughing at something Darcy said as she sits next to him, perched on a barstool.

"Babe!"

I'm halfway to the bar when Kendra's voice stops me, and I spin around to find my friend, Jack, and Sawyer sitting around a table for six.

"Where's Jenna?" I ask, pulling out a chair and taking a seat, hooking my shoulder bag over the back.

Other than for the briefest of moments, I haven't looked at Sawyer, but I can sense his eyes on me.

"In France," Jack replies absentmindedly, picking up his beer and taking a pull.

Turns out, Sawyer isn't the only one staring since the Blades center can't tear his gaze away from the bar—or more specifically, his sister.

"Stop staring!" Kendra nudges her elbow into Jack. "They're just friends, and Darcy flies back to the UK tomorrow night. You can't blame them for wanting to catch up." On an eye roll, she sets her attention on me. "The Storm has a four-day rest period, and Jenna's brother has a big game in Paris. She flew over to watch him."

I nod once and pick up the cocktail menu, anything to prevent my eyes from landing on the one man I want to look at.

"He plays pro rugby, right?" I ask, fully aware he does since Jenna told me before. But again, anything to keep me distracted.

Jack wraps an arm around Kendra, pulling her into him and kissing the side of her head. She giggles, twisting her hand in his shirt.

"Yeah, plays in the Top 14 league." She pauses and eyes Jack with a playful smile. "He's pretty hot."

His attention immediately snaps from his sister to her. "I am here, you know."

He brushes his lips over hers, and they share a kiss that belongs in the bedroom. In a moment of weakness, I glance over at Sawyer.

My senses were right.

He's dressed in a gray henley with the sleeves rolled to his elbows. His enticing green eyes, framed by dark lashes, study me intently. I'm wearing the same dress as the night we hooked up, although it wasn't intentional. In a hurry to get changed and out the door, I grabbed my favorite outfit and threw it on, only to connect the dots halfway into town.

Sawyer picks up his pint and takes a large pull, condensation dripping down the glass and over his fingers. I know I could look away, focus on the drink menu in front of me. Yet I can't pull my attention from him, nor can I quell the familiar tingles as they dance across my skin.

It's likely only a second or two, but it feels like forever when Sawyer sets his drink down and points at the menu gripped in my hand.

He tips his lips up, harboring satisfaction at the effect he has on me.

Cocky asshole.

I'm half tempted to ask him if he enjoyed his snoop session in my garage and if he makes a habit of going through people's things in secret, but that would run the risk of having a conversation about my former motocross career—something I've buried in the back of my memory and not talked to anyone about. Not even Kendra.

"Are you planning on ordering a drink from that or just babysitting it all night?" Sawyer asks, dipping his head at the menu.

I narrow my eyes and push back my seat, breaking Kendra and Jack from their make-out session.

I look around the table, smiling sweetly at the broody captain opposite me. Injecting brightness into my tone, I say, "I'm going to grab a mimosa. Can I get anyone—"

"Yeah, I'll take another beer." Sawyer lifts his half-full glass from the table, taking another sip.

He never has two pints on a night out, but again, I think better than to admit I previously noticed that little fact about him.

"IPA?" I ask, maintaining my sweet smile and nodding at the brand stamped on his glass.

"Sure thing," he replies, reaching into his pocket—no doubt for his credit card.

But before he has time to hand me his Amex—and I assume it is black—I'm across the room with my bag and standing at the busy bar, a couple of people down from Archer and Darcy as they continue talking.

Five minutes later, I'm still waiting on service. There's a ton of people here tonight, but I swear some of them get served before me.

Lifting my arm, I wave my card in the air, determined to attract a bartender's attention.

"You look like you could use a little help."

When a tall shadow crowds me from behind, I close my eyes slowly. I've succeeded in my bid for attention all right, just not in the way I wanted.

Sawyer

To my left, I've got my center getting into it with his girl. Straight opposite me, I've got my goalie flirting like crazy with my center's sister. And in my hand, I've got my empty pint glass, ready to smash beneath the force of my palm.

Why?

Because standing maybe twenty feet away and with her back to me, I've got a pink-haired twenty-six-year-old Collins getting hit on by a good-looking guy who, I'm guessing, is a similar age to her.

I clocked him the second Collins reached the bar. Initially, he was sitting at a high-top table with some friends, but the minute he noticed her, he seized his opportunity.

At first, he was behind her, crowding her space and whispering something into her ear like a creep. Now, he's standing by her side, leaning against the bar and pretending like what she's saying is the only thing that has his attention.

For the past ten minutes, I've reminded myself I have no say over what she does, who she sees, and which bed she chooses to sleep in each night. I have zero hold over her whatsoever.

If she hates the attention this dude's showing her, she's doing a damn good job of hiding it. I'm not idiot enough to know Collins enjoys sex, maybe even the occasional fling with a guy. And since last November, it's only gotten more painfully obvious that she'll never be short of options.

Guys way younger than me—and likely more confident to make their move—will forever be at her disposal. It's not just the way she looks tonight in that hot-as-fuck dress she peeled off in front of me, nor is it the casual waves in her hair and striking makeup that draw the guys in. It's her demeanor. Her badass attitude and total self-control that make them—and me—putty in her hands.

He probably thinks he's breaking down her walls and getting to know her on a level that swings the pendulum in his favor for tonight—perhaps even a date, if he's lucky.

But he isn't.

I doubt Collins Mackenzie has ever let a guy see the real her —a tornado could never be that vulnerable.

Could she be vulnerable with me?

"You okay there, buddy?"

I glance toward Jack's voice, lifting the glass to my lips and forgetting it's empty.

Kendra's eyes dart to Collins, and she offers me a look that screams sympathy.

A sharp tug pulls in my chest, and I set the glass down on the table, exhaling silently.

"All good, just running over plays from this morning's practice," I lie.

Neither of them buys my bullshit, and honestly, neither do I as a long stretch of nothing passes between us.

"Fuck it."

In a single motion, my chair is across the dark wooden floor, my empty glass in my hand, and I swear to God, I hear a low cheer from Jack as I make a beeline for Collins.

"All okay, Baby Girl?" My voice is gruff but assured as I set my glass beside her and pray she doesn't kick me in the balls for the nickname.

Eyes wide and a perfectly manicured brow arched, she turns around to face me. I haven't even acknowledged the blond dude since I reached the bar, but I can feel the weight of his stare as I focus solely on Collins.

I can't make out if she's more pissed or shocked right now, but I can definitely tell she's both. And like each time before, her reaction fortifies my need, daring me to challenge her in the way I know she likes.

This girl doesn't want a man at her feet. She wants a guy who'll toss her around the bedroom and tussle for dominance.

"Is this your, er …"

"Boyfriend," I finish for the blond-haired guy as he shifts awkwardly next to us.

Collins's eyes drop to my hand as I wrap my palm around her hip, turning her to face me fully.

I know the sparkle in her eyes isn't from the twinkling lights pinned to the ceiling above us; it's fueled only by the charge we both feel when I touch her.

She lifts her gaze back to mine, and I watch the way her throat works on a swallow.

"I've been waiting on our drinks for a while," she finally says.

Without saying a word, the guy takes the hint and returns to his friends, pulling a smirk from me while I stare down at her.

She bites on her lip, a subtle flush warming her cheeks. I know she's fighting a smile, and I know a part—or maybe even all—of what just happened pleases her.

"You gonna beat on your chest like a caveman now?" she asks in a steady tone that's all fake.

I shake my head slowly—pleasure, satisfaction, and realization rolling through me.

I want this girl.

"Come home with me." The words hang between us, and my lungs tighten while I wait on her response. "We both know that wasn't the last time."

For a brief second, I see my need reciprocated in her expression, and then it's gone. As quickly as it appeared, she wipes it from her face, shutting me down in her trademark way.

Collins shrugs and breaks eye contact, attempting to garner a bartender's attention. "We can't sleep together again. It's not a good idea."

Despite the disappointment settling in my gut, I squeeze my palm still wrapped around her hip. "Give me one good reason why, Collins."

A staff member acknowledges her, gesturing to give him a minute, and finally, I have her eyes back on mine.

She blows a breath into her cheeks, another shot of vulnerability crossing her features. "Because I don't do sex when it can get complicated."

She reaches up on her tiptoes, and I lean down to meet her height.

Glossy lips tease the shell of my ear as she says, "And especially when that complication involves a man who I can tell wants more from me than I can offer. I don't know exactly where you expect this to go, but it doesn't involve catching feelings."

Satisfaction inflates my chest. It's the first time she's been truly honest with me, lowering her defenses even a fraction.

I lean into her ear, the charge between us at an all-time high. "Aren't you a little bit intrigued by this? I know I am. I want to know where this can go."

She shakes her head, dismissing the notion immediately. "We already turned that stone over. You're just horny."

"Maybe I am, and I don't see anything wrong with that. Are you horny, Baby Girl?"

She inches back from me, brown eyes narrowed at the nickname. "Yes. But it's nothing a toy can't cure."

My dick stirs. Images of Collins with a vibrator between her thighs is all I can see.

She drops her eyes to the front of my pants, releasing a satisfied noise. The sound only drives my need further.

"Come home with me," I repeat. "Let me be your toy. You can ride me all night and call all the shots on what we do."

She tenses, my suggestion turning her on. She's tempted—I can see it in her eyes, written across her face as she looks off to the side.

I'm so close to winning her over that I can feel it, the word *yes* balancing on the tip of her tongue, when Archer laughs loudly—a pop of reality snapping her walls back up.

"No," Collins denies me for a second time, though this response is even less convincing than the first. "Like I said, I don't think that's a good idea."

THIRTEEN

SAWYER

When I recall the worst games in my NHL career to date, I generally think about the ones played in Colorado.

As an athlete, my biggest weakness is—and likely always will be—my psychological approach. If I'm in a good headspace and locked in on the ice, it's all about the game and nothing else. Even if we're down by four in only the second period, it doesn't matter. I'm focused, never wavering from the task at hand.

Over the years, the team's psych has encouraged me to mentally prepare for games by running through my strongest performances, virtually playing out my best moves, passes, shots, and even hits. A lot of those moments have happened on the Philadelphia Bolts' home ice. I don't know why, but this arena brings me good juju. It was the first game I played where I felt a fraction of myself after Sophie's death. It's also a place where I've scored the most goals, and as a defenseman, that's the kind of shit you never forget.

Tonight, I'm playing on that exact ice, and we're up one, deep in the third.

No thanks to me.

This is not an away series I will remember, other than for the way my head has been firmly up my ass the past few days.

The puck spills from Jack when he's boarded by a Bolts defenseman. I just fucking stand there. I see it sliding toward me, but my skates don't move. Well, they do, but way too late and slowly.

Jack's one of the most chill guys I've ever played with, but even he's nearing the end of his patience when he throws his arms out just as the Philly center intercepts the puck and breaks for a turnover.

They score, drawing us level and ending Archer's recent run of shutouts.

He's pissed. I can feel his eyes as they bore into the back of my head.

As I skate off the ice for a switch-out, it's clear Coach is feeling the same kind of way, shaking his head as I flop onto the bench and remove my mouthguard.

With one eye still on the game, he turns to me. "The fuck is going on, Bryce?"

Would this be a good time to tell him I'm playing like shit because of a girl I can't get out of my fucking head?

She blew me off—for a second time. But unlike the first instance at Lloyd's last November, this isn't about my ego; my feelings run way deeper.

"Just not at it tonight," I groan.

Emmett, who got handed a penalty two minutes earlier—which didn't fucking help my cause—knocks on the plexiglass next to me.

What's going on? he mouths.

I shrug and turn back to Coach, who's looking straight at me.

"If I put you back out there for the final three minutes, do you think you can move faster than my gran?"

I deadpan, knowing he's not wrong. I've been slow as fuck.

"You're playing like you're carrying some kind of injury," Coach's tone is exasperated, reflecting how I feel.

With zero excuses and consequently no answer to his statement, I replace my mouthguard and stand, ready for the switch when his hand lands on my shoulder.

"I don't know what's going on in that head of yours, Bryce. But you're the captain, and you need to lead by example. That includes keeping any personal issues out of the rink."

News flash: they didn't stay out of the rink.

I played like shit, but somehow, Matt Rice—our assistant captain and winger—managed to bury an impossible slap shot, clinching the *W* we badly needed to keep our run of recent form going.

"Well played." Archer slides up to me as I pull off my left glove and shake hands with some of the opposing players I've known for seasons.

"You know they say sarcasm is the lowest form of wit, right?"

Archer chuckles from beside me, shaking the Philly coach's hand. He knows this team well and gets especially pumped for games here since this is his hometown and boyhood team.

"You cost me a shutout," he replies, voice playful, though I can sense his frustration. "What's going on, man?"

I stop partway down the tunnel as the rest of the team files into the locker room. I should be happy—even fucking relieved —that my performance tonight didn't cost us the game.

The tunnel is almost empty when I pause on chewing the corner of my guard and pull it out of my mouth completely.

"Collins," is all I say, uncertain of the best way to explain what's circulating in my head.

A rogue grin tugs at Archer's lips. Maybe he knew exactly what was going on. Maybe he tore his attention away from Darcy for a split second and clocked my hand on Collins's hip.

"What about her?"

I scrub a hand over my mouth, a brief wave of nausea washing through the pit of my stomach. "I think … I think I want her."

He shifts his weight, the same smile still across his face. "Tell me something we haven't already worked out. I could see that when she blew you off last November and again the other night."

He misses fucking *nothing.*

I pull off my helmet, scratching at the back of my neck. "No, you aren't listening. I *want* her. For more than sex. I'm really …" I fill my cheeks with air. "I'm completely into her. I can't stop thinking about her. My boy is enraptured by her, and, goddamn, man, so am I. I thought I could let it go, you know? Keep it together and not let feelings get in the way." I puff out a single harsh breath. "Seeing that guy with her the other night …"

"The blond dude?"

I nod once. "Seeing him make a move on her? I couldn't stomach the thought of her going home with him. I think … I think the only bed I want her in is mine."

Archer looks off to the side, discomfort painting his face.

I knew he wasn't the right person to talk to about this. Jack would've been my better option. Archer has never been into feelings, especially when it comes to women. He's a great guy and a damn good friend, but this kind of conversation just isn't in his wheelhouse.

"Shit, Sawyer," he replies, "I don't know what to say. Are you telling me you're in love with her?"

"No," I bite out, my frustration at this entire situation growing constantly. "I'm just saying, whatever I'm feeling, it's strong. When we hooked up, I had feelings. She was the first woman since Sophie that I really connected with on some kind of level and in a totally different way from what I've ever had before. She challenges me." I giggle like a fucking teenager. "You were right when you asked if we'd slept together that night I took her home. We did, and it was one of the best nights of my life. Not for her though. She told me I was an average lay."

His eyes shoot up before he doubles over with laughter. "Jesus, I would never fucking recover if any girl said that to me."

He laughs harder, and I wait—with added petulance—for him to stop.

"And after her saying that, you're telling me you've fallen even harder for this girl?!"

I offer him a tight smile. "Essentially, yes."

"Jesus. You really are fucked."

"Thanks. Really fucking helpful," I reply.

Archer's laughter calms. "What is this about Ezra? You said he's enraptured by her or something."

I think back to the meal at Jack and Kendra's and the look on his face. The sounds of his laughter and squeals as they filled the street with him riding on the back of her bike. The look on Collins's face at the table that night when I'd told Ezra we couldn't go over and again when I said he couldn't keep coming over to her garage. She wasn't just disappointed for him; she was genuinely gutted herself. I could see that. I could feel the warmth radiate from her.

"It's difficult to explain, but he comes alive around her. It's hard not to fall harder for the person who makes the world a better place for your child."

He's not a dad, but I know my goalie gets it.

"So, what are you going to do?"

I laugh without humor. "She doesn't feel the same way. It's likely she'll leave town in the next few months, maybe even weeks. If I carry on down this line, then I'm on a one-way ticket to getting hurt. Still, it didn't stop me from asking her to come home with me on Wednesday. I'd even posed as her boyfriend to deter the lecherous asshole from moving in on her."

Archer makes an agreeable noise, and it guts me.

He pauses briefly before speaking. "Total transparency. From what you're saying, I think your feelings are already at risk."

"So, what's your advice?"

He smirks in response. "Well, hopefully, mine is better than the gem you gave me about Kassie and Shane."

I roll my eyes and wait for him to have his moment.

"Tell her how you feel."

I shake my head, nausea rolling through me again. After Sophie, I made a deal with myself that it was just Ezra and me—a team. "I don't know if I can do that."

Archer lifts a brow, unconvinced I have a realistic alternative. "You think you get anywhere in life without taking risks? Of course you fucking don't."

He has a point, and ordinarily, I'd agree. But this doesn't feel like a risk, more like emotional suicide. Especially after Wednesday night's failure.

"I think you need to tell her," he reaffirms. "If she tells you to take a fucking leap, then, yeah, it will suck, but at least you'll have an answer." He pauses and eyes me carefully. "But I care about you, man, and this is cutting you up in some way. Also," he tags on, "I value shutouts, and that was a fucking shit show out there tonight. So, let's just say we're both fully invested in you getting your shit together."

FOURTEEN

COLLINS

CAMERON

Can you cover an extra shift this Tuesday?
Simon wants to take an extended leave.

ME

For his vacation in Mexico?

CAMERON

Yes. He's put a lot of extra overtime in recently,
and I think he could use the break.

With a raised brow, I type out a response to Head Dickface—the name I'd love to use for his contact, but unfortunately, it's too high risk that he might see it and fire my ass.

Simon has worked multiple double shifts, but so have I, though I don't see Cameron offering out extended leave to me. Maybe if I was still blowing him, it would be different.

I'd rather never vacation again in my life.

Besides, I could use the additional pay since the inheritance from my grandparents is almost gone and my savings is looking depleted.

ME

All right.

CAMERON

Cool. Will need to be a seven a.m. start since we're stacked the entire day.

Finger poised over my phone, I'm about to tell him I'll be there at eight and no earlier when my intercom buzzes, and I set my phone down and head for the door.

"Sorry, you likely have the wrong apartment," I immediately say. I'm not expecting any packages, and I rarely have visitors, aside from Kendra or Jenna.

"That would be impossible since I've already tried every other option."

I'm partway back to my phone when I spin on my heel at the sound of Sawyer's voice.

I race back over, my pulse kicking up a notch. "What are you doing here?"

There's a short pause before he speaks again, his voice unsure. "Trust me, I've been asking myself the same question for the past ten minutes. Can we talk?"

My best guess is, he's here about the photo album I caught him looking through when I took Ezra out on the bike or the way he posed as my boyfriend last Wednesday night.

I'm not as pissed about it as he maybe assumes—on both counts, that is. There are far worse pictures he could have found than a few motocross highlights.

And as for last Wednesday night … I push away the feeling that raced through my body and threatens to reappear at the memory of him claiming me in front of that overbearing blond guy.

With a shaky hand, I press the speaker, my heart still beating fast. "Is Ezra with you?"

"No. He's at school."

"You know, when I gave you my address, it wasn't so you could show up at my place, unannounced."

A heavy breath blows through the speaker. "Can I come in or not?"

On an involuntary grin, I press the button to buzz him in and unlock my door, pulling it open.

A few seconds later, Sawyer appears, dressed in a backward red Blades cap and training gear—which includes gray sweatpants—and white Nike sneakers.

Taking the stairs three at a time, he pauses when he reaches the top and finds me dressed in a long black Metallica T-shirt and sleep shorts, although he probably can't tell I'm wearing anything since they're basically hot pants.

Sawyer scratches at his temple. "I … ugh …" He trails off, eyes diverting to the floor.

"Assumed I'd be dressed?" I smirk, feeling exposed despite the fact that he's literally had his face between my thighs.

With restless eyes and hands, his cheeks pinken, the smattering of freckles across the bridge of his nose more prominent.

He shifts his weight and scuffs the floor lightly. "I wanted to talk about what happened."

I take a couple of steps back and hold my door open. "Are we talking about what happened in my garage or at the bar?"

"Both," he drawls, his Southern accent doing things to me.

"Well, let's discuss it inside, where half the building can't hear us and my nipples aren't in danger of cutting glass from the cold."

He flushes again.

God, this is way too easy.

Once inside, I guide us toward my simple but more than serviceable kitchen. With a butcher's block countertop and stainless steel shelving, it's not your regular kind of kitchen—way different from Sawyer's luxurious gray marble and polished cabinets.

He stops in the middle of the room and spins around to take my small open-plan space in. A black leather couch and TV sit in the only real living area I have, other than my bedroom and bathroom, which lead off to the left, although the doors to both rooms are closed.

He shoves his hands into his pockets, still unsure of what to do with them. He looks nervous, and I can't help but wonder if this is really about him snooping through a few photos or saving me from an asshole.

Taking pity on him, I grab my robe from the back of a chair —which is tucked under my small dining table for two—and throw it on. Though I'm not about to break the tension and speak first, I want to hear what he has to say.

After a long moment, his eyes connect with mine, his face a multitude of emotions. I hold my breath, even more curious about what's going through his mind.

"First, I wanted to say I'm sorry for going behind your back and looking through those pictures. I'm normally not the kind of person to …" He pulls off his cap, pushing a firm hand through his obviously unwashed hair before replacing it back on his head.

Why is that simple action so damn sexy?
Stop it, Collins.

"I'm not the type of guy to invade someone's privacy," he finishes. "Also, I wanted to thank you in person for the way you'd been with Ezra. I get you wanted us to keep our distance, and I genuinely didn't think he'd ever meet you, let alone become obsessed with you and your bikes." He laughs and pulls at the back of his neck, wincing. "When I say obsessed, I mean more curious and …" He releases his neck, and his hand slaps against his thigh.

I'd laugh if I didn't have secondhand cringe on his behalf. The guy can barely string three words together right now.

"Don't worry about the photos," I say, and his face immediately eases. "As for Ezra, I meant what I said—he can come around to my garage anytime he wants. I think it's great that he's so passionate about something."

Heat warms my chest at the memory of his excitement. He rode on the back of my bike like a pro, laughing and giggling with the wind whipping at his face.

Sawyer nods once. "I think that's why I'm shocked at the way he's rapidly developed an interest in, er … the bikes, not necessarily you. I mean, you're nice."

He huffs out a laugh and, honestly, I want the ground to open up and swallow us both.

"I get what you're saying," I offer.

Sawyer smiles, hands returning to his pockets. "You're nice to him anyway."

I quirk a brow and spin around to the coffee machine, pulling two cups from the shelf situated above it. "Since you showed up at the ass crack of dawn, how about a coffee?"

"It's nine thirty, not exactly early. I stopped by on my way back from morning skate."

I turn back over my shoulder. "Do you want one or not?"

"Yes, please," he replies, walking toward me.

I turn back away, the tingles I frequently fight to suppress showing up once more.

"I wasn't finished with what I came to say."

His hot breath tickles the back of my neck, and I pause on making the coffee.

"Go ahead," I breathe, hitting Start on the machine.

A coffee aroma filters into the space around us.

"Look at me, Collins," he says.

My pulse kicks up another notch, tingles invading all of me —from my fingertips to my toes.

A strong hand wraps around my hip. Through my robe and shirt, I shouldn't be able to feel the warmth of his palm or remember so clearly the last time it was there, holding me in place while he asked me to leave with him.

But I do.

"Look at me, Collins," his gruff voice repeats.

The coffee machine cuts off, and with his grip firmer, he turns me toward him.

We're close, our bodies inches apart. The tingles turn to an ache, settling between my thighs, and I hate that he has this effect on me. To the onlooker, I might be a little wild, but underneath, I'm always in control. Every guy I touch is safe, uncomplicated, and poses zero threat to the way I live my life. And consequently, my fleeting presence in theirs doesn't leave anyone hurt. I don't want to hurt this man—or his son.

Like he's pulling me in, my eyes lock with his, and we both breathe rapidly.

"What did you want to say?" I barely recognize my own voice, which sounds way higher than usual.

Sawyer's eyes flash to my lips and then back to mine. If he tried to kiss me, I'm not sure I'd be able to stop him. Though, since he thinks I don't kiss, I doubt he will.

The truth is, what I said that night was bullshit. I do kiss, and I've kissed a lot of guys over the years. It wasn't too personal because there were no feelings involved. Even after one or two dates and some sex, kissing them was just another act.

But kissing Sawyer, I know that would be different.

The kind of different that would make me wonder when he'd do it again.

The kind of different that made me back away at the bar.

"Let me take you out, Collins. I saw the conflict in you last Wednesday. You wanted to leave with me again, and I know, deep down, you want to explore whatever this is." His voice doesn't waver on a single word—a sharp contrast to the man who was falling over his sentences a few minutes before.

My head's spinning the second the request leaves his mouth. "I'm sorry, what?"

A tender smile traces his full lips. "You heard me, Collins. Let me take you out. For food, a movie, a motorcycle show, even for a walk somewhere. All I'm asking is for your undivided attention to be on me, just for a little while."

FIFTEEN

SAWYER

Other than at the bar last week, this is the closest I've been to Collins since I had her in my bed, naked and wrapped around me.

She still smells the same, and the way her chest moves rapidly fills mine with warmth.

I affect her.

I've always known that I had some kind of impact on her—the way her skin reacts beneath my touch, the brief flashes of vulnerability, the rise and fall of her chest. Even when she adjusts her collar as my breath tickles her neck.

"What do you say, hmm?" I ask, my face showing way more confidence than I feel.

Collins has said three words since I asked her out, and that was a request for me to repeat what I just said. A little like in the cocktail bar, I know I caught her off guard, and honestly, I like it. She hasn't had the time to gather herself and manufacture a witty response. The Collins in front of me is real, raw, and … fucking gorgeous.

Aside from the photos from when she was younger, this is the first time I've seen Collins without makeup. She's probably chalked my initial nerves up to the sight of her wearing only a T-shirt—and, yeah, it stopped me in my tracks. Her legs are just as I remember them—shapely and smooth, fair skin I want my tongue to explore all night. Though it's her natural beauty beneath the shine of a mid-November morning that really stole my breath, ripping it from my lungs as she stood at the entrance to her apartment.

The second I walked into her space, I was reeling, wondering which door her bedroom hid behind. How many guys have had the privilege of seeing her like this—all soft, bare skin and wild hair?

Turning up unannounced was a borderline dick move, but a little like my need to figure out this girl—beyond the flashes of real she shows me—I was powerless to drive straight home after skate. Archer's advice has been on repeat in my mind since the game against Philly, and now I have to shoot my shot.

The faint murmur of traffic is the only sound we can hear as Collins breaks eye contact, and I catch her chin, bringing her focus back to me. I'm so done with suppressing my urge for this girl, my need for her attention.

I don't know what this is between us, between her and my son. It's indescribable and more than I've felt in a long while.

"Are we talking, like, a date?" Her eyes reach mine on the final word.

I catch another glimpse of vulnerability as it passes through her. Ordinarily, I'd hate it. The thought of her feeling uncomfortable or exposed stirs a protective alpha feeling within me, one that lay dormant for years. Though, in this moment, I can't say the look in her eyes is one I don't welcome. I want her to be torn over spending time with me. I want more than the flat-out *no* I frequently hear.

Between my thumb and forefinger, I grip her chin more firmly. "You can call it what you like, Collins. Two friends hanging out or a date. I'll take whatever you give me."

She exhales slowly, chewing on her lip as she ponders a response. "I thought we agreed never again."

Just hearing her refer to that night pumps blood to my dick. The adrenaline surging through my veins urges me on, daring me to push this a little further. I want to test her, just like she does me.

I lean toward her, a smug grin pulling at my lips. "The only attention I get from you is the same kind you pay everyone else, probably even less. I want something from you that's just for me, and I gotta be honest, Collins—I think you do too."

Her head's spinning out—I can tell. I've switched from a guy falling over his words when he arrived to one holding her by the chin while he tells her what he wants.

"I think you're kidding yourself," she replies with confidence I know is fake. "I don't date."

"You do, Collins. You're just telling yourself you don't. It's all narrative, barriers, and bullshit. Plus, weren't you meeting a guy that night we first met at Lloyd's?"

Chin still in my hold, she rolls her eyes. "I met him at a bar with the intention of a hookup. And then I found out he was married and cheating on his wife." She pauses for a second. "Just your standard asshole guy, I guess."

"That's honestly what you think of us, isn't it? Either asshole or a crap lay—maybe both."

She shrugs, her trademark response hardening my dick.

"Stop shrugging," I demand.

She does it again and grins wide. "I'm sorry. I just love pushing your buttons. It's fun."

I lean in a little further, pleased when I see the way her skin pebbles. "I think you do it to distance yourself from me. It's a safety mechanism and your default setting."

I know I'm taking a huge leap—for myself and Ezra. A large part of me fears this could all end in disaster, though a smaller— and louder—part drives my actions to follow Archer's advice.

"I have to work early each morning," she replies.

"I can have you home well before bedtime."

She flushes at that, and I release her chin, my hands going straight to my pockets, curling into fists as I wait on her decision.

"Will you tell Ezra?" Collins asks.

"Why?" I question.

She twists her lips to the side as she looks away, and I let her have a second. I'm intrigued about everything that goes on in her mind, but especially now, when it comes to thoughts of my son.

"I'll go on *one* date with you, but I don't want to complicate things with Ezra. If I keep on the way I'm going, I'll be looking for a new job, likely outside of New York."

I hoped she would agree to a date, and I fully expected her to offer me only one. What I didn't anticipate was the way she'd prioritized my son in all of this.

I feel myself falling further, my lips desperate to touch hers.

The final words of her sentence sit less comfortably though. Thoughts of how temporary she likes to keep everything in her life stick in my throat. It's true; I don't know what this is between us—though I sure as shit wouldn't be putting myself on the line like this if it didn't feel real.

"What do you mean, *keep on the way I'm going*? Is something wrong?" I ask, expecting to be shut down straight away.

She blows out a short, sharp laugh. "Just me being me, pissing off bosses and generally being a pain-in-the-ass employee. Plus, rent's getting expensive here, so I'll probably give notice on the lease."

I can't tell if these are genuine issues or if she's already talking herself out of seeing me.

I opt to play it cool. "So, what I'm hearing is, you're not just a brat with me?"

The tension building between us is seismic, crackling each time one of us moves an inch.

"What I'm saying is, I'll go out with you, but I won't promise anything beyond that."

I work to keep my body language unaffected. "I can take us somewhere private so you won't be recognized or photographed."

She quirks a questioning brow. "If I cared about that anymore, I wouldn't have let you touch me or pose as my boyfriend last Wednesday night. Besides, if they catch a photo of us again, then I'm sure I'll be forgotten in a week or two."

I remain silent. I don't like the thought of this girl being forgotten, not one fucking bit. She's anything but forgettable.

"I guess this is what you have to ask yourself, Sawyer: are you okay with Ezra potentially seeing us alone together and asking you questions?"

He already has, right after he searched for your social media profile.

"If he sees something and asks, I'll tell him we're friends," I reply. "Because that's the truth, right?"

She offers a tight nod. "Yes."

Her breath fans my face, a familiar scent washing over me, fueling my desire to take her mouth and prove the bullshit in that statement.

We aren't friends.

"You have to protect Ezra first," Collins adds, softness in her eyes.

I have so much I want to say. I don't know if she's an only child. I don't know if she has any experience with kids or even wants them someday. But judging by the way she is with Ezra, she'd be a fucking great mom.

Ripping myself from unhelpful thoughts, I pull a hand from my pocket and test the water, grazing my index finger along the side of her hand.

"I'll pick you up on Tuesday at five. That way, you can be

home earlier, and I can get childcare for Ezra without him needing to stay over at his grandparents."

Collins opens her mouth, but quickly closes it, her thoughtful expression replaced with a familiar mischief. "You also don't want to stay up past your bedtime. I can't imagine how tired I'll be when I'm your age."

I narrow my eyes. "Are you saying I'm old?"

She rests a condescending palm on my shoulder, though the warmth in her features contradicts her actions, and I feel the connection she seems hell-bent on denying pass all the way through me.

"Yes, Sawyer. Yes, I am."

SIXTEEN

COLLINS

I'd say ninety-nine percent of the time, Head Dickface—aka Cameron—is full of shit. Unfortunately, just not today.

He wasn't kidding when he said the shop schedule was stacked, and to make everything worse, each bike I've worked on has been a shit show. I swear some of them haven't had a service in years despite what their owners said when Simon booked them in before he took leave—if he even asked, that is.

I've replaced three wrecked drive chains this afternoon alone, and by the corroded state of the one I'm working on right now, I'm guessing this will be my fourth.

Reaching into the pocket of my overalls, I pull out my phone and check the time.

Half past four. Shit. Sawyer will be at my place in thirty minutes.

My insides flip for the hundredth time since he asked me to go out with him a few days ago. Since my mouth ran away with itself and I answered yes, I've been countering anxious thoughts with the reassurance that this is the only time we'll go out.

You said no more when you slept together, and now you're going on a date with him.

Sawyer Bryce isn't your type, Collins. He's a family man. His brownstone home screams it, along with the old photos of him and Sophie posted online.

So, I had a snoop session too. Sue me.

"Collins, there's another customer out front. He needs you to look at the transmission shift," Cameron yells from his office, where he's been parked all day.

With the scissor lift still taken by another mechanic who doesn't really need it, I'm crouched by the wheel of the bike I'm servicing.

I spin on my heel to face Cameron. "I needed to be out of here, like, ten minutes ago."

His face is scornful as he rises from behind his desk and approaches, hands in the pockets of his freshly pressed pants, not an oil stain in sight.

"I need you until at least six." He thumbs over his shoulder toward the waiting customer.

I push down my anger, temptation to quit right on the spot dangling on the tip of my tongue. "Can't you take care of a transmission issue?"

Cameron flushes. Ah, yeah, he can't. Because he doesn't know a hydraulic fork from a brake cable.

"He specifically asked for you. Said a Reel you posted about this issue recently went viral and people were leaving comments, saying you worked here or something."

Yeah, I know; someone must've recognized the shop floor. I wanted to take the Reel down when I saw the comments, but others were finding it helpful, so I kept it going and figured it was too late anyway.

At least Cameron isn't pissed I used the garage to film in.

I stand, rubbing my oily hands down my thighs, and he tracks the movement, causing me to recoil.

I can't believe I slept with this guy.

"I have to leave," I reiterate. "I need to be somewhere."

Cameron narrows his eyes. "I said today was going to be stacked, and it is."

"Not my fucking fault you can't fix a basic issue or manage the staff schedule," I say to myself.

"I'm sorry. What was that?"

Maybe not to myself.

"Nothing," I snipe and reach for my phone. "I need to make a call."

When Cameron doesn't take the hint, hovering over me like a prison guard, I pull up Sawyer's contact and type out a quick text, a shot of disappointment hitting me.

ME

> Hey, look. I don't know if you're on your way to my place, but I'm not there. Can we reschedule?

It's barely twenty seconds before a reply arrives, the contact name I gave him making me smirk.

OLD MAN

> Where are you?

ME

> Stuck at work. It's crazy, and I'm the only one who can fix the bike that just came in.

OLD MAN

> I'll be there in ten.

Panic and those goddamn tingles shimmer through me simultaneously.

ME

> Wait. I just said we need to reschedule. I'll be at least another hour, maybe more.

OLD MAN

I can wait.

ME

How do you know where I work?

There's a long pause, maybe five minutes, and then my cell buzzes on the floor next to me just as I'm finishing up on the current bike, which, thankfully, didn't need a replacement drive chain.

OLD MAN

I just do.

ME

More snooping on me?

OLD MAN

Stop being a brat, or I won't take you where I have planned.

I catch myself grinning wildly at my phone, now alone since Cameron retreated to his office a few minutes ago.

ME

I'm not really at work. I just made up a lame excuse so I could avoid you.

OLD MAN

No one likes a liar, Collins. Now get on with your work so I can spend some time with you, just like you want me to.

"ESSENTIALLY, THE LINKAGE WAS MISALIGNED, WHICH WOULD

explain why you couldn't shift smoothly. I've adjusted it and run her through the gears, and I'd say she's ready to go."

Mr. Smith, the customer who follows me online and specially requested me when he came in, heaves a sigh of relief. "So, you don't think there's any permanent damage to the transmission or something more serious?"

I shake my head and lead him out of the garage, heading back to the service desk. "No. It was a simple fix in the end. I mean, any longer, and things could've gotten worse, but we caught it in time."

"That's great news," he replies. "How much do I owe you?"

I shake my head again and push through the door. "It was a ten mi—" I stop mid-sentence when my attention immediately lands on a broody hockey player sitting on a black plastic chair toward the back of the room.

With his left leg balanced on his right knee, Sawyer folds his arms across his chest, a smug grin playing on his lips.

He knows he looks hot. Black funnel-neck coat, black jeans, and dark gray sneakers. He's let the scruff across his jaw grow out a little, and as I approach the desk to finish up on Mr. Smith's paperwork, I push back thoughts of how it would feel between my thighs.

He might not be adventurous in bed, but he sure as shit can make me come on his tongue.

"You were saying how much?" Mr. Smith snaps me back into the room.

"Huh? Oh, yes. One second." I'm flustered, reaching across the desk and grabbing the nearest pen.

Signing off on the work, I take a quick glance at the dark-haired man standing in front of me. I can tell he's anxious over money, and the bike sitting in the garage is obviously his pride and joy. I wonder if being out on the open road brings him a sense of calm, like it does me. I wonder how far he traveled today to seek out my help.

I swipe a line through the total box. Cameron can go fuck himself. "No charge, sir. I'm only too happy to get her running for you."

Out of the corner of my eye, I catch Sawyer dropping his leg to the floor, bracing both elbows on his knees, watching intently.

I flush for no good reason.

"Are you sure, Collins?" Mr. Smith asks, looking unsure and hopeful at the same time.

"Ten out of ten," I confirm, folding the service invoice in half and placing it in an envelope.

"If you have any further issues with shifting, I suggest another adjustment to the linkage. It can take a couple of tries before getting it right."

I hand him the envelope, and he reaches out, taking it with gratitude before heading to the exit.

"Well, you have yourself a great day, miss."

"Were you supposed to charge him?" Sawyer asks the second the door closes behind Mr. Smith.

"Yes. But my boss doesn't need to know about it."

Sawyer rises from his chair and walks across to me, his smug grin more visible, along with the length of his scruff.

He isn't wearing a hat today, his glossy, dark hair begging for my hands.

"Do you ever play by the rules?" he asks, leaning against the counter.

I can feel the heat as it warms my cheeks. "Rarely."

An appreciative rumble emanates from his chest. "But you can be kind."

I throw him a questioning look.

"You could've charged him, but you didn't."

I'm not from a wealthy background. My parents died, leaving me with next to nothing, and the money my grandparents left was everything they'd had in the world, including a few pensions. But my family were good people, and my parents had scrimped and saved to pay for my expensive motocross habit. When my grandparents died and I was left alone, riding open roads was one of the only ways I could find peace, and when I was eighteen, I rescued my first Road Glide and carefully put her back together—a little like myself, I guess.

"Where's your head at, Collins?" Sawyer asks, now standing in front of me.

I was so deep in thought that I didn't notice him round the counter.

"I can be kind when I want to be," I breathe, instantly affected by his proximity and cologne.

His smile turns sweeter, although the playful edge remains. "How about you maintain your streak of kindness, grab your jacket, and let me take you out?"

I glance down at my overalls, and when I raise my eyes back to his, I see the desire behind them.

"Let me quickly change out of these and freshen up."

He reaches up and tucks a lock of hair behind my ear, the rough pad of his thumb grazing the shell.

"You do that. I'll go warm up my truck."

SEVENTEEN

SAWYER

JACK

All right, so I want to plan a house party to celebrate Kendra making Team USA. It's been a long time coming for her, and I can't let the moment pass silently.

ARCHER

Curious question, but is there anything you do silently?

JACK

All are invited, except Archer.

ARCHER

When you say "all," does this include your sister?

JACK

So, I checked with Jon, and he tells me they can call up the farm team goalie. Apparently, the death of ours won't be missed.

ARCHER

Taking the high ground. When is this party you speak of?

JACK

I'm thinking this Saturday since we head on a seven-day away series straight after.

JACK

And, yes, Archer, her entire football squad will be there for you to fawn over.

ARCHER

I've turned over a new leaf. Playboy days are behind me.

ME

The only thing he's turning over is your sister.

JACK

Yeah, Jon says we don't need our captain either.

On a chuckle, I briefly glance up at the entrance to Smooth Running, a good kind of anxiety swirling in my stomach. My right knee bounces beneath my truck's steering wheel as I wait for Collins.

ARCHER

picture of him shirtless and working out

JACK

I was about to ask if you guys wanted to meet at Rise Up, but I guess you're busy posting to your OnlyFans page, Archer. What about you, Sawyer?

This afternoon isn't a secret. Still, I haven't told anyone I'm taking Collins out. Likely because until I got here and saw her, I wasn't sure she wouldn't stand me up.

ME

I'm down for the party on Saturday. I can get a sitter for Ezra. I can't meet up right now though.

ARCHER

He's balls deep in Collins.

Manifesting that shit.

JACK

Wait, are you actually?

ME

No. But I am about to take her out.

ARCHER
HOLD THE MOTHERFUCKING PHONE.
JACK

Details, Sawyer. Immediately.

ME

You both need to calm the fuck down. I'm taking her to the Botanic Garden. It's stunning this time of year, and I figured it would be a good place to talk.

ARCHER

Best place to fuck is the Japanese Hill-and-Pond Garden. There's a large Acer tree by the lake and barely any footfall, even in the daytime.

JACK

You're unbelievable.

ARCHER

Thanks.

ME

I don't think that was a compliment. I'm not fucking anyone against any tree, especially one where you've been.

> I'm also regretting this entire conversation.

ARCHER

> If it helps, I fucked her on the ground. It was kind of romantic. The fallen leaves got in the way and into places they probably shouldn't …

JACK

> "Playboy days are behind me." Sounds likely.

ARCHER

> So, back to this party. Is your sister coming or what?

JACK HAS LEFT THE CONVERSATION.
ARCHER

> Did I go too far?

ME

> Obviously. I get we joke around, but you should let him know that you understand Darcy is off-limits. Now that she's single and moving to a strange country, he's probably feeling protective.

In my peripheral vision, a glass door swings open, and I catch Collins as she steps out of the building.

This girl is effortless, dressed in black from head to toe. Her tight jeans cling to her toned thighs as she heads across the parking lot toward my truck. She's wearing a fitted sweater and boots, finished with a fluffy scarf and a cropped leather jacket.

I wonder why she chose to dye her hair pink and not black. I know she's a natural blonde; it's obvious from the color of her eyebrows, although I couldn't tell from the rest of her body since she's bare below the waist—an image that's burned into my memory.

When she taps on the glass for me to unlock the truck and let her in, I hit the switch and shake off my daze, too busy reminiscing and fantasizing over the way she looks.

"You can put your tongue away. Old men who stare give me the creeps," she jests, lifting herself onto my passenger seat and dropping her mini backpack onto the floorboard.

I turn my body toward her, resting my forearm over the steering wheel. "Is this how it's always gonna be—gibing about my age every chance you get?"

Her eyes drop to the open text chat, my phone still in my hand. "If you're lucky enough."

I quickly lock my phone—after noticing Archer hasn't replied anyway—and pocket it.

Collins clips her seat belt and stares out the windshield. For a beat, I see unease in her eyes, and I follow her trail of vision.

Through the shop's glass windows, I see a dark-haired guy, likely in his mid-twenties, rounding the counter and taking a seat at the front desk. He's dressed like a manager.

"Is that your boss?" I ask cautiously.

She rolls her lips together. "Yep. Cameron—aka Head Dickface."

I blow out a single laugh. I shouldn't be surprised at the nickname. This girl probably has one for me too. "You like him then?"

She shoots me a look of disdain. "I slept with him before he got a promotion, and now it's awkward as fuck."

The second Collins says it, her face drops like she knows she shared too much.

Every muscle in my body contracts—jealousy, hurt, discomfort, white-hot anger surging through me. Did she compare him to me? Has she been with him since that night we were together? Fuck, is she dating other people right now?

My best efforts to disguise the abundance of emotions roaring through me fails, and I close my eyes slowly, my forearm slipping down the steering wheel until its firmly gripped in my palm.

"Sawyer, look at me," Collins says quietly, her voice way softer than normal.

"I'm good," I lie. "This probably isn't even a real date. You should be able to talk to your friends about other guys."

And now I'm voluntarily friend-zoning myself.

A warm palm lands on my right thigh, and I slowly open my eyes at the feeling of her touch—one I find myself craving way too often.

"Look at me," she repeats, reminding me of the time I asked her to do the same in her apartment.

I do as she asks and see nothing but kindness.

"There's nothing going on between me and Cameron. There never was. He's a dickhead to me and I probably accept more than I should because I love working with bikes. I have zero interest in ever going back there with him."

This time, I'm slammed with a tidal wave of relief, followed by intensifying anger. "What do you mean, he's a dick to you?" I half growl, my dormant alpha male further stirring to life.

She grins, and I can't work out if it's because she likes my protective nature or if she enjoys seeing me wound up, period. "You don't need to defend me or anything."

"On the contrary." I bristle. "I defend people I care about, whether I'm dating them or not."

Eyes wider than before, Collins goes to reply, but then stops.

I shift the truck into gear, thinking better than to say any more. Still, I'm not retracting my comment because I mean it. I do care about her. I care if someone's mean to her or treats her like shit. No one gets to do that. She might be hard on the outside, but I'm slowly seeing all the softness that lies beneath the impermeable exterior she portrays.

"Where are you taking me?" she finally asks as I pull out of the lot and onto the road.

"Ever been to the Botanic Garden?"

She shakes her head. "No. Is that where we're headed?"

I take a left. "Yeah. We should catch the light as it fades behind the trees. It's really pretty this time of year. Then I got us tickets to the opening night of the light show they hold each year."

She smiles, one that's sweet and all warmth. "I only have this thin jacket and scarf."

Taking another left, I side-eye her carefully, unadulterated satisfaction purring through my veins. "Guess you'll have to use one of my Blades jackets I keep in the trunk."

I expect her to kick back against the idea, but she doesn't as she turns to look out the passenger window, daylight already starting to fade.

Something shifts between us—I can sense it as it settles inside my truck. Acceptance, comfort, maybe even a silent admission that she likes me on a deeper level. The idea of Collins wearing my jacket is simple and hardly a big commitment, yet it feels seismic, and I feel borderline adolescent as the visual of her wrapped in something that carries my scent plays out in front of me. I already know which jacket I'm going to pull out—the one I frequently wear to early morning skate. A couple of hours of her wearing that should keep it smelling like her for weeks as I drive to the rink at the ass crack of dawn.

In spite of the warmth that fills my chest on the drive to the garden, I can't shake the underlying knowledge that, in all likelihood, this is temporary. Collins, in my truck, riding and spending time with me—it's all subject to a time limit.

Her priority is living her life and doing all the things that make her happy, and I can't say I blame her for that. I guess we only live once.

I only wish that priority included me.

EIGHTEEN

COLLINS

O h Jesus, fuck, he smells good.

Did I secretly hope he'd lend me his jacket?

Yes.

Am I pissed at myself for being so weak?

Also yes.

It smells like his bed, all Sawyer and fresh cologne. I've witnessed other women talk about "man smell" and how it drives them wild, although I never understood what they were talking about. That is, until I got too close to the Blades captain. And now I'm wearing his jacket, his initials stamped across my chest.

Standing at the rear of his truck, I focus on the zip, entirely too distracted by my heightened senses to realize part of the lining is caught, and that's why it won't budge.

"You need some help with that?" He points at where I'm struggling.

I haven't looked him in the eye since we arrived at the Botanic Garden, and I'm all kinds of off my game. This is not my usual MO. Collins Mackenzie is self-assured and calm in most situations. The last time I can remember feeling like this was when Gretchen Roberts stole the SuperMini World All-

Stars title from underneath me on the final turn of the final race.

"I got it." I fuss, pulling on the zipper that just—won't—fucking—*zip*.

"Here, let me help."

The instant Sawyer's warm, rough fingertips touch mine, I pull away, the back of my knees hitting the truck bumper.

"I said, I got it," I bite out, pissed at myself for being so snappy when all he wants to do is help.

In a move I really wasn't anticipating, he steps forward, hands finding mine once more.

I catch a softness in his green eyes, brows slightly raised in question. I don't flinch or try to move away as he frees the zip and starts fastening the jacket, his hands over mine as they slowly ascend my chest.

Since the Botanic Garden has an event tonight, there are a few people around us, but I don't concentrate on anything other than the feel of his skin on mine. I think that was what surprised me the most the night we hooked up—how my skin could vibrate with such intensity without the need for the usual toys I liked.

These past five weeks since I left his place in a hurry, I've been proactively suppressing—and avoiding—situations like this. Yet now, I get the feeling Sawyer isn't going to back down so easily, and that thought catapults a shot of need in me that I can't deny.

"Are you going to chase me down until you get what you want?" I whisper, my throat tight.

The zip was fastened a good few seconds ago, though Sawyer holds his hands over mine.

His eyes fall to my lips. "Is that what you want, Collins?"

My breathing is shallow and quick. "You can't ask me impossible questions like that."

He bites down on his plump bottom lip, and I'm unsure if

he's fighting the urge to kiss me or smile. "Now you know what it feels like."

"What do you mean?"

His hands leave mine, finding the back of my thighs, lifting and perching me on the end of his tailgate. I want him to step between my legs and kiss me. Every single fiber in my body wants it. Even if I know it's a really bad idea.

Sawyer's eyelids fall shut, and he exhales deeply. "Because I feel like I'm in an impossible situation with us—I'm chasing you even if you don't want me to." He opens his eyes, nothing but honesty behind them. "When I asked you to come home with me a second time, it wasn't purely so I could wrap you around me again. At the risk of repeating myself, all I want is your time and attention, all to myself. At first, it was a fascination with the pink-haired girl who had said I wasn't her type. And now … now it's a need, Collins. So, yeah, I'm going to chase you because I have no choice."

I want to run my palms across the scruff of his jaw, pulling his face closer to mine.

"And what would you consider a successful catch?" I ask, ears throbbing with my pulse.

Sawyer takes the smallest step back, hands finding his pockets. He looks uncomfortable at my question, maybe because he doesn't think I can cope with his potential response. "That's enough questions for now. Come spend some time with me."

OKAY, SO THE BOTANIC GARDEN IS STUNNING.

And incredibly romantic when lit up in this way. The trees twinkle with warmth, the lake glows red, and even some of the pathways are lit by dancing multicolored lights.

"Is my jacket doing the job?" Sawyer asks as we pass under a long tunnel wrapped in white string lights.

We've been here around an hour, and night has completely fallen. Despite me saying I wouldn't be bothered if he was recognized with me, I am grateful for the darkness, as it camouflages us far better than if we were here in daylight.

I snuggle further beneath my scarf, Sawyer's scent penetrating it as we continue to walk around the Japanese Hill-and-Pond Garden.

"It is. Thank you," I reply, pockets of air puffing into the atmosphere as I speak.

I look across at Sawyer, and he smirks.

"What?"

He shakes his head as we come to a stop by a huge Acer tree, this particular variety I know to be rare. I didn't go to college, and I don't have a fancy education, but Japanese culture—and food—is something I have studied in my own time.

He glances at the tree, shaking his head. "Nothing. Just something Archer said earlier."

I quirk an inquisitive brow. "You guys were talking about the Acer tree?"

"Not exactly." He winces and takes a seat on a white bench a few feet down from the main pathway. The position provides a view of the lake as a color-changing cycle begins, lighting the water in a beautiful way.

There's a comfortable silence between us that doesn't scream to be filled with small talk. Perhaps it's the calm environment, or maybe it's the company. I don't know, but I feel the urge to do something alien.

Share.

"The year after my grandparents died, I visited Tokyo. It was only for two weeks, but I feel like it changed me."

Sawyer twists his body completely around to face me. "In what way did it change you?"

I smile at the memories. "For a young girl, I'd traveled around the US a lot and then to a few other countries." I eye him carefully. "I used to compete in motocross at a high level."

Sawyer rolls his lips together. None of this is new to him, of course.

"But the traveling combined with an expensive sport took every last cent my parents had." I cast a quick glance at the lake, now glowing pink. "Mom and Dad always wanted to visit Japan. Dad had this obsession with their culture and history, but mainly the food." I chuckle, remembering the times he tried to make sushi and failed.

"When they passed away in a car accident, they didn't leave a lot behind since they'd had debts up to their eyeballs and our house was a rental, all because I'd been hell-bent on pushing my obsession with motocross, desperate to be number one."

Sawyer doesn't say a word. I can feel his eyes locked on me as I look out onto the lake.

I clear my throat of emotion. "Anyway, after they died, I quit competing and sold all my equipment. I resented the sport and how much it—and my all-or-nothing attitude—had taken away from them, including my dad's wish to visit Japan one day. From that moment on, I promised myself I wouldn't take life too seriously, and I *definitely* wouldn't take it for granted. Life is too short to be stuck in one place, grinding away at the same nine-to-five job. I designed my life specifically around freedom and the ability to up and leave whenever I wanted. When my grandparents died and left me a nest egg, I went about making the most of the life I wanted to lead and never looked back."

A couple more seconds pass in comfortable silence.

"Look at me, Collins," Sawyer eventually says, his voice firm but gentle.

"You always say that," I reply, doing as he asked.

"That's because you rarely do."

I fight back the shrug I always seem to give him since I have no damn clue what to do when he's around.

"When was the last time you shared yourself with another person like that?"

Don't. Fucking. Shrug.

"I can't remember. Kendra probably knows the most at this point, but I didn't tell her everything about me and never about my past in motocross. I've always struggled to open up and especially about my younger self. I was a selfish kid and I'm not proud of it."

Sawyer edges closer to me; I'm unsure if it's deliberate, but I like the way it makes me feel.

"The only person I see in front of me is a good one. Thank you for sharing with me."

His warm breath reaches my face, tickling my lips, and I wet them on reflex.

"I'm not unhappy, you know. In life. I'm probably happier than most people." I've zero idea why I feel the need to qualify it, but the words tumble from me regardless.

He cocks his head to the side, studying me in a way that's hot as fuck. Like, in this moment, I'm the only person who exists in his world.

"I can't imagine choosing to be solitary is a happy place, but if you say so."

I mirror his actions, cocking my head too. "Does that mean you're unhappy? There's only you and Ezra."

Sawyer shakes his head, a tender smile in response to his son's name. "I'm happy, but I never discount the opportunity for my life to get better, feel fuller."

Since I shared a part of my past with Sawyer, I find myself wondering why his blood family isn't more involved in his and Ezra's lives. Did they die, like mine? Really, it's his private business. But like a lot of things with this man, curiosity gets the better of me.

"How come you don't see your parents?"

He draws in a deep breath. I wouldn't say thoughts of his family hurt him, but by the look on his face, there's a lot of emotions going on right now.

"Let's just say, my family isn't exactly close. I don't really talk to my mom, dad, or brother who still live back in Louisiana, where I'm from. I didn't have a terrible childhood or anything like that; it was more a case of being detached. They didn't come to my ice hockey games. They weren't interested in supporting much in my life. They'd prefer to go out with friends or on vacations."

He drops his head, and I can tell whatever he's about to admit is hurtful to him.

"My older brother is an asshole who got involved with some bad crowds, and my parents don't make an effort for anyone but themselves. When I moved out for college, they never really called me or asked how I was doing. I guess you could say I'm just used to going it alone. When Ezra was born, Sophie and I tried to rekindle a relationship with them so they could see him. It didn't work, and they let us and Ezra down multiple times. That's when I called it completely and said *never again*."

To my surprise and despite what he's saying, Sawyer smiles. "Dom and Alyssa are more like the parents I didn't really have. I guess I found my own family in them."

I nod along, feeling and understanding all Sawyer's saying. Perhaps we're alike in more ways than I first thought—though our circumstances are different, we're both without our blood parents.

I look out onto the lake, feeling a sense of hurt on his behalf. "I'm sorry your family wasn't what you deserved. People can let you down when you need them the most."

"Is that why you don't kiss? Fear of growing attached and being let down?" he asks quietly.

The immediate need to shut down this conversation swells in my gut.

"I do kiss."

His brows knit together, blue lighting cast across the lake glowing on his high cheekbones. "Just not me then."

He hasn't forgotten a moment of what we said or did that first night we hooked up, has he?

I pull in a breath. "I can't sleep with you or kiss you, Sawyer. I …" I trail off, panic rising.

He edges closer on the bench. His hand sliding down the back until it's only millimeters away from my shoulder.

Sawyer reaches up, cupping the side of my face in his palm. I know my cheek is cold, but it burns from his touch.

"Hand over a little of that control, Baby. You can trust me with it."

Another inch closer, and I'll be doing just that—kissing him.

"Aren't you scared?" I ask. "You've lost people too. You could start falling for me, and then I could just up and leave."

"Oh, Baby Girl." He runs the callous pad of his thumb across my bottom lip, smiling knowingly at me. "For a girl who thinks she has it all worked out, you just don't get it, do you?"

Even if I wanted to reply, I couldn't.

Sawyer closes the remaining distance between us, whispering against my lips, "I already am."

Just like I knew I would, I let him kiss me. Every single bone melting until I can't be sure I'm upright.

His hand slides further along the bench until it leaves the wooden frame and wraps around my shoulder, pulling me into him.

This kiss is sweet with no tongues, a dance and test of each other's limitations. Or maybe just mine. But I know what I want, even if a part of me screams to ignore it.

A whimper races up my throat, the appreciative sound urging

him on. His smooth tongue lightly traces the seam of my lips, and I part for him like a goddamn river breaking its banks.

Sawyer smiles into the kiss, satisfied with how easy it was to have his way with me.

I pull away from him, chest heaving, blood pumping, tingles everywhere—especially between my thighs. "You see, this is exactly what I mean. Kissing you is dangerous."

A soft laugh bubbles from him, and he ducks his head, kissing the underside of my jaw. "I want to do a lot more than just kiss you."

I feel my thong grow damp. "You know we can't do that."

He kisses my jaw again. "For the same reasons you told me we couldn't kiss?"

I feel my defenses fly up. I need to shut down this conversation before it ventures into unsafe territory like discussing the feelings I know I'm rapidly developing for this man. "No. Because last time was only above average." I blurt out in a panic.

He looks hurt, and I hate that.

"I was more than a six, and you know it."

Shaking my head, I shuffle a centimeter away from him. "No, that was the truth. It was … vanilla?"

Sawyer narrows his eyes. "You're being totally serious, aren't you?"

I nod once, despising my response. My hesitancy to sleep with him again isn't centered around his abilities in bed, and I know it. There's only one way I'd let Sawyer take me back to bed, and that's if feelings weren't involved for him and Ezra wasn't at risk of getting pulled into it. The worst-case scenario would be him seeing us in a compromising position and wondering if I was his dad's girlfriend after all. I could never do that to him or Sawyer.

Regardless of my nod, Sawyer looks determined, reaching out and twisting a lock of my hair around his finger. "Hypothetically speaking, if we slept together again, what would you want me to do?"

Oh Jesus.

The ache in my core borders on unbearable, and I bite my lip, trying to center myself.

"I guess, first, I'd like you to not fall any further for me. Sex, combined with emotions, makes things complicated."

He visibly deflates, and I feel shitty for it.

"So, you only want a no-strings type of arrangement?"

"Yes. I think you're hot as fuck, and I can show you what I like in bed. But for everyone's sake, this can only be about sex. If you don't think you can do that, then I get it."

Sawyer's eyes search mine—pain, frustration, annoyance, and then acceptance passing through them like a carousel. "If it were only me, I would risk my feelings to be with you in any way you wanted. This isn't just about me though, and I can't only think of myself; I have to think of my son too. He's perceptive—maybe more than I've previously given him credit for— and I don't want to sneak around behind his back. If we were just fuck buddies, that's what we'd have to do." Sawyer tucks the piece of hair he was playing with behind my ear. He doesn't look certain of his next words, an internal war taking place in his mind. "And I don't think I can do that."

I don't reply because there isn't anything else to say. He's right. The cold facts are here, between us, swirling in the freezing Brooklyn night sky.

This is the right decision.

This is for the best. For me, for Sawyer, and especially for Ezra.

I'm not mom material; I can barely hold down a job, for Christ's sake.

My time in New York was slowly coming to an end anyway, and this way, no one gets hurt.

So, why does it already feel like I am?

NINETEEN

SAWYER

It's been three days since I dropped Collins off at her place and watched as she disappeared inside her building.

I guess I should've seen it coming when I asked her on a date. Getting my hopes up for more than a few hours in her company was ill-advised and fucking naive. Not once had she ever led me on or given the impression that she wanted a relationship. Still, all I needed was for her to relinquish even a modicum of control and trust what I knew we both wanted.

When I had started dating Sophie, I was in my early twenties and a little like Archer is now—into parties and various women. I hadn't expected to find someone special, but then—bam—I met her one night, and we hit it off in a way I'd never experienced. Our conversations were free and easy, and to my surprise, we both wanted the same thing—a relationship and to see where it took us.

A year later, we were married, and my life had done a complete one-eighty in all the best ways. I had a family in Sophie, including Alyssa and Dom.

When Sophie died, I grew bitter toward the concept of love and a happily ever after. The closest I got to witnessing it was through Kendra and Jack. Those two are meant for each other, like fated mates. I guess I always believed there was one person out there for you, a single personality that matched yours perfectly, like unique puzzle pieces slotting together. And if for any reason you were torn apart, that was it. That was your one chance, gone forever.

That November night, I wasn't looking for anyone. Dating just wasn't in the cards for me and especially not with a girl who —in any way, shape, or form—was the complete opposite of Sophie.

Collins has repeatedly told me I'm not her type—despite the fact that she finds me attractive. But the truth is, up until last November, she wasn't mine either.

Until she was.

With her bratty mouth and free-spirited attitude compared to my calm demeanor and family-oriented life, she thinks we're incompatible and doesn't believe two people so opposite could work out. Granted, she hasn't said those words out loud to me, but I can tell that's where her head's at.

The truth is we fit together perfectly. We already proved it.

That one kiss confirmed everything. Even if she wants to deny it, she can't. I have *never* shared a kiss like that before. The kind of kiss where you can't figure out if it's real or fantasy. The kind of feeling that lasts a lifetime but is over way too soon and you search for the next opportunity to experience it.

When she parted her lips, I felt more in a single stroke of my tongue against hers than I'd thought a brief second in time could offer.

And I know she felt it too.

I told her I was falling because I couldn't lie, and the moment those words left my mouth, I expected Collins to freak out. I pictured her expressions playing out like a visualization exercise with my sports psych. I saw none of that though—no horror, no panic, not even a flinch—when she let me take her mouth with mine so I could show her just how much I was feeling.

Right now, I should be gutted at her rejection, but I'm not. No-strings sex is the opposite of what I want with Collins and I know that's not what she wants either.

She asked me if I was going to chase her, and I told her I already was.

Nothing about that statement has changed for me. A fuck-buddy arrangement isn't going to cut it.

All I need to do is I show her how it could be between us.

And I absolutely fucking will.

I don't think Collins has ever had a guy put her at the center of his world, and maybe that's why she's never felt the pull to stay in one place for longer than a short-term rental agreement.

I want that to change, and I want to be the reason for it. All I have to do is figure out a way to show her that once she drops her anchor somewhere, it's okay to let it bury itself in the seabed and take root. It's okay to stand on the shore and watch the tide go out. Sometimes, the biggest waves and the best rides aren't always the ones taking you out to sea.

"You realize there's an entire gym full of equipment, right?" Jack strolls over to where I've been pounding the treadmill for the past forty minutes.

Deep in my own thoughts, I lost track of time.

I reach out and slow the program to a fast walk, sweat dripping from my forehead and onto the track below.

I don't reply as I lift my Gatorade from the cupholder, taking a large pull before setting it back down.

"You also realize it's okay to not wear a shirt when you work out?" He continues talking, inspecting my soaked white Dri-FIT. "Your shirt is pointless since I can already see your nipples."

The treadmill slows to a cooldown pace, and I draw in a deep breath, concluding I've likely gone too hard for what was supposed to be a light conditioning session.

"So, we going to talk about Tuesday night, or are you going to keep us all hanging?" Jack asks right as Archer sidles up beside him, also not wearing a shirt.

With his drink bottle, he points at my chest. "You know that shirt is covering nothing, right?"

I hit Stop on the program and huff out a breath, ripping the shirt over my head in one motion. "Here. Now you have a better view."

They both smirk like two bratty adolescent twins.

"I didn't come over to admire your torso, impeccable as it is. I heard the words *Tuesday night* and took it as my cue to join the conversation." Archer leans toward me like it's classified information. "Give us the details. Did you f—"

"No, I didn't fuck her by, against, beneath, or anywhere near the tree," I drawl. "We did talk though."

"Annnnd?" Archer motions his hand in front of him, asking for more details.

I scrub a palm over my face and step down from the treadmill with my towel and shirt, wrapping them around the back of my neck. Then I grab my bottle of Gatorade. "And we kissed," I confirm.

I swear I hear a muted shriek of delight from Jack.

"Right before she told me she was down for a no-strings arrangement and nothing more."

"Nice." Archer nods. "An ideal situation."

I deadpan, "Did you hit your head on something and completely forget our conversation last week?"

"Are you gonna go for it then?" Jack cuts in before Archer can respond. "The fuck-buddy arrangement?"

I shake my head and walk over to the Olympic bar. Archer drops his bottle and automatically gets in position to spot me.

"Nope."

Throwing my bottle, towel and shirt on the floor next to me, I complete the first rep, holding the bar above my head for a couple of seconds.

"I'm not going to sleep with her again until she admits she wants more than just sex."

I complete the next rep, and Archer takes the weight, allowing me a chance to look at my center.

Eyes wide and a hand cupping his jaw, Jack waits for me to continue.

I sit up on the bench as Archer drops the bar back onto the rack.

"The kiss was … it was pretty fucking special, and I'm not about to walk away from something like that. I'm not moronic enough to do that."

"Do you think she feels the same?" Jack asks, expression full of concern, and I know it's for me and because he cares. "If she told you she didn't want to get into anything after you kissed, then is there a chance she doesn't feel the same?"

"I also told her I was falling, and she didn't freak out at that. In fact"—I rub my palms down my black athletic shorts—"that was right before we kissed."

"So, you think she's playing hard to get?" Archer says, coming to stand in front of me.

"Nah. She doesn't know what to do with it—with the fact that I want her and she wants me. It's all alien to her." I release a deep chuckle and pick up my Gatorade, taking a sip. "Hell, this feels alien to me. I haven't felt like this since …" I trail off.

"Sophie?" Archer finishes for me.

I nod once. "Yeah."

Jack scratches at his chest. "So, what are you going to do?"

My cheeks ache from the smile spreading across my face, and they both mirror my expression.

"What any decent guy who wants a girl would do—engineer as many opportunities as possible to show her why I'm exactly what she wants but is denying."

Jack raises his brows, excitement rolling off him. "Can we be of any help with your plans?"

I push a hand through my damp hair, thinking over my options. "Do you know if Collins is coming to the game tomorrow night?"

"I don't know," he replies. "But I can make it so that she does."

Ezra rarely comes to the arena anymore, although he does like going to the Scorpions games since they're our rivals and fights usually break out on the ice—the perfect opportunity for him to wave his foam finger around. Because Dom's a sucker for a rivalry, he and Alyssa will no doubt come along and Ezra stays with them on game nights anyway. Last-minute tickets to the family box are easy to secure when you're the captain.

A part of me feels uneasy about him seeing Collins, but he also thinks we're friends—at least I hope we're that right now. If she vanished from his life completely, he'd ask questions and likely be hurt. Plus, I know she'd miss him too. And those thoughts drive me forward.

"Okay, great," I reply. "The plan is to clinch the *W* on the ice and head to Lloyd's straight after."

TWENTY

COLLINS

Since the Botanic Garden, nothing has felt the same.

The more times I replay the conversation between us, the harder it is to convince myself that the way things ended that night was right.

Walking away from a guy shouldn't be this difficult, especially when we were nothing in the first place. We're just friends.

Keep telling yourself that, Collins. Friends don't kiss on benches by the lake, and a friend definitely shouldn't make you feel the way Sawyer did with a single stroke of his tongue.

He wants more, just like I knew he would. He wants commitment and long evenings of cuddling in front of a movie. He wants cocoa on cold days and snowmen built in the backyard on wintery mornings.

He wants a woman—not to replace Sophie, but to play a motherly role in Ezra's life.

Each time I'm in his presence, I can't help but feel like a life like that might be something I want, too, especially if it was with someone like Sawyer. But the pressure to offer him that kind of stability—a permanence I've spent my adult life resisting because, inherently, that just isn't me—causes me to pull back every time we get close.

Maybe it's right person, wrong circumstance. I don't know. I've considered the possibility that, one day, I'll look back on my life, alone and old, and regret the decisions I made when I was younger.

But if I get involved with Sawyer and Ezra and ultimately get cold feet, I know I'll regret hurting them more.

So, why is this fucking difficult? I'm a lone wolf; it's what I'm used to. And why does the thought of Sawyer eventually meeting a woman who gives him everything I know he wants hurt in a way I never expected it to?

Because he isn't the only one who's caught feelings.

When he pulled up outside of my place to drop me home on Tuesday, I hesitated in the silence before I reached for the door of his truck.

Right there, on the tip of my tongue, were the words I so badly wanted to say. *You want to come upstairs?*

They were the hardest words to swallow down. Five words that gutted me when they reached the pit of my stomach. I knew if I asked him, he'd say yes, but only under the condition that we gave us a go officially.

When I turned to leave, he grabbed my left arm, swiveling me back around to face him. Of course, we'd see each other again, but never in the same way. This chapter between us was finished before it got started.

And that was all because of me, and the way it hurt was only made more painful by the kiss I'd promised we'd never share, but I went ahead and let him anyway, even after he admitted his feelings.

He wanted to know what I liked in bed; he wanted to see that part of me, the part I was convinced he'd hate. Though now, all I can think about is the way I'd take us both to the brink of ecstasy and how amazing it could be, if that kiss was anything to go by.

The absolute best thing to do would be to stay away, to see Kendra, Jenna, and Darcy away from the rest of the friend group. To do what I do best and drive distance between myself and my feelings. I can even quit the job I know I'll likely lose anyway and move to New Jersey—a place I've yet to visit. Hell, I can even head to Europe, or go back to Japan, or maybe even give Australia a try.

I could be in so many different places right now; still, I'm not. Because sitting in this family box, next to a twelve-year-old boy who is fast turning into my best friend, and watching the Blades host the Scorpions is exactly where I want to be.

Last night, while I was curled up on my couch, watching *Stranger Things* and eating my body weight in comfort snacks, Kendra called, demanding I got to the next game so she could see me.

This girl has a habit of dragging my ass out to places.

She was likely expecting an excuse. Instead, she got a Collins she never knew existed. The dam walls broke, and I sobbed into my corn chips and dip. I told her everything—from the kiss to what I'd said when he asked me to give us a shot.

I don't know if Sawyer knows I'm here, sitting next to his son and former in-laws, and I don't know how he'd feel about it either.

He'd probably be pissed at me for spending more time with Ezra and meeting his family when I told him I couldn't have a relationship with him.

The game is one to one and deep into the first period when Ezra taps me on the shoulder, a foam finger on his other hand. "If you could only pick one, would you want my dad to lift the Stanley Cup, or would you want a brand-new Harley delivered to your garage, free of charge?"

I lightly drum my fingers against my bottom lip. It's a genuinely tough decision. "What model and color are we talking about?"

In the past half hour since we all sat down for the game, Ezra has told me stuff about bikes I never knew myself. According to Alyssa and Dom, he's switched out Fortnite for motorcycle magazines and has an obsession with the latest biker documentary just released on Netflix.

"Oh, that's easy," he replies, voice animated. "The CVO Road Glide ST in black."

My lips form a *O* as I blow out a hot breath. "Yeah, she would be something else."

He folds his arms across his chest, sitting back in his seat. "If one of those were on the table for me, Dad would never lift the Stanley, period."

I snort out a laugh, attracting attention from Kendra and Jenna, and they smile sweetly, both of them enamored with the boy sitting beside me.

"I think I'd sacrifice the bike for your dad's dreams," I reply quietly.

Leaning down to grab his popcorn, he topples it over, cascading across the floor.

His shoulders slump, but he doesn't let the accident deter him from his thoughts. "You would? I mean, you'd pass up the CVO?!" he exclaims, disbelief in his voice.

I pick up my bag and unzip it, pulling out a bag of jelly beans. "I think, sometimes, life is about compromise or just finding the joy in others living their dreams."

I can't lie; these past few days have been emotional for me, and the look in Ezra's green eyes as he absorbs my words brings a glaze to mine as I recall the conversation in the Japanese garden. It was the most vulnerable I'd been in a long time, and I liked how it felt.

Ezra draws in his bottom lip, fixing his attention on the game as the first period ends and the players skate off the ice, number twenty-nine tipping his head over his shoulder toward our box.

As Alyssa finishes cleaning up the popcorn, I open the candy and offer it to Ezra. "Want some?"

He takes the packet from me and shakes it. "There aren't any red ones left."

I catch sight of Kendra. Shaking her head in a way that depicts awe, I know she's recognizing another passion I share with Sawyer's son.

"I, um … might've already eaten those ones." I wince. "Red jelly beans are kind of my favorite."

He deadpans, pure adolescent-style. "So, you thought you'd try and pass the rejects off on me?"

I reach down into my bag, pulling out a second—this time unopened—packet of jelly beans. "I mean, I have these, too, if you're interested?"

His eyes light up as I open the bag and spill a few out onto the small table separating our seats.

"Green ones are gross. I hate them with a passion," Ezra says, finding the first red one and popping it into his mouth, followed by a second.

"Don't have too many of those. You'll ruin your dinner when we get home," Alyssa calls across to us, and I throw her a reassuring wink.

I can't be sure if she thinks something's going on between Sawyer and me, but if she does, I don't see an ounce of animosity in her eyes. They're good people, family-oriented and so caring of Ezra.

Despite their welcoming nature, I couldn't feel any more out of place or unsuitable for the Blades captain. Family life like this is an alien concept to me.

My stomach knots as I tip a few more out before resealing the packet. "Go ahead and finish them up."

"You aren't going to have one?" Ezra asks.

I shake my head, leaning down closer so only he can hear. "I'm not all that hungry. You take these for dessert later."

I pass him the bag, and he takes it, slipping it into his jacket pocket, which is hanging on the back of his chair.

"For saying you're old, you sure act like you're a college girl. Are you sure you aren't lying to me?"

He quirks a brow, and I blow out a laugh, garnering attention from everyone around us.

"I'm sure. And less of the old. That's something we reserve only for your dad and his wrinkles."

He screws up his freckle-smattered nose. "Yeah, he's practically ancient. I can't see anyone loving him now."

My heart shatters into a million fucking pieces. Right here, in this loud, jam-packed arena, it breaks clean apart.

I clear my throat as the players skate back onto the rink. "Do you want him to meet someone else?"

He sinks into his seat, a crimson flush rising onto his face. "At one point, I kind of figured you and my dad were ... I thought my friends were right and you were his girlfriend. But then I asked him, and he told me you were just friends." He turns to me, question in his gaze. "Is it because he's too old, or do you have a boyfriend already?"

"I don't have a boyfriend, Ezra," I reply, voice muted.

He shrugs his shoulders. "Must be his age then because I can tell he likes you, and Dad never likes girls. I think he misses Mom too much."

Butterflies swarm my body. I know Sawyer likes me; he's not made that a secret. Though hearing it from his twelve-year-old son? Now, that hits in a completely different way.

I want to tell him I like his dad, too, but I hold back. I'm here as his dad's friend, and that's it. I'm here with my friends, and that's as far as it can go.

"I miss my mom," he continues. "But if you asked me which of Dad's dreams I'd want to come true, I think I'd choose someone who makes him happy instead of him lifting the Stanley Cup."

TWENTY-ONE

SAWYER

Climbing into my Lamborghini, I can't help the smile as it pulls at my lips. A few weeks back, I'd have been as clueless as Alyssa, but Collins recently shared a concept for the new Harley model on her IG Stories, and naturally, I watch those too.

Like a fucking stalker.

Warmth floods my chest. I should probably be a little more concerned that my boy will be up all night, but all I can concentrate on is the image of him sitting alongside Collins, sharing a bag of candy and talking about motorcycles.

MeHe's happy though, right?

ALYSSA

Yes. LOL. Absolutely bouncing.

ME

I guess that's all that matters. He'll burn himself out and fall asleep soon.

ALYSSA

She's nice.

ME

Who?

ALYSSA

Sawyer, you know precisely who. Collins. She's good for Ezra. All he did was talk to her the entire game. She likes him too—I can tell.

I crank the engine on my car and grip my cell in my left hand.

What are the chances of her showing up at Lloyd's tonight? Jack asked Kendra to practically force her down there.

Though I should know by now that my girl doesn't do *anything* she doesn't want to.

ME

All cards on the table … I like her a lot. But it's not that easy.

Within seconds, Alyssa's calling me, and I pick up, my phone automatically connecting to the Bluetooth as I pull out of the players' parking lot and head for Lloyd's.

"Hey," I say.

"Talk to me, please," Alyssa says immediately, her voice low, ensuring the conversation is private.

I pull up at a stoplight and blow out a long breath, anxiously drumming my fingers on the steering wheel.

"Recently we went on a date and back in October we spent the night together. I guess you could therefore argue we've been seeing each other. Although that isn't really accurate. I want her. I have feelings for her."

Alyssa hums like none of what I just told her comes as a surprise. "Your feelings aren't reciprocated?" she asks, her tone a touch flat, likely disappointed on my behalf.

When the light turns green, I head down the street.

"I wouldn't say that either. She's into me; she's just not into relationships. I'm working on things, and that's all I can say right now."

"So, you're chasing after her?"

I pull into the secure parking lot I use each time I come to Lloyd's and swing my car into a space.

"Would you call me an idiot if I said yes? It's the first time I've wanted a woman since Sophie, and honestly, it feels different this time."

"Well, Collins is a lot different from my daughter. Younger, for one thing, and very confident too. I don't think you're an idiot for going after what you want, Sawyer. You've been alone for so many years, and you need someone to grow old with. I—"

She breaks herself off, and I grow cold with anticipation.

"Finish what you were going to say," I ask.

She clears her throat quickly. "I just don't want you getting hurt. How old is she exactly?"

"Twenty-six," I reply, wincing slightly.

I know nine years makes a big difference at this stage in life, but at the same time, I see our age gap as more of a technicality. Yeah, sure, there are elements to Collins that scream younger, like her carefree attitude, lack of responsibilities, and pink hair.

There are also parts of her that leave me in awe over the mature ways she handles life. She's making decisions for herself, and I really and truly don't think she gives a fuck what anyone thinks or says about her.

I speak again before Alyssa has a chance to tell me it won't work out because she's too young for me. "I want her. I want to see where this can go because there's something special between us and I know she can feel it too."

A brief moment of nothing passes between us, and my palm tightens around the steering wheel. I'm not looking for Alyssa and Dom's permission to date anyone—and I don't need it—but I do respect their opinion. There are few people I can point to with confidence and say they have my best interests at heart. Jack, Archer, Kendra, and likely Coach. Alyssa and Dom are on that list. They have known me for years. Alyssa especially knows my limitations, and she saw the way Sophie's death tore me in two.

A gentle sigh blows through my speakers before she tells me precisely what I want to hear. "Then go after your heart, Honey. And just in case you need to hear this, go after her for Ezra too."

WHEN I PUSH INTO LLOYD'S, THE PLACE IS PACKED. PEOPLE ARE crowded around the main bar area, and footage from our win over the Scorpions is playing on every overhead screen. It was a big game tonight against our rivals and one we took control of right from the start. With Jack taking the starting center role last season, he's grown into the position his stepdad used to play and is now running the show in the slot—and, being honest, everywhere else on the rink.

Now that I'm thirty-five, thoughts of my retirement are never far away from the forefront of my consciousness, and neither is where the captaincy will go when I eventually hang up my skates.

Jon Morgan might not be Jack's blood dad, but I see all the qualities in him that Jon had as captain of the Scorpions for so many seasons. He'd make a better captain than I ever have.

Jack's also got his personal shit together. Unlike me.

As I walk farther into the bar, my eyes are scanning for Collins—from the seating areas to the hallway leading to the restrooms—though I come up empty.

"Hey! Is anyone going to serve me?!"

There's only one pink-haired girl that voice belongs to. I turn in a circle as I reach the ropes cordoning off the private area.

Standing at the far end of the bar with her arm extended in the air, my girl in black competes for the attention of anyone who will serve her.

"You know there's a private bar we can use, right?" I say on my approach, voice filled with flirtation and my body thrumming with a sensation I only feel when she's around. Its intensity tonight is off the charts as I take in her black ankle-cropped leggings and Guns N' Roses T-shirt. It's long and faded, and the way she tied it to just above her navel has me fighting to keep my eyes focused on her face.

Exasperated, she drops her arm to the bar top and rocks back on her heels, casting me a quick glance I know is designed to mask her interest in me.

Too bad for her, the flush in her cheeks tells me otherwise.

"I wanted a mojito. Jensen Jones's wife, Kate, is here with Jon's wife, Felicity. She told me they were top-tier, but the private bar is out of every ingredient, so I came to get one here." She waves her hand around again, sighing defeatedly.

I step a little closer, the need to flirt all-consuming. "You're telling me, a girl like you—the big explorer—has never had a mojito?"

She turns to me, looking grouchy, the pink staining her

cheeks just as prominent. "No, Sawyer, I haven't. Ordinarily, I don't drink a lot, but tonight, I felt like alcohol was needed."

I lean against the bar, my body blocking her exit. It isn't deliberate, but the fact that she can't escape kicks my heart rate a little higher.

"Want to talk about what's got you all worked up?"

She bites the inside of her cheek, eyes dropping briefly to the floor and then coming back up to me. Pools of deep brown silencing everything around us. "Sometimes, you just need to let it all go."

I pinch my brows together, confused. "Relinquishing a little control?"

This time, Collins edges closer, though I can't be sure why. "I'm just wired on thoughts, Sawyer. I need to relax."

Not taking my eyes off her, I raise my arm, and a few seconds later, a bartender approaches.

She rolls her eyes in response, and a single chuckle radiates from my chest.

"What can I get you?" the bartender asks, looking between us both.

I couldn't give two fucks who sees us in public together at this point. If someone else takes photos and Ezra catches wind, then I won't avoid telling him. I'll be up front because, right now, I have very few alternatives. I believe that what I have with Collins is special. And I'm sure me going after her is what Ezra wants too.

"Can I get a Diet Coke and two mojitos? Thanks," I ask.

The bartender nods once and disappears.

"Wait. Two?" Collins asks, the scent of her breath urging me to cover her mouth with mine.

I grin like a fucking idiot. *I never smile this much.* "You wanted to relax, no?"

She shrugs and then laughs, knowing how much that riles me up.

"Alyssa called me and said I have a very hyper twelve-year-old at home. Won't go to sleep. Allegedly, he's on a sugar kick, courtesy of a jelly bean overdose."

She snorts a laugh as two mojitos and a Coke are set down in front of us, and I hand the bartender cash, instructing him to keep the change.

I pick up one of the cocktails and mix the mint leaves around with the single black straw, offering it to her.

Collins takes it from me and wraps her lips around the straw, holding me captive with her eyes.

Fuck, Jesus.

That night we spent together, she didn't suck my dick, but in this moment, it's all I can think about as she swallows her first sip.

"Good?" I ask. Only able to manage a single gravelly word.

In a move I don't expect, she holds the glass out to me, nodding once. "I think so. Give it a try."

I tip my chin at the other mojito sitting on the bar. "I could just try this one."

She continues holding the glass out to me, her other hand maneuvering the straw around so I can use it. "I mean, you could. But that one could taste completely different."

Without saying another word, I duck my head and take a pull from the cocktail.

She instinctively wets her lips. I know she's horny—we both are. I know we're desperate for round two, and I know she wants more than just to fuck me. I thought the chemistry between us in the Botanic Garden was fire. But this, tonight? The charge settling around us is enough to power Brooklyn for a month. On the ice, I feel alive, my body ready for anything, responsive and tuned in. Though it's nothing compared to the arousal coursing through my veins right now. Collins has always had this effect on me. It's just, now, I'm struggling to keep a lid on acting out what I want to do.

And right now, that's pinning her to the nearest wall and fucking her goddamn brains out.

Six out of ten, my ass.

"So?" she finally asks.

I take one more sip and pull back, and she sets the glass on the bar. We're barely speaking, and I like that since I've come to realize Collins's words often contradict her body language.

"Delicious," I finally add.

She wets her lips again, and my willpower to keep away—the voice of reason and protection that said no to sex without strings—snaps. Alyssa's words from the conversation we just had drives me forward too.

There can be nothing bad about the way I'm feeling.

Grabbing her hand, I lead her down a dimly lit hallway directly behind where she was standing. I know we've abandoned our drinks, but I couldn't care less.

"Sawyer, w-what are you doing?" she asks from behind me, her voice quiet, but I can hear it since we're away from people and the beating music.

"Taking control," I growl, coming to a stop and spinning her around until her back meets the wall.

I'm pressed up against her, and I know she can feel the effect the past few minutes have had on me as my dick presses into her navel.

Collins looks up at me. All the fire and sass she usually carries are gone, and in their place is need.

I take a slow, deliberate look down her body and grip her chin with my hand, my other on her hip, holding her firmly. I know she likes to be held in this way.

"Last time we fucked, I went too easy on you. That's not what you like though, is it?"

She continues to stare up at me, and I release her hip, slapping my palm hard against the wall above us.

"Is it, Collins?" I repeat, tagging her name on because I want a fucking answer.

And because I know dominance turns her on.

"You like a power struggle, don't you?" I speak again, my voice raspy. "Is that what would rank me higher than a six? If I pinned you against a wall like this and fucked you while you told me it wasn't enough? You'd demand I screwed you harder, and when I was finally nailing you with your legs spread wide and your pussy aching from the force of my cock, you'd come all over me. Wouldn't you?"

My splayed palm above her head forms a fist.

"Talk to me, Collins."

"I would."

Two words, breathless and needy, set my blood on fire.

This is how she likes it.

"Come home with me," I plead. And it is a plea. It sounds like one as it tumbles from my lips, and it feels like one as my gut swirls while I wait for her response.

I try again. "Come home with me, and I'll fuck your brains out. I'll give you the best night of your life."

Nothing.

"Collins," I say way louder than I want, my forehead dropping to hers on an exhale. "Let me take you home, Baby Girl."

I feel the way she melts into me as her hands frame the sides of my face, and she lifts my head and rises on her tiptoes.

"Sawyer, you told me you couldn't and wouldn't go for no strings."

I'm powerless to prevent the whimper as it leaves my throat. "I know, but if that's all you'll give me, I'll take it. What we have is too strong to ignore and I'm going to hang in there until you see it too, or when you're ready. I'm yours to do with as you want, for however long you're around. Maybe I am being an idiot and setting myself up for heartbreak, but I have to risk that

you'll catch up with my feelings. I have to go after what I want."
I press my hands over hers. "And what I want is you."

TWENTY-TWO

"*And what I want is you.*"

Over and over, Sawyer's demand replays in my head while my body melts into his, screaming the answer I desperately want to give.

I want this. I want him.

My limbs begin to tremble, the weight of my answer bearing down on us both.

If I sleep with him, will it be as more than just a fuck buddy? Or is he truly giving me a no-strings arrangement?

I open my mouth to answer and then hesitate.

"I'm so confused," I whisper.

Hands still framing his cheeks, he covers them with his own and presses our palms into the sides of his face, eyes dark with more than just lust. "What's got you confused, Baby Girl? Tell me what's going on in that pretty head of yours."

The nickname licks through my body in a delicious wave, making me pool with need. I hate nicknames—always have. Mike used to call me Honey, and it never sounded natural, coming from him. But the way Sawyer calls me Baby Girl? I'm trembling all over again.

"You," I breathe. "You've got me all twisted up. Well, you and your son, to be exact. What are you doing to me?"

He just smiles, one that reaches his ears and sparkles in his eyes. "Some say my boy and I are the Dream Team."

I close my eyes and swallow thickly. "I want you so badly."

"How, Collins? How do you want me? Are we talking just my cock or more?"

I squeeze my eyes tighter.

"Open for me, Baby. Open." His voice is soothing and persuasive.

Although persuasion is not what I need.

Courage.

That's what I am searching for. An emotion I've never been short of, although it's deserted me right now as I step into unknown territory.

When I crack an eye open, his handsome face stares straight back at me, brushing his thumbs over mine.

"Attagirl," he croons. "So fucking beautiful."

I pull a hand from underneath his, and it falls to the waistband of his black dress pants, his white button-down shirt casually tucked into them.

His eyes drop to where I'm fiddling with his black belt, trying to unloop it, and he smirks. "You want my cock, Collins?"

I nod once. "Yes."

With his belt unfastened and hanging open, I begin working on the button and then his zipper.

Sawyer looks off to his left and down the dark hallway. At the top, people are entering and leaving the restrooms.

"I can't fuck you here."

I drop my head into the crook of his neck, releasing a soft moan. "Then take me home with you, like you want to."

His forefinger finds my chin, lifting my head back up to face him. "I need to know where I stand. Before I push inside you, I have to know where my head should be. If it's just sex, then I need to disconnect and fuck you." He draws his bottom lip between his teeth, biting hard. "But if it's more than that …"

His eyes fall to my lips, and memories of the kiss we shared at the Botanic Garden cause me to throb all over.

"But if it's more than that," he repeats softly, hopefully, "then I want to feel it all. I want to be all in and put my trust in you not to break me the first chance you get to leave town."

The past few weeks pass before me like a slideshow. Sawyer and me outside of Rise Up. He and Ezra arriving at my garage, Ezra helping me detail my bike, then riding through the streets of Brooklyn together, Ezra giggling behind me. Sawyer asking me at the bar to come home with him, turning up at my apartment and asking me for a date. Me sitting next to him on the bench while we exchanged pieces of our past before we shared the best kiss I'd ever had. Sawyer telling me he couldn't just be fuck buddies. Me tucking jelly beans into Ezra's jacket pocket. It's all there, clear as day. Begging me to take a leap and start dating this man for real.

"Can you do something for me?" I ask, twisting the end of his belt around my hand.

He drops his lips to my jaw and kisses me twice. "Anything."

"Show me what it would be like if I said it was more than just a fuck."

We don't say goodbye to anyone as Sawyer takes me by the hand and leads me out of Lloyd's and into the November Brooklyn night. His belt is barely fastened as we race for the exit.

As we cross the street and head for the parking lot he guided me to several weeks back, I feel a very different set of emotions.

I'm nervous.

I know my hand is trembling slightly, but I fight to keep my persona confident. I asked him to show me what it would be like if I was beneath him as his girl because I can't curb my curiosity any longer.

I said no to him more times than I'd wanted, and tonight, I have to crack the door open and take a glimpse at what "more" with Sawyer Bryce would look like. And I don't take this lightly, not for me, Sawyer, and especially not for Ezra.

Swinging the passenger door open to his black Lamborghini, I duck under his corded arm to get in, but a palm wraps around my wrist, spinning me back to face him.

"To be absolutely clear, if you get into my car and come home with me tonight, I'm not holding back, Collins. With your body, your mind, or in my own head. I'm giving you everything."

I step toward him, not feeling the cold in only my T-shirt since we didn't even head to the booth to collect my jacket or bag. Kendra will figure out that I left and take them home with her.

"That's what I'm hoping for," I whisper into the silent lot.

Sawyer closes his eyes, hand tightening on the doorframe. "Actually, I don't think I can wait to get you in my bed."

Lust takes over any nerves. "Tell me what you want me to do."

He tips his chin at the black leather passenger seat. "Sit on there and face me."

He releases my wrist, and I do as he commands. Dominant Sawyer is everything.

"What now?" I ask.

He runs a palm across the scruff of his jaw before glancing quickly over his shoulder, checking to see who's around.

We're all alone.

Standing right in front of me, he slowly drops to his knees, hands finding the inside of my thighs, spreading me wide.

"Rest your foot on here." He taps the door sill with his hand. "I need you open for me, Baby Girl."

"But I haven't even—"

A loud rip echoes in the lot, bouncing off the concrete pillar walls separating the spaces.

"You just ripped my leggings?!" I exclaim. "That's …"

On his knees in front of me, Sawyer waits for me to finish my sentence.

But I don't speak, and when he tears the seam even wider, material hanging loosely around my thighs, I don't feel any of the cold, only the heat from my desperate pussy.

"You're already so wet, coating my knuckles, Collins." He brings the back of one hand to his mouth and licks me off him. "And so fucking sweet."

When he edges closer to me, I lean back on my elbows, thankful I'm petite enough to fit across the bucket seat.

The sound of him licking me from his hand drives me forward. I want his mouth on me.

"Tear my thong too," I command. "Tear it clean off my cunt and eat me."

Both hands grip my flimsy black thong, his eyes on me and lips shining from my release.

"It's been way too long since I saw this pretty pussy."

In one slow ripping motion, Sawyer pulls it apart, his tattooed forearms straining deliciously.

I'm totally exposed as I run my feet wider and sit up a little more.

"Eat," I command, taking some of the power back.

Sawyer buries his face between my thighs, swiping his tongue through my pussy, from my asshole to my clit, circling it twice. Then he sucks it into his mouth, and I clamp my knees around his head, taking my weight onto one elbow and thrusting my hand through his tousled hair.

"Yes," I pant. "Right—fucking—there."

He sucks me harder and faster, and I grow wetter, feeling my release flow into his mouth. I'm not coming yet, but I'm close. The strokes of his tongue are determined and perfectly placed.

I push his head into me further, wanting more, and with a whimper, he gives it to me, entering me with his tongue.

"Fuck me. Fuck me with your tongue," I shout.

He pulls back, and I open my thighs.

"Get on my hood."

"W-what?"

"You heard me," he groans against my pussy. "Get on my hood."

"But I'm so cl—"

He cuts me off when his hands circle my thighs, lifting me off the seat and carrying me to the hood of his car before setting me down. "I can fuck you better with my cock."

"But—"

"Don't argue with me, Collins." He unzips his pants and pulls his belt open. Sinking his fingertips into the tops of my legs, he pulls me to him. His face softens as he pushes his boxers down, and his angry, hard cock springs free. "I'm showing you what it's like to be my girl and exactly how you would be treated." He notches himself at my entrance, wrapping my legs around his waist. His tip pushes in, and he stops, eyes on mine.

"I'm still on birth control, so do it. Give me everything," I bite.

In a single thrust, he slams into me, filling my pussy full.

"Oh fuuuuuck," he moans, hips pulling away and pistoning back in.

"Is that all you have?" I goad, offering him a bratty smirk.

One hand wraps around my throat, fire burning bright in his green irises. "Oh, Collins, you haven't seen anything yet. I'm gonna fuck you so good on the hood of my car."

Thrust.

"Then …"

Thrust.

"I'm going to throw you around my bedroom all damn night."

Thrust.

My jaw hangs open at the way he plows into me—without mercy but still with expert precision. Tonight, this man is *definitely* not a six out of ten.

"I prefer to be tied up, edged, and whipped." My confession hangs between us as Sawyer stills his hips.

"What was that?" A devilish smirk spreads across his face.

I reach forward and palm his ass, pistoning him into me. "I said, I like to be tied up, edged, and whipped."

He fucks me, and I release all over his dick.

Sawyer drops his head to see where we're joined, watching me come hard—not only from the way he just fucked me in a public place on the hood of his car, but at the thought of living out my kinks with him.

"Dirty. Fucking. Girl," he moans, capturing my mouth with his. "Does my girl have kinks?"

I gush all over him again, and he slams into me, my grip on his ass tightening.

"I like to be played with in bed. Tease me, and I'll see fucking stars. Play with my senses too."

On a guttural groan that has me crying out his name, Sawyer spills inside me, face falling to the crook of my neck and a gentle whimper leaving his throat.

A good few beats of silence pass before our breathing jointly evens out, and he picks his head back up to look at me, his large palm wrapping around the back of my head, fingers toying with my hair.

"That has to be at least an eight, right?" he asks hopefully.

A giggle bubbles out of me. It's sweet and a complete juxtaposition to the filthy words we shared a few seconds ago. My hand moves from his ass to a button on the collar of his shirt, opening it and giving me a better view of his tattooed chest and pierced nipple that I love to play with.

"You fucked me so good, Baby," I praise.

His dick twitches inside me, and he pulls out, tucking himself back into his pants, leaving me agonizingly empty.

"Let me get you back to my place before I fuck you here again." He runs his hands over my arms. "It's freezing, and I need you warm and under my sheets."

I go to push off his hood, but he cups my face in his palm.

"Collins."

"Yeah?"

Sawyer blows out a breath. "Is it okay for me to think of you as mine yet? Or do you need more time?"

I pause for a brief second, possibly too long for him, as he speaks again. "It's fine. I can wait a little longer."

Leaning forward, I place a chaste kiss across his lips. It's the first time I've initiated a kiss between us, and I sense the relief as it washes through him.

"I don't know. But I can tell you this," I say softly, heart beating in my ears. "My place might be on a monthly contract, but I have absolutely zero intention of leaving. Right now, I want to be around you and your amazing boy."

TWENTY-THREE

SAWYER

"Ride my dick, Baby Girl. I want to see those perfect tits of yours bouncing above me."

I'm positive we've both lost track of time since we burst through my front door, and I flung her over my shoulder, carrying her up the stairs toward my bedroom.

"You want me to fuck your cock, Sawyer?" Collins asks, voice laced with desire.

"I want you to bury it inside that tight pussy and rock over me until you're seeing stars," I reply, rolling off her and onto my back.

She rises onto her knees and straddles me, gripping my cock in her palm and pumping it a couple of times before slowly sinking down until I'm seated deep inside her.

On the first rock of her hips, I throw my arms behind my head, gripping the roots of my hair and pulling the strands hard. Not counting the orgasm I gave her in the parking lot, she's climaxed multiple times since I got her back in my bed, and I'm determined to hold off on blowing my load for as long as I can.

She moves over me a second time, casually fucking my cock.

Collins braces her palms on the tops of my thighs, and she

moans. When she throws her head back it adjusts the angle of her body and the way her pussy grips me, the sensation sending crushing pressure to the base of my spine.

I can tell she likes it more than the first night we spent together—the noises from her mouth and pussy leave me in no doubt. She's comfortable with me tonight, taking what she wants from my body and not fighting the undeniable connection between us.

Still, I want more. I want to prove myself to her—inside the bedroom and out of it. I want her to realize I can be the only guy she needs.

"I'm coming all over your dick," she gasps, eyes back on mine. "Want to see?"

I lift up onto my elbows as she moves her hips over me and then lifts off, and I see it—her release streaming from her, flowing over my dick and down to my tight balls.

"I've never known a girl who could get so damn wet," I praise. "Tell me you only get this wet with me."

She doesn't answer, and I choose to ignore any potential disappointment. Just because I asked the question doesn't mean I'll get a response—or the one I want to hear.

Sensing she's tiring, I grip her hips and keep our rhythm steady. I'm not nearly done with her tonight.

"What's your favorite position?"

She looks down at me, the pink flush on her cheeks growing darker. "The hot seat."

I interlace my fingers with hers, and she continues to ride me.

"That seems a little tame for a girl who likes to be whipped."

Despite my comment, I still have every intention of giving her what she wants, and with her still riding my dick, I drop her hands and edge across the bed, sitting on the end and placing my feet flat on the floor.

We're face-to-face as I sit up and take my weight on

extended arms. "For the hot seat, you need to spin around and spread your thighs over mine, Baby Girl."

I can't be sure if she registered what I said since she continues to face me, slowing the rocking of her hips to almost a complete stop.

Pieces of her hair stick to her slick forehead, and her eyeliner is smeared in a similar way to that first night.

Just how I like it.

It's obvious she has something to say but is fighting it.

"What is it?" I ask.

She shakes her head subtly, blown pupils filled with emotion.

I lean down, taking her left nipple into my mouth. There's only so far I can push her to open up, and I'm concluding the long game with Collins is the way to winning her heart.

"My body wants to go fast with you, fuck you hard and in all my favorite positions, but my head won't let me do that." Her voice is laced with the same level of emotion I saw in her eyes a second earlier, and I pause over her nipple.

When I bring it back between my teeth, she stops me with a finger under my chin. And like I've done with her countless times before, she tips it up to look at her.

"I haven't stopped thinking about that night, you know. I mean, I tried to forget about it and move on, but deep down, all I wanted was to have you back inside me."

Even though we aren't moving anymore, I'm still hard and inside her, and I drop my forehead against hers, closing my eyes. "As someone a little older, let me offer you a few words of geriatric wisdom."

She snorts a laugh, and my heart beats faster at the sound.

"It's okay to change your mind about someone or something. What you thought you wanted twelve months ago might not be what you want now. It's okay to pivot."

She looks atop my head, running her hands through my hair;

the feeling ricochets throughout my body, and goose bumps break out across my skin.

"Is that what you did with me? I know you haven't been with anyone in a while and haven't wanted to start anything up since …" She trails off. "Well, since your wife …"

I move beneath her, needing to feel the way her tight pussy clamps around my dick.

Collins breaks out into a delicious shudder, her arousal coating the insides of my thighs.

"Total transparency. I haven't ever wanted anyone like this. Not the way I want you. I don't chase after anyone, Collins. I don't take risks with my or my son's feelings either."

I thrust up into her gently, and she whimpers.

"But I believe in what we have. So, yeah, I guess you could say I'm pivoting. I pivoted when I saw you last November, and I'm pivoting again after I initially told you I couldn't do no-strings sex. I know this is right for me, for you and for Ezra. And I'm willing to wait for you, Collins."

Her eyes soften further, and again, I can tell she wants to say something but is struggling. I grant her a reprieve and wrap my hands around her hips, swiveling her around into the hot seat position.

"Now take what you want and let me see just how much you enjoy being fucked like this."

RIGHT AFTER I TOOK COLLINS IN HER FAVORITE POSITION AND she came hard, I emptied myself inside her and pulled her into my chest, settling us under the sheets, and we fell into lazy conversation.

We didn't talk about us or the nonstop mind-blowing sex we'd just had. Instead, she wanted to talk about Ezra and his love for motorcycles. She wanted to know if he'd ever shown an interest in bikes or if it was new. That was when I confessed I'd been watching her Instagram page too.

Being Collins, she naturally teased me and called me a stalker, but I didn't miss the way her breath hitched when I owned up to watching every Reel she'd posted since setting up her page.

And that was where we stayed, tangled up in my bed with her head resting on my shoulder—my fingers sifting through her soft hair—until we fell asleep, and I woke a few minutes ago to the sun rising and peeking between the gaps in my blinds.

I've gotten further than I did the first night, in that she's still here, her head in the crook of my arm, one small hand splayed across my stomach.

She didn't remove her makeup, her eyeliner now way more smeared than it was when she rode me.

When she looks in the mirror and notices, she'll probably be embarrassed, just like she was a few weeks ago when I crept to my en suite door and I heard the faucet turn on and Collins quietly scolding herself. As I stood there with my ear to the door like a fucking creep, I heard her talk about how she promised herself she wasn't "going to do this." By "this" I assumed she meant sleep with me.

I half-wince, half-smile at the memory, hoping this morning's different. I hope she sees the smears and smudges around her eyes as a testament to the way I rocked her world last night. Collins had asked me to show her what it would be like if she said yes to more with me, and I went all out to give her that.

In a half hour, I need to get up and head for morning skate before we go to Jack and Kendra's for the party he's arranged to celebrate her selection for Team USA.

I war with myself. While she's asleep, I know she'll stay longer—in my house and in my bed. But if I wake her, there's a chance she'll want to leave, though at least I'll get to speak to her before I have to go.

All I want is to be inside this girl constantly; I need it like I need the air in my lungs. Yet I also want to know everything about her without secretly flicking through a photo album. She's shown me parts of her, and I know there's so much more to see. My initial attraction to Collins was manifested in the way she fascinated me, and that feeling has only gotten stronger.

Fuck it.

"Baby," I whisper into her hair, "I gotta head to skate."

She shifts, releasing a muffled yawn that fans across my chest.

Jesus Christ, I'm so done for.

"Like, right now?"

The hand resting on my stomach descends toward my naked lower half, and I roll over to face her, cupping her bare ass in my palm and pulling up so we're face-to-face, heads resting on the same pillow.

"I have a few minutes to spare."

Collins wraps her leg over mine, asking me to come closer even though we're only inches apart.

"Do you know how different this morning looks from the first time I had you in my bed?"

She giggles softly, happiness radiating from her. "Yeah, well, this time, the sex was at least an eight."

"You're going to be the death of me—you know that?" I say, kissing her shoulder. "Either that or you're going to make me really late for skate."

She palms my already-hard dick. "What can I do to convince you to fuck me again?"

An incredulous laugh bursts out of me, and I roll on top of her, bracketing her head between my forearms. "Baby, you've already got me wrapped around every finger you possess. If you can convince my coach that his captain's time is better spent working out with his girl in bed, then I'll slide inside you right now."

Maybe I'm still drunk on lust or semiconscious from the best sleep I've ever had, but when the words *his girl* leave my mouth, her eyes bug out.

I pull back a couple of inches, trying to work out what's going through her head. "I … I didn't mean to assume you and I are—shit, I'm sorry. I got ahead of myself for a second."

You call her your girl just in your head, Sawyer.

Her eyes scan my face. She doesn't look freaked out, but I can tell there's something eating at her.

"Are you going to Jack and Kendra's tonight?" Collins switches the subject, and I feel a combination of relief and anxiety, wondering what she's thinking.

Still hovering above her, I kiss the end of her nose. "That was the plan, although Ezra spent last night with Alyssa and Dom and will stay there again tonight, so I want to spend some time with him today."

It's on the tip of my tongue to invite her out with us when she clears her throat and the spell of last night is broken.

She looks around the room—maybe for a way out, possibly for her clothes. I'm not sure. All I know is, I'm not ready for her to leave.

"Are you going tonight?" I ask, feeling like a teenager asking if his crush is going to the school dance.

Collins looks at me like that's exactly how I sound—a lovesick puppy desperate to know when he'll see her again.

"I am, but I have to work overtime today at the garage, so I might be late."

"Want me to pick you up?" I rush out. "From work, your place, wherever you're going to be?"

She cups my face, a smile pulling at her lips. "I can make my own way to Kendra's, although"—she pauses and smirks—"if you're a good boy, I might let you give me a ride home."

TWENTY-FOUR

SAWYER

"I'm so fucking proud of you, Kitten. I genuinely can't think of anyone more deserving of their place on Team USA, and I know you're going to kill it."

Standing in front of the fireplace in their living area, Jack sets a kiss on his girlfriend's forehead. The entire friend group is here—me, Collins, Jenna, and Archer.

Jenna pumps her fist in the air, ready to make a run toward Kendra, but Jack holds his hand up, asking her to wait a second.

Sitting on the opposite couch, Archer leans forward, resting his elbows on his knees, one brow raised at me in question. Next to him, Collins wears the same expression, as does Jenna.

Jack swallows thickly, his body language anxious. Reaching out, he takes Kendra's left hand in his, interlacing their fingers, but not speaking.

"A-are you okay?" Kendra asks, cocking her head to the side and studying him carefully.

Jack swallows again.

Oh fuck. He's gonna do it.

He smiles, trying to get ahold of his nerves. "I didn't plan on doing this right now, but you know me—my mind runs away with an idea, and I can't help myself." He pauses and inhales a deep breath, his eyes meeting hers. "Especially when it comes to you."

On the final word, he dips his right hand into his pants pocket, pulling out a small black box.

Kendra's free hand covers her mouth, muffling her gasp.

"Fuck me, our boy Jack is getting motherfucking married!" Archer exclaims, and every head snaps his way.

He sinks back into the couch, cringing at himself. "At least … I *think* that's what's happening."

"You really are a twat at times, aren't you?" Jack shakes his head at our goalie, although I can tell he's amused as he slowly drops to one knee, eyes returning to Kendra.

"Wait." She stops him with a hand underneath his arm. "There's only one time I want you on your knees for me, and this isn't it. Look me in the eye while you ask me." Her voice is barely a whisper, and the room is deadly silent as we all look on.

Jack takes their still-joined hands and hovers it over the box. "Pop the lid, Kitten."

I steal a quick glance at Collins—a palm over her mouth and her eyes glassy—and I witness a little more of her hardened exterior melt away in the face of pure love.

And that's what Jack and Kendra have—the kind of love written about in books.

When Jack releases her hand and Kendra opens the box, the gateway to her emotions bursts open, tears rolling down her cheeks.

"Is it a ruby?" she asks.

Jack plucks the yellow gold band from the box, a single large ruby set on top. "Matches Scarlett."

While Jack grins and a laugh bursts from Kendra's chest, I conclude Scarlett is some kind of inside joke I do not want to know about.

"I've had it for a few months now, Kitten. I was convinced

the right time would be when we headed to your mum and dad's for Thanksgiving, but then I got this urge to ask you tonight, in front of all our friends and in our home. Plus, your brother has been calling me nonstop since I got the ring, wanting to know if I popped the question. I think, deep down, I knew you were it for me the second I laid eyes on you in college. Even if you barely knew my name." He pockets the box and wraps his hand around the nape of her neck, bringing her forehead to rest against his.

As she takes her hand back, they both hold the ring between them, and Kendra releases a gentle sob. "I always thought you were hot, especially your accent."

Everyone laughs briefly, including Jack.

"I bided my time and waited for you to work out that you deserved an upgrade to someone who would treat you like the queen that you were. And I was lucky enough for that guy to be me."

Jack removes his hand from the nape of Kendra's neck, tipping her chin up to look at him. Just as she wanted, they're eyeball to eyeball, and it's the most intimate proposal I've ever seen, only something soulmates could pull off.

"Marry me, Kendra. Let's forever eat chili late at night and quote *Friends* while sitting on the couch. Let me ply you with Yorkshire Tea and take you to some of the best bakeries in England. Let's make a home in the US and maybe, one day, fill it with our children. And even if, you grow to hate clotted cream and get tired of sitcoms, let me stand beside you as you take different paths in life. As Ross would say, we can *pivot* together."

The second that word leaves Jack's mouth, my eyes are back on Collins, and this time, she has hers on me.

A tear falls from her left eye, shining in the soft light of the apartment, and she quickly swipes it away.

I've never seen Collins cry. I need to go to her, my arms itching to wrap around her frame and pull her into my body.

But this is Jack and Kendra's moment, so I keep my ass firmly planted on the chair, my attention locked on the girl I shared my best night with.

"Yes," Kendra replies.

The single word sends my starting center into full golden-retriever mode as his eyes grow wide and he quickly pushes the ring onto her left finger, the fit as perfect as they are together.

"You hear that?" He tips his head toward the ceiling. "I'm marrying Kendra Hart and making her a Morgan!"

"Yeah, you are, Baby!" Kendra wraps her arms around Jack's neck.

He picks her up, looping her legs around his waist, and spins her around in a circle.

Archer and Jenna immediately leap to their feet, flying across the room to congratulate them, and I take a second to let them all hug it out before I join them myself.

"I think you need to copyright your pivot moment so no one else uses it."

I turn my head away from the group to find Collins standing in front of me. Her eyes are still glassy, but her face wears a cute smile.

I rise to my feet and hover over her while the others continue going crazy.

My left hand palms her hip, and I grin down at her, loving the way she relaxes beneath my touch. "Maybe I should copyright it; it definitely has an impact."

The temptation to lean down and kiss her is overwhelming, as is the tent forming in the front of my jeans.

Collins drops her eyes to the bulge, her lip pinned between her teeth when she looks back up at me. "We should go congratulate the happy couple," she whispers, her voice full of lust.

I nod once and summon all my willpower to release my tightening grip on her hip and, consequently, break the spell between us. Although I'm already running through options and my best opportunity to get her alone—as soon as fucking possible.

"Lead the way, Baby Girl."

"Where are you going to get hitched?" Archer asks.

He, Jack, and I stand in the kitchen while the girls gather in the living area, inspecting Kendra's ring for the hundredth time.

Collins is animated, excitement written across her face while she holds Kendra's left hand in front of her.

You can't convince me this girl doesn't believe in love.

Jack speaks, pulling my attention back to the boys. "How much do you know about your coach?"

Archer side-eyes me, and I throw him a blank look, unsure what the location of where they get married has to do with Jack's stepdad.

"Errr …" Archer scratches at his temple. "I guess I know a bit."

Jack shakes his head, smiling around the lip of his beer bottle before taking a quick pull. "One thing you need to know about Jon: if anyone—and I mean, *anyone*—he knows is due to get hitched, he wants to organize the entire thing from start to finish."

I take another look at my goalie, not entirely sure I'm hearing Jack right. Either the single beer he's had went straight to his head or I'm hallucinating from zero sleep, courtesy of banging Collins all night.

I reach forward and take the bottle from Jack's hand, setting it down on the counter beside me. "That's enough alcohol for you; we're heading on a seven-day away series tomorrow, and I want my center in good shape against Dallas."

Jack frowns and grabs the bottle back. "I'm being serious.

The guy is addicted to weddings. I haven't even told Mum and Darcy I planned on asking Kendra, for fear of Jon turning up at my door with five wedding planners and a fucking six-tier cake. Only person who knows is Ollie, Kendra's brother."

"Oh, Darcy's going to be pissed when she finds out you didn't tell her beforehand," Archer chimes in, a devilish smile tracing his lips. "Your sister is a little like me in that way."

Jack sets his own bottle down behind him this time, one brow raised as he turns back to Archer. "And what way would that be, Moore?"

The use of Archer's last name has my goalie grinning harder, loving how easy it is to goad Jack about Darcy.

He shrugs and crosses his ankles, leaning back against the fridge. "I'm just saying, we share a lot in common, is all. When she's around, I can tell she wants to talk with me; we vibe with each other."

Blowing air into my cheeks, I'm powerless to prevent the explosive laugh, and I bend over and release it. "I'm sorry." I hold up a hand. "Give me a second." I point in Archer's direction. "It's just his reference to vibing. Seriously, this entire conversation is awkward as shit." I laugh again.

When I rise back to my full height, two pairs of eyes bore into me. The first pair—Jack's—holds nothing but disdain. The second—Archer's—sparkles with amusement.

After a second or so, Jack folds his arms across his chest, attention momentarily flicking over my shoulder and toward the girls as they continue talking in the other room. "Let's get this all out in the open, shall we? Especially since Darcy is now single—"

"Wait, she's not with Liam anymore?" Archer interrupts Jack.

"You know damn well she isn't," Jack replies with an eye roll. "As I was saying"—he pins Archer with a stern look—"it's obvious you're hot for my sister. So, here's your chance to admit it without hiding behind jokes."

Jack falls silent while he awaits Archer's response.

Running a hand across his mouth, Archer quickly realizes his best friend isn't fooling around.

He drops his head between his shoulders and inhales a long breath. "I'll admit she's pretty."

"And?" Jack adds.

"And … nothing," Archer finishes. "She's pretty, and she's fun to be around, but I'm not the type of guy who would suit her. She likes guys who are serious and want long-term. Plus, I think Coach would put my balls in a vise if I buried my dick in his stepdaughter."

I can't be certain, but I'm ninety-nine percent sure Jack is about to puke on his kitchen floor.

"I-I literally have no words for you right now," I say to Archer, glancing over my shoulder and catching Collins as she disappears down the hallway, no doubt heading for the bathroom.

"Yeah, me too. Other than to say, I really regret bringing up this entire conversation," Jack agrees. "Although I will say this: you're wrong about Jon putting your balls in a vise."

Archer looks mildly hopeful, although I can't say I share the same optimism on his behalf.

Jack leans closer to Archer. There's a tinge of playfulness in his expression, but you can't mistake the serious edge. "It'll be a joint effort with me."

Archer's shoulders shake, silent laughter rippling through him. This guy isn't intimidated by anyone, yet despite knowing how reckless he can be, I can tell he gets the message loud and clear—*don't touch Darcy Thompson.*

"So, what you're saying is, you both want to touch my balls."

"For fuck's sake," Jack drawls. "No, I don't want to touch your hairy balls. I do, however, want you to stay away from

Darcy because she just had her heart broken, and she doesn't need a fuckboy messing her around for a one-time thing."

TWENTY-FIVE

COLLIN

I feel … a little tipsy.

The surprise proposal set the drinks flowing, and like I'd said to Sawyer last time we were in Lloyd's, I am not a girl who drinks a lot.

I'm also freakin' tiny, so I can handle booze about as well as a toddler.

Searching through my bag for gloss, I find myself giggling at the eight out of ten I gave Sawyer this morning, along with the smug look on his face when I said it.

Truth is, it was more like a nine, but I don't want him getting ahead of himself.

I've got the gloss wand to my mouth when a soft knock sounds against the bathroom door.

"Just a second," I call back, quickly swiping a clear layer across my bottom and then top lip.

The knock sounds again, and I close the cap, dropping it into my bag and heading to unlock the door.

"Sorry," I say, pulling it open to find Sawyer leaning against the opposite wall in the hallway, one foot propped up behind him, his black dress shirt open at the collar and dark hair effort-lessly styled.

I thumb over my shoulder, working to keep my eyes on his face and not on the tattoos painting his forearms. I recently noticed Ezra's name inked down the inside of his left arm and found myself wondering if it was a recent addition since I hadn't seen it before.

"I was just finishing up applying my gloss."

Not saying a word, Sawyer drops his arms and pushes off the wall, quickly crowding me in.

He shoves one hand into his pocket and tips his head toward a door behind him. "Join me in there for a second?"

I peer over his shoulder, heart thumping against my ribs. "What's in there?"

"A bedroom."

With his spare hand, he takes one of mine and turns on his heel, pushing the door open to reveal a four-poster king-size bed, dressed in crisp white sheets, with floor-to-ceiling windows on the opposite side.

With its monochrome feel, the room is pretty simplistic, only a single dresser along the nearest wall and a nightstand on either side of the bed.

Sawyer spins around to face me, leaning over my shoulder and pushing the door closed with a soft click. "I want to have a little fun, Baby Girl."

My eyes grow wide as excitement courses through me, heat already pooling between my legs. "Be more specific."

Up until now, Sawyer hasn't removed his hand from his pocket, so when he does and a pair of fluffy black handcuffs appears, my heart rate hits a level that has me fighting to stay upright.

I fucking love being restrained.

Sawyer casts his eyes up to the bar connecting the four posts on the bed, licking his lips as he clearly thinks over his plan.

"Where did you get those?" I point to the cuffs.

His attention falls back on me. The room is dim since its only light source is the city beneath us, the street lights accentuating the sparkle in his eyes. "I followed you to the bathroom but got the wrong door, ended up in here. While I was waiting for you to finish up, I found these"—he dangles the cuffs in front of him—"in the dresser."

I quirk a brow. "I thought you said you didn't usually go through people's things?"

He smiles in response, taking a step toward me and opening the first cuff, the sound of the metal firing off sparks across my skin.

"I don't, but when I saw something fluffy hanging out of the drawer, curiosity got the better of me."

He's inches away when he opens the second cuff. "And knowing how much you like to be tied up ..." His hand falls to the button on my black jeans, popping it open and then moving to my zip. "Well, let's just say, I'm keen on discovering just how kinky Collins Mackenzie really is."

Both hands tug my pants and thong down in a single, quick motion, and just as fast, one arm loops under my ass, picking me up.

I suppress a surprised squeal as he carries me over to the bed.

"What are you going to do?" I ask breathlessly.

With his spare arm, Sawyer swings the cuffs over the bed frame and then lifts me higher. "Secure the cuffs around your wrists, and I'll take your weight."

Overrun with need, I struggle to focus on the cuffs and securing them, but after a few seconds, I manage.

Sawyer pulls my pants and thong over my ankles and throws them to one side, fire smoldering in his eyes as he hooks my legs over his shoulders and looks at me with awe.

I'm suspended and completely at his mercy.

And so damn close to coming already.

My pussy is lined up with his mouth, and as he licks through me for the first time, he never removes his eyes from mine, hands clamping around my upper thighs, spreading me wider on his broad shoulders.

I throw my head up toward the ceiling, straining against the cuffs. "Oh—fuck—yes," I cry out, probably a little too loud since our friends are only a couple of rooms away.

"I want to know something, Collins," Sawyer growls after another lick through my wet pussy. "You tell me you like it kinky in the bedroom, but has anyone ever made this dripping cunt squirt?"

Of their own volition, my thighs clamp around his head. My needy desperation for him to lick me again drives me wild.

"No," I croak out. "I'm not a squirter."

He takes my response as a challenge, parting my thighs wider with his hands and driving his tongue deep inside my entrance.

He momentarily comes up for air, sucking my clit and releasing it with a pop. "If I make you squirt, do I get a ten?"

I double down on the task he's obviously setting for himself. "I don't squirt."

Sawyer sucks me back into his mouth, two fingers entering me and curling to find my front wall.

My head lolls forward, the pressure of an orgasm building, release already flowing freely. "I'm going to come really soon," I breathe.

Sawyer pulls away from me, his voice full of wonder. "You're dripping down your thighs, Collins. You are definitely a squirter, and tonight, I'm going to prove it to you."

Gathering some of my release onto his fingers, Sawyer tips my pelvis toward him, exposing my ass and circling it slowly.

"I remember you telling me you didn't offer your ass to anyone." He circles me again, and I buck my hips, pulling against the restraints. "Does that include me and my fingers?"

I'm so turned on, I can barely form words.

Sawyer teases my hole gently. "Speak, Baby Girl. We likely don't have long before someone comes searching for us."

"I … I want you to t-touch my ass," I plead in a broken voice.

Fuck, this isn't you, Collins. You like to be tied up and dominated, but you're never *this vulnerable.*

And definitely *never this goddamn needy.*

"Make me squirt, please," I plead once more.

Something akin to alpha-male dominance flashes through his eyes, and his lips tip up into a wicked grin. "The key to making you go off is this."

Slowly, he pushes his pointer finger inside, working me into a frenzy. Then, with his other hand, he concentrates on my pussy, attacking both holes in the best way possible. I feel the pressure —the delicious, undeniable pressure—as he strokes my G-spot and ass in a perfect rhythm.

"When you feel like it's time for me to get on my knees, tell me," Sawyer instructs.

"On your knees?"

He strokes me again, and more arousal leaks from my pussy, streaming down my inner thighs.

"I want to catch every drop you squirt in my mouth, and from my knees will be the best way to do it."

"Put another finger in my pussy," I command. "I want to feel so damn full of you."

Sawyer wastes no time adding another finger, and when he slips a fourth inside me, all I can hear is his moans in response to the way I suck him in.

"Squirt for me, Collins. Hand me a little piece of control. Let go and let me drink you in."

Two more strokes of his fingers, and the first shot of my release hits his lips. Quickly, he drops below me, removing his finger from my ass and using that hand to support my body while continuing to stroke my G-spot with the other.

"You can go harder than that, Collins," he croons, massaging my confidence in the same way he does my clit.

I moan, releasing a pleasured whimper I could muffle if my hands weren't suspended above my head. Instead, I work to keep myself as quiet as possible as, over and over again, I squirt into Sawyer's mouth, and he swallows me down, licking his lips after each release.

When I've given all I have to give, he stands and pulls his fingers from me, wrapping his free arm under my ass and offering his soaked fingers out. "Suck."

I open and do as he demands.

"Good fucking girl," he praises. "Now, tell me again how you can't squirt."

I'm speechless, rendered to nothing but a puddle as my pussy throbs from its high and my brain desperately tries to catch up to what the fuck just happened.

Sawyer reaches into his pocket and pulls out a key to the handcuffs. "Let's get you down."

"Sawyer …" My eyes flare wide when, over his shoulder, I watch the door handle depress. "Sawyer," I pant, still breathless and recovering. "Someone's—"

"OH JESUS, FUCK!" Archer announces, his head craned around the door, eyes practically falling from their sockets.

Sawyer groans into my stomach, pulling me further into his body and throwing an arm across my breasts. "For the love of God, Archer. Get out and wipe your memory clean!"

TWENTY-SIX

SAWYER

COLLINS

You know when I told you I was into kink, exhibitionism wasn't on that list. The look on Archer's face will be burned into my memory until the day my body is turned to ash.

ME

I know, Baby Girl. Mine too.

COLLINS

You didn't even see his face; you had your head buried in my stomach.

ME

Imagining it is traumatic enough.

COLLINS

I don't think I'm ever going to recover. I'll never be able to look him in the eye again.

ME

Try a seven-day away series with him.

COLLINS

Please tell me he hasn't told the others what he walked in on!

ME

No, but he has been insufferable.

I peer across the hotel bedroom and at Archer as he takes his usual afternoon nap before a game. With his arms braced behind his head, he even looks cocky in his sleep.

ME

Although insufferable is his usual setting.

COLLINS

Of all the people to catch us, I do think Archer was the best option.

ME

Why?

COLLINS

Playboy. He's probably been in a similar position himself at some point. I bet he has a few skeletons in his closet.

I think back to his run-in with Shane and Kassie.

ME

True that.

Is it bad that I'm already thinking of ways I can get you in that position again?

COLLINS

Not happening.

As her latest message comes through, I can't help the sense of unease. Is she serious? No more sex? I want so much more with her. I'm a patient guy, especially when it comes to the people I care about. But I need to know where her head is at.

ME

It might be a really bad idea, bringing this up now and over text, but I have to know, Collins. Do I even stand a chance with you?

COLLINS

You're right; this is a really bad idea—and bad timing too. I want to talk to you about us when you get home. There's so much I have to say.

My stomach roils, threatening to empty itself out onto the plush hotel carpet.

ME

That's another four days away.

COLLINS

I know, and I'm not trying to be deliberately evasive. I just need this time to figure everything out in my head.

I like you, Sawyer. I like everything about you.

Tension dissipates from my body, although not entirely, and a smile slowly creeps onto my face.

ME

Why don't you let me take you out when I get home on Sunday morning? How about some breakfast?

COLLINS

I'm working overtime again at the garage.

Something about the number of hours my girl works doesn't sit right with me. I get that she's passionate about bikes and her job, and I get that Brooklyn is an expensive place to live, so she needs the money for rent, but I don't hear of other mechanics picking up hours like she does.

I consider typing out a message to that effect but quickly

think better of it. Poking my nose into her business will *not* get me on the right side of Collins Mackenzie.

Archer stirs in the bed next to mine, and as he mumbles something in his sleep, an idea blooms in my head. Not far from her garage is a place called Lustful Luxuries.

ME

All right, how about I take you out for lunch? You get an hour, right?

COLLINS

I do, and, yes, why not? So long as it isn't stuffy or snooty.

ME

Oh, Baby Girl, I can confidently confirm it's neither of those things.

COLLINS

We're going with the nickname then.

ME

I don't see you objecting to it anymore.

COLLINS

No, I am not.

"Do you think Jack and Kendra have used the handcuffs yet?"

Still smiling like a fool, I lock my screen and set my phone down on the duvet next to me.

Turning to Archer, who has fully woken and is lying on his side, facing me, hands clasped between his head and the pillow, I balk at the thought of Jack getting it on.

"Why in the world would you be thinking about your center and his fiancée having sex?"

Archer rolls onto his back, interlacing his fingers across his chest. "I'm not in that sense. I just can't believe you got away with it."

"We got away with it because you haven't said anything—thank Christ."

He runs his pinched fingers across his lips, zipping them shut. "This mouth is forever sealed."

I tap my phone screen once, checking the time and how long we have until the team bus pulls up. "Is that a promise?"

He pushes his head back into the pillow, a grumble rising from his throat. "I'm always the butt of your jokes. No one takes me seriously around here." He swings his legs over the edge of the bed and sits up, facing me. "And I can be one hundred percent trusted and serious when I need to be, you know? Not everything is a game to me."

I mirror his actions until we're facing each other. "Name one thing you take seriously," I say, lips trembling with amusement since I'm only goading him, just as he does with everyone else.

To my surprise, he flushes—full-on fucking flushes; hot pink takes over his face and chest since—once a-fucking-gain—he isn't wearing a shirt.

Collapsing back on his bed with a thud, he stares up at the white ceiling. "Never mind."

Well, color me intrigued.

"Archer," I demand, "what the fuck have you done this time? Please tell me you haven't gotten it on with Kassie again."

Archer's jaw tics, his eyes remaining locked on the ceiling. "Nope. No danger of that."

I flop onto my back in a wave of relief. "At least you learned the error of your ways with her. Maybe you'll be a little more careful about who you hook up with in the future."

"No danger of hooking up either."

I'm back in a sitting position, relief replaced with concern. Not just in response to his statement, but the way he said it. I go to speak, but he cuts me off.

"I don't want to talk about it because it's pointless. So, can we just change the subject, please?" He pushes a stressed hand through his hair.

My concern increases. "Is everything okay, man?"

He puffs out a humorless laugh. "Yep. Everything is just peachy."

"Oh, well, now I definitely believe you."

He twists his head to face me, and it's then I see just how serious Archer Moore can be. In all the seasons I've played with him, I've never seen him look like this.

"It doesn't matter how many times you ask me; I'm not talking about it. I might be a lot of things, but contrary to popular belief, I'm not an idiot. I know where the line is. So, can we just forget this conversation ever happened?"

"If that's what you want, I—"

"Yeah, that's what I want," he bites out, shooting off the bed and heading for the dresser over on the far side of the room.

Pulling a drawer open, he grabs a couple of tops and walks them over to a training bag slung on a chair in the far corner. "I'm going to hit the gym for an hour before we head to the arena. Want to join me?"

I mull it over, thinking it might be a good way to get us back on track, when my phone buzzes next to me, and Ezra's face lights up the screen.

I pick it up and wave it at Archer, indicating I can't make it to the gym.

He throws a top on and gives me a thumbs-up. "Say hi to my little buddy Ezra," Archer calls over his shoulder, swinging the door open and closing it behind him.

"Aren't you supposed to be at the arena?" Ezra gets straight into it the moment our video call connects.

I guess a *hello, how are you* would be asking too much of a preteen.

"Will be in an hour. How was school?"

He rolls his eyes and dumps himself down on Alyssa and Dom's couch.

"Ezra, shoes off, please!" I hear Alyssa call from behind him.

Ezra rolls his eyes again and then fidgets—I'm guessing pushing them off with each foot in the way he does at home. "School was school. What are we doing for the holidays?"

I shrug since, just like Thanksgiving, I'm not a fan of Christmas. The only effort I make is for my son. "I guess the same as last year—dinner at Alyssa and Dom's and then back home for dessert and board games."

"Borrring!" he exclaims, which earns another scolding from Alyssa.

I run a palm across my face. "Well, you come up with something, and we can discuss if it's possible. Remember, I have games all around that time."

Ezra looks off to the side and then back at me. "Can we … can we go see Collins and her garage for Christmas?"

I scratch at my chin, not sure how the fuck to answer. She doesn't really have family, so I can't use that as an excuse—and I don't want to. Seeing Collins on Christmas Day would be the best gift.

Still, I need to play this safe for everyone. I can't just go and invite ourselves over to her place.

"She's likely already made plans, and I'm not sure detailing her bike is on her agenda that day."

My son visibly deflates, and I do the same. It's no lie that all any good parent wants is to see their child happy.

And Collins makes him exactly that.

"She loves bikes just as much as me, and I want to spend the day at her garage, so I think you're wrong, Dad."

It's possible I am incorrect, and a large part of me hopes I am.

I roll my tongue across the roof of my mouth, figuring out what the hell I should do. She wants to talk when I get back to

Brooklyn, and while Lustful Luxuries isn't exactly the place to hold a meaningful conversation, I'm confident my bed will be after I use whatever we buy on her later that night.

I rein myself in. *Jesus, Sawyer, you're talking about Christmas with your son.*

"All right," I say, and Ezra's face lights up like the damn Rockefeller Center Christmas Tree. "Let me talk with her when I get back home."

TWENTY-SEVEN

COLLINS

Fucking finally, a day off.

The plan? Fucking nothing. Veg out, watch the *Alien* movies, and eat my body weight in all the delicious snacks that are no good for me or my waistline.

I've worked myself into the ground these past few weeks, picking up any shift available and covering for colleagues and their vacations.

TV remote in hand and a bowl of Cap'n Crunch balanced on my lap, I'm poised and ready to start my day of nothing when the intercom buzzes, and I drop my head between my shoulders.

If this is Cameron showing up to find out why I haven't replied to his earlier text, asking how to replace a brake cable, I swear to whoever lives up there that I will throttle him with said cable.

That, or shove it somewhere.

Cap'n Crunch now turning to mush, I haul myself off the couch and head for the intercom, connecting the line just as it buzzes again.

"Yes?" I answer, exasperated.

"Ooh … all right, ma'am, what's got your panties in a

twist?" Kendra's voice sings down the line, way too enthusiastic for a morning.

I immediately hit the button to allow her access and unlock my door, heading back for my couch and settling in with my cereal.

She'll let herself in.

"Nothing like a warm welcome," she says, dropping her bag by the door and kicking off her sneakers.

Unlike me, Kendra is a neat freak. I wouldn't exactly describe myself as messy, more that I thrive in organized chaos. Apart from when it comes to my garage. That is a different story.

She flicks her eyes up to the dirty dishes by the sink.

"Don't even think about it. I can rinse them later. I have the entire day to myself, and right now, I'm watching *Alien*."

Kendra takes a seat next to me, leaning over to peer into my bowl. "I used to eat those when I was eight."

"I want no judgment," I respond around a mouthful. "I'm answerable to only myself and my waistline."

She flops back into my soft couch, chuckling. "Isn't this film a bit … heavy for a morning?"

Dropping my spoon into the bowl with a clatter, I slide it onto the small coffee table in front of us. "Did you stop by for a reason, or is it National Pick Collins Apart Day?"

Kendra just smirks at me, mischief all over her face. "No. Actually, I was on my way back from early morning conditioning, and I thought I'd drop in and ask the question both Jenna and I are desperate to know. She'd be here, too, if she didn't have lunch with her boyfriend's parents."

Now I'm intrigued.

Picking up the remote, I hit pause on Sigourney Weaver and turn back to my friend. "You know, I don't need to know the Blades schedule. I can tell just by how annoying you are whether Jack is around or not. You find ways to bother me when he's away rather than racing back to have endless sex with him when he's home."

She lifts a finger in the air. "It's funny you should mention sex because that was the first thing I concluded when you and Sawyer snuck off together on Saturday night."

"Squirt for me, Collins."

The delicious memory of Sawyer swallowing me down hits right between my thighs, and I cross my legs, desperate to hide its effects.

"Is that your question? Where we disappeared to?"

"Uh-huh."

Buying myself some thinking time, I fidget with my hair, readjusting my messy bun.

"We needed to talk after the date at the Botanic Garden, so that's why he came to find me. Sawyer pulled me into your spare room, and we talked everything over."

She's not buying it—I can tell as she twists a lock of blonde hair around her pointer finger. "Who knew that two people talking could turn the biggest playboy in the NHL white as a sheet just from witnessing said conversation?"

I drop my hands from my hair, slapping both thighs simultaneously. "All right, we fucked. Well, I say fucked, but it was …" I pause, heat rising through my body.

"Did it involve a pair of fluffy black handcuffs by chance?"

"How did you know?"

"Because …" She rises from the couch and heads for her bag, pulling the exact pair from the front pocket and dangling them in front of her. Nothing but amusement is in her voice as she says, "Whichever one of you decided to cover your tracks clearly forgot which drawer they had been kept in. Last time we'd used them, they were not stored in the middle drawer."

Ugh, in my haste and panic, I threw them back in the dresser and pulled on my pants.

"So, tell me"—Kendra props a hand on her hip—"did he cuff you to my spare bed and make you see stars?"

"Not exactly." I press my lips together, more memories flooding back. "He suspended me from the bar across the top and then ate me out until I saw stars."

Jaw agape, she drops the cuffs, and they hit my hardwood floor. "H-he had you hanging from the bed while he …"

I nod once.

"Lawwwwd," she drawls, returning the cuffs to her bag and walking back over to me, taking a seat. "I mean, how did he hold you up?"

"He balanced my legs on his shoulders so my pussy was in his face." I hold a palm in front of my mouth. Christ knows why I do it. The girl doesn't need a map.

"That is so … damn hot," she sighs. "But I'm glad you didn't break the bed."

My head darts to look at her, and we both burst into fits of laughter.

"Archer walked in on us as we were finishing up. He saw my tits, the works."

Kendra doubles over, clutching her stomach. "Oh my God, it hurts; it hurts. My stomach muscles are burning," she gasps between breaths.

"Yeah, well, I wasn't laughing when I walked out of the spare room. I couldn't even look at Archer for the rest of the night."

And I couldn't. I wouldn't say we're strangers since we're part of the same friend group; we've laughed and joked around a bit, but flashing myself at him was not something I had planned on Saturday night. Obviously.

"Well, he hasn't breathed a word to anyone, so I think your secret's safe with me and him."

I smile appreciatively.

"Though, seriously," she continues, "Sawyer's into kinky stuff, like you? You two are a match made in heaven."

The temptation to deny we're perfect together is right there, dancing on the tip of my tongue. I swallow it down and instinctively nod in agreement. "I don't know exactly how kinky he is, but let's just say, he both surprised me and blew my mind that night."

Kendra's lips twist in question. "So, are you two"—she crosses her index and second finger over—"dating?"

When I go back to fiddling with my hair, Kendra reaches up and takes my hand in hers. It's a move I didn't expect, but it's comforting.

"Go for it, Babe. I can tell you really like him."

On a long sigh, I bring my eyes to hers. I can't remember the last time I sought reassurance from someone. Or more importantly, the last time I needed it.

"When he gets back to Brooklyn, we're going to talk. I really like him, but I'm scared of what a relationship will mean."

She squeezes my hand harder—more reassurance that soothes my worries. "A relationship is, and can look like, anything you want it to be. It doesn't mean you have to lose yourself or what you love."

I think back to what I had with Mike. He hated bikes and was uncompromising about it too. I could never imagine Sawyer being that way. Then I think about Ezra and how I love spending time with him.

"Is being with Sawyer what you want?" Kendra breaks the short silence that fell between us.

I find her eyes again and see the warmth in them. "I think it really is."

TWENTY-EIGHT

COLLINS

In the end, Kendra stayed and watched the first two Alien movies and used up her "entire weeks' worth of snack allowance"—her words, not mine—in nailing all of my popcorn stash, which was sizable. I told her now that she was engaged, she'd entered the "comfortable" phase in her and Jack's relationship, which earned me a death stare.

Since I'm working all hours God sends and I now have depleted cupboards, I'm pulling on my boots, getting ready to go to the store, when my intercom buzzes for a second time.

"There's no more popcorn left, Babe. Go home and eat your own stash," I say into the speaker, convinced it can only be one person.

"Collins? It's Ezra."

I pause on grabbing my bag and jacket from the stand by the door and immediately buzz to let him up.

I swing my front door open and head down the first flight of stairs. I'm partway down when he comes into view. Dressed in his red uniform for the private school Sawyer once told me he attends, he has a heavy duffel bag hanging off his shoulder.

"Hey," I say, stopping just a few steps above him.

His green eyes crease with a smile. "Do you live in the penthouse?" he asks.

I drop down a couple more steps until we're at the same height. "This isn't the type of building to have a penthouse," I reply, a touch of confusion in my voice, wondering why he's here.

Ezra looks around the stairwell, casting his eyes across the exposed brick that's also featured in my apartment.

He adjusts the heavy bag—which is no doubt piled with books—and I reach out and lift it off him.

He rolls his shoulder back in relief. "I wanted to ask you a question."

"Okay … but let me ask you one first, if that's all right."

"Shoot."

Just as he reaches out to take his bag back, I loop it over my shoulder, the weight almost toppling me backward. He definitely has his dad's strength.

"I've worked out how you found where I lived since I had shown you that time you came over to my garage. What's got me puzzled though is, how did you get here?"

Eyebrows pulled together, he chews nervously on his bottom lip, scuffing the floor lightly with his shoe. "I got a ride."

I rear back a little, studying him carefully. He's trying to hide something, and he isn't a great liar. Another characteristic we share.

Neither of us speaks, and I'm determined not to be the first one to break the silence. Despite having zero experience with kids, I have very vivid memories of my own childhood. When I was Ezra's age, I was stubborn. Everything my parents and grandparents did was for my own good, yet I was convinced they were actively working against me. I don't necessarily see the same level of defiance in Ezra, though I can tell he's holding out on me.

His face turns sheepish. "Promise you won't tell Dad?"

"Ezra"—I shift the heavy duffel bag up my shoulder—"I can't withhold things from Sawyer—you know that. Although I am worried about what you're not telling me."

He looks off to the side and then down at the floor again.

I duck down a little, attempting to capture his attention. "Ezra?"

"One of the eleventh graders from the high school has a motorcycle, and he offered me a ride on it the other week, but Dad was picking me up. Then, today, after school, he offered again."

His eyes flare when he looks at me and no doubt registers the horror on my face. "But he has his license and everything, and he didn't go fast," he rushes out. "Alyssa and Dom said I could ride the bus home today, and when Carter offered, I figured it was okay?" He ends his little speech on a question, clearly seeking my approval.

I can't give it to him.

It's difficult to pinpoint a single emotion as so many of them trickle down my spine when I think about Ezra getting on the back of a teenager's bike and riding across Brooklyn. Fear, dread, anger toward Carter—who should have known better. Crushing panic takes hold, weighing so heavily that the bag on my shoulder suddenly feels lighter than air.

I introduced him to bikes; I took him out on one. Did I not do my job correctly and make it clear that while riding was fun, it was also incredibly dangerous, especially when the person you were with wasn't experienced or careful?

I crane my neck to look behind him, feigning to search for something. "Where are your leathers and helmet? Or did you hand those back to Carter when he dropped you off?"

Ezra flushes—hard.

Again, we fall into silence, and this time, I don't need him to speak. I already know the answer to my question.

"If you want a ride back from school one day, I can come get you, okay? Just …" I trail off, not wanting to ream the kid out and embarrass or shame him. "Getting on bikes without the proper protection is really unwise."

He nods and reverts back to chewing on his lip. "Dad's going to kill me, isn't he?"

I smirk. "I'll be careful with how I deliver it, and I'll make sure to tell him you know the score now."

Right at that moment, I hear Ezra's bag vibrate.

"Damn, I bet that's Grandma or Grandpa asking where I am."

Pulling the duffel off my shoulder, I unzip the front pocket and check the screen, handing the vibrating cell out to him. "It's Alyssa."

He shakes his head profusely, motioning to me. "Can you speak to her? Say I'm with you. I'm less likely to get into shit that way."

I quirk a brow at his language and hit Accept.

"Hey, it's Collins. Ezra's with me."

"Collins?" Alyssa says, understandably sounding surprised.

"Yeah, Ezra just turned up at my place."

"Why? Wait, how did he get there?" she asks, sounding more and more frantic.

Ezra's eyes bug out, a pleading look not to tell her anything. He obviously heard what she said.

Right or wrong, I offer Ezra a reprieve. "He got a different bus after school and stopped by my place to say hi."

Pulling back my jacket sleeve, I check the time. "I have to do some grocery shopping, but I can take Ezra with me and …" I look up at the twelve-year-old boy, who's anxiously shifting from one foot to the other. "And we can go for pizza and drop him back at your house later this afternoon. If that works?"

The grin that breaks out over his face could brighten even the cloudiest December day.

"Are you sure?" Alyssa asks.

"Yeah, more than happy to do that, and I promise, this time, it won't involve jelly beans."

She snorts a laugh, the sound reassuring, maybe even accepting, and for the second time today, I like the way it feels.

"Okay, well, tell him to be good, and we'll see you a little later when you bring him home."

"THERE'S NO WAY YOU'RE GOING TO—OH NO. MY BAD," I SAY, watching Ezra sink the largest slice of thin crust I've ever seen.

"Thishh is weally, weally gwood." He points to his insanely full mouth before finally swallowing. "Pepperoni is king."

"No kidding," I reply, hands clasped under my chin, a wry smile plastered to my face.

I never met Sophie, although I know what she looks like from pictures posted on the internet. I see a lot of Ezra in her—his smile, for one, and the way his eyes crinkle at the corners. However, Ezra's mannerisms remind me so much of Sawyer. From the cocky way his lips tip up when he goads you to his tendency to flush at the tiniest thing.

I'm not a huge fan of hockey, but it's common knowledge that Sawyer Bryce carries a reputation as the grumpy Blades captain. At first, I thought that was his whole self, that the persona the media portrayed was an accurate representation of the man off the ice.

I couldn't have been more wrong, and when Ezra smiles, the similarity I see between Sawyer and his son proves that point entirely.

Ezra motions to my plate. "Are you going to eat that slice?"

"Probably not." I push it toward him, and he immediately folds it in half, sitting back in the booth and devouring it in a couple of bites. "I'm saving myself for ice cream."

He stops chewing. "Ice cream? Dad always says if you don't finish your meal, you can't be hungry enough for dessert."

Reaching across, I snap up a menu from the end of the table and flip to the ice cream sundae page. I've been to this place a lot since I moved here—before now, only ever on my own—and I know the ice cream here is the best in town.

"Yeah, well, when it comes to treats, what your dad doesn't know can't hurt him …" I flick my eyes up to Ezra as he finishes a final bite of pizza. "Right?"

"Yes, ma'am!"

Five minutes later and with dessert on the way, I realize Ezra never asked me the question he had when he showed up at my place.

Picking up my soda, I take a sip and set it back down. "What was it you wanted to ask me earlier?"

He takes a pull on his strawberry shake. Memories of when we met back at Rise Up flush a comforting feeling through me. I guess it was the first time he discovered bikes, and maybe it was the start of a lifelong passion for him.

"Dad said he would talk to you when he got home, but I didn't believe him. So, I came over to ask you myself."

I've got to hand it to this kid; he's direct, and he knows what he wants. Add it to our list of commonalities.

"Go ahead," I instruct, feeling a little nervous about what's coming.

He releases a long sigh as two identical chocolate sundaes—topped with whipped cream, Oreos, a wafer and sliced cherries—are set down in front of us.

Ezra doesn't move to grab his ice cream, choosing to focus on me instead. "The holidays are right around the corner, and I was wondering if I could come to your garage and we could detail your bike." He twists his hands together on the table, lips following suit. "Alyssa and Dom normally cook dinner, and then we play board games. I don't know if you're seeing your family, although I kind of got the idea that maybe you don't have a whole lot of people, like we don't. Christmas is fun and all, but I think it would be better if we—"

"I'd love to," I softly interrupt his rambling. It took me exactly zero-point-two seconds to accept his invitation since it didn't need any thought. Detailing my bike on Christmas, with Ezra, sounds like the best way to spend the day I generally don't bother celebrating since I'm nearly always alone.

"For real?!"

I nod and smile. "Sure. Why not?"

He snaps his fingers, delighted. "All right! You could come back for dinner afterward."

I wince, not wanting to overstep. "Well, yeah, maybe. Let me check with your dad."

He waves a hand in front of his face, like that's the craziest idea he's ever heard. "Eh, he's desperate to see you. Probably kiss you too."

With a wafer halfway in my mouth, I practically choke on it.

Ezra balks at my reaction. "What? I already told you he likes you." He taps his pointer finger against his temple, leaning toward me. "I can tell when a boy likes a girl."

Feeling more than uncomfortable, I seize the opportunity to turn it around, leaning forward myself. "Oh, yeah? And are there any girls you like?"

A Sawyer-style flush paints his freckled cheeks. "No!"

Satisfied that there is, in fact, a girl he likes, I push his sundae toward him, a smug grin all over my face. "Okay, I *definitely* believe you. Now, eat up so I can get to the store and then drop you home before I land myself in trouble with your grandparents for keeping you out too long."

TWENTY-NINE

SAWYER

It's possible I just set the record for the fastest airport exit in human history. Jack had nothing on me as I hauled ass from the runway, racing through security and out into the parking lot.

I need to see Collins.

Seven days is nothing compared to some of the extended away series we travel for, and already, I'm thinking about how the fuck I'm going to make it through those since this one was damn torture.

The only relief came partway through the week when Collins messaged, letting me know Ezra had turned up at her apartment and she took him for pizza and ice cream. I was suiting up when I got the text. Imagining the two most important people in my life sitting in a booth somewhere, Ezra's beaming face as he shared a pizza with my girl, was the best possible game prep I could've wished for.

I killed it that night on the ice. The only place I'd have chosen over the rink would've been a seat next to one of them in the booth or maybe just the chance to be a fly on the wall, witnessing the effect those two had on each other.

Collins Mackenzie is incredible. Sure, she's beautiful, smart, and her own unique brand, just as she portrays to the outside world. But as I peel the layers back, I see so much depth to her—a side I think she subconsciously denies herself from revealing. The kind of caring side I'm convinced is exclusive to my son—and I hope to me too.

Realizing I'm in love with the woman while sitting in her workplace parking lot was not on my bingo card. In fact, none of this was. Yet it's happening, and not an ounce of me is mad or intimidated by it.

As I sit in my truck—my luggage in the trunk since I didn't even bother to take that home—I watch her go about serving customers and filling out paperwork from behind the front desk.

From this distance, I can't see her face, though I know she's smiling—she has to be. Motorcycles are what makes this girl happy. Witnessing the passion as it rolls off her in waves is what makes me happy. Because I can relate to that feeling with hockey. When Sophie died, that passion dulled, at one point turning into something that felt more like resentment—since if I hadn't been away from home at that time, I might've been able to save her.

Collins has reignited that passion. Hell, I even smiled during a press interview last night. Jack, the fucker, feigned passing out when he saw the footage.

Swinging my door open, I close it and lock the truck up, striding toward the entrance as Collins disappears back inside the garage.

The bell above the door rings as I push into the reception area, pulling off my Blades cap and running a nervous hand through my hair. I'm desperate to talk about us and what she wants.

Christ, please be me.

"Can I help you?"

I'm halfway to the seating area at the back when a male voice stops me in my tracks, and I spin around to face him.

I've no doubt this is her boss, Cameron, wearing a crisp white shirt and black pants. He even dresses like an asshole and uses way too much hair gel. I can smell it from here.

Taking a couple of steps back toward him, I tip my chin at the door leading to the garage. "I'm here for Collins."

His brown eyes study me carefully, slick black hair shining under the fluorescent lights. I can't be sure if he recognizes who I am, and equally, I couldn't give a fuck.

"I assume you're another one of Collins's Instagram followers, looking for a free bike service or health check?" he asks, voice full of cynicism.

Ten seconds in his company, and I don't like him; he gives me the fucking creeps.

I scrub a hand over my unshaven jawline, puffing out a soft breath. The temptation to do just as I did in the bar that time and claim I'm her boyfriend is overwhelming, but I resist, opting for the truth.

"I don't own a bike. I'm here to take her out."

He balks but tries to hide it. "As in a date?"

"Yeah," I reply, not that it has anything to do with him.

Cameron scratches the side of his neck, clearly displeased. "Well, you'll need to come back when she gets off her shift at, like"—he pushes back the cuff of his shirt, checking his watch—"after five."

I mirror his actions, pushing up the sleeves of my coat and black henley. "She has a lunch break in, like, twenty minutes, no?"

Casually, he readjusts the collar on his shirt. The move is condescending. How the fuck does a girl like Collins stand working for a guy like this? Thoughts that she actually slept with this prick surface, and I push them away.

Don't punch her boss, for fuck's sake, Sawyer.

"You want to take her out for a date on her lunch break?"

No, fucker. I want to see her as soon as motherfucking possible, and if that means grabbing an hour with my girl before she has to return to work for your sorry ass, then that's what I'll do.

I smile, patience wearing thin. "Yep. I just got back from a week away, and I want to see my girl." The *my girl* part slips out unintentionally.

His brows shoot to his hairline. "So, you're a thing?" He huffs out a doubtful sound. "I think you're getting ahead of yourself, buddy. Collins doesn't get serious with anyone. Not even NHL players."

Ah, so he does recognize me.

My level of calm now rapidly dwindling, I shove my hands into the pockets of my jeans. "Maybe it just took the right guy to come along."

Unless Collins told him, Cameron has no idea I know they once had a thing. His face tells the story though as he rocks back on his heels, getting a better view through a window into the garage.

"I'm not a huge hockey fan, but I know who you are. And since your face is always in the press, I'll save you the potential of public embarrassment." His face is all smarm as he resets his focus on me. "Watch out with that one. She's got a habit of bedding men and leading them on, only to toss them aside a few days or weeks later."

My blood boils as my hands curl, straining inside my denim pockets as they fight to form fists. "You sound like you speak from experience," I reply, acting none the wiser, my voice not revealing how pissed I am at the way he speaks about a girl he clearly knows nothing about.

"Huh, yeah, you could say that. At one point, I thought Collins liked me for my personality. Turned out, she just wanted to ride my dick."

I'm across the room and in his face in a split fucking second. "Don't talk about Collins that way. In fact, never speak about her again."

Yep, alpha Sawyer has officially reentered the chat.

His eyes flare, and he holds up one hand. "Whoa. All right there, buddy. I'm just giving you a friendly warning to get out before it's too late—or at least adjust your expectations."

On a clenched jaw, I debate what his cocky face would look like with a broken nose. "You think I'd take a warning or even listen to a guy who treats his employees like shit? You know what I think? I think you wanted more, and she turned you down, so your ego got bruised, and now you abuse your position as her manager, making her work all hours God sends as a way to nurse your wounds. That's right; she's told me all about you."

I take a step back, and he doesn't say a word, his self-assured face never wavering.

"Now, given that she barely uses her vacation time and you clearly like taking advantage of her passion for bikes, this is how it's going to go down."

Behind the desk, I clock an oil-stained set of overalls, and I casually move around Cameron, pulling them off the hook and tossing them at him.

Stunned, he catches them against his chest.

"You're going to change out of those ugly-as-fuck dress shoes and pants and into something that tells me you actually give a shit about your staff and possess even a modicum of work ethic. Then you're going to cover my girlfriend's shift …"

Shit, I said it.

"And she's going to take this afternoon *and* tomorrow off work," I finish.

He scoffs. "Are you for fucking real? I've got a business to run."

I turn on my heel, practically yanking the front door off its hinges. I'll wait for Collins in the truck.

Before I step outside, I pause and tip my head to look at him. "Call in a colleague to put some hours in—hell, close for all I care. Because there's zero chance of her showing up for work tomorrow morning. Not when I have her in my bed."

THIRTY

COLLINS

Well, the end of that shift was fucking weird.

One minute, I was servicing the air filter, rushing so I didn't overrun into my lunch break, and the next, a sour-faced —albeit that part wasn't weird—Cameron was standing next to the bike in his overalls, telling me to clock out for the day and take tomorrow off too.

I wasn't about to argue, especially since I knew Sawyer was sitting in the reception area, waiting for me.

Except he isn't here.

And feeling some kind of way over the prospect that he stood me up, I reach into my jacket pocket, ready to text Sawyer, when his red F-150 pulls up outside the front entrance.

As I pull the door open and approach his truck, I can't decide which emotion is stronger—excitement at the mystery date he's taking me on or relief as I realize he turned up after all.

"Hey, Baby Girl," he immediately greets me as I open the passenger door. He stretches across the center section and plants a kiss on my cheek. "I missed you."

I clip myself in and turn to him, waving a nonchalant hand in front of me. "Eh, I would say the same, but I was too busy seeing the other man in my life."

Sawyer pulls off his aviators, playfully smirking. "By 'other man,' are you referring to a twelve-year-old showing up at your apartment, unannounced?"

I think back to the time Sawyer did exactly that, trying to convince me to go out with him. "Hmm," I muse, reaching across and tapping him on the shoulder. "Like father, like son, I guess."

Sawyer presses his lips together. "Thank you for taking him out for pizza and ice cream, he hasn't stopped going on about it." He pauses and twirls his sunglasses around, thinking. "I also appreciate the way you handled the ride he took over to your place. You were right to remind him of the dangers and you dealt with it way better than I would've done."

I offer a tight smile. "He wasn't annoyed that I told you then?"

Sawyer shakes his head on a low chuckle. "No. I don't think it's possible for you to annoy him, that's my specialty."

Uncertain if his next action is driven by the conversation we just had or my hot-as-fuck leather pants I know he loves, but when Sawyer takes my chin between his fingers and pulls my mouth to his, I conclude the source behind his motivation to kiss me really doesn't matter.

He feels incredible.

I dissolve beneath him, a tiny whimper escaping me when his tongue teases the seam between my lips.

"Open for me, Collins," Sawyer quietly requests. "Let me taste what I desperately missed these past seven days."

The moment I do, he takes the kiss deeper, snaking a hand under my ass.

I press my palm against his chest, all too aware of the last time we got into it around people. "Listen, I'm down for more later, but not right in front of the garage. Cameron could see."

A heady rumble reverberates in his chest, his tongue licking into my mouth, fingertips sinking into my pants. "I don't think you need to worry about that asshole anymore."

Using the hand still planted on his chest, I push back slightly, eyes narrowed in question. "Give me the specifics, Bryce."

He chuckles, going in for another kiss.

I push back further, waggling a finger at him. Okay, I'm flirting, but still partially serious. "Uh-uh, not until you tell me exactly what you mean by that."

He lifts his shoulders and chuckles again, knowing full well I'm getting a taste of my own shrugging medicine. "I meant nothing by it. He just knows where the boundaries are."

I decide to test out a theory, wondering if my sudden afternoon and day off have anything to do with the man sitting next to me, still trying to steal kisses. "We'd better hurry up and head to wherever you're taking me. I don't want to be late in getting back for my asshole boss."

He pauses with his lips over mine, the feel and scent of his breath making me tingle in the familiar way only he can evoke. "You and I both know the only place you're going to be for the next thirty-six hours is my bed."

The tingles intensify, tightening my core.

"Won't Ezra be home tonight?"

He tips his head from side to side, thinking it over, though clearly not seeing me staying as a problem. "He will."

I draw my bottom lip between my teeth. "Is this where we talk?"

Moving away from me and shifting into gear, Sawyer doesn't say anything as he pulls out of the parking lot and heads down the street, taking a couple of lefts until we reach a quiet suburban area.

He kills the engine and leans across the center section, unclipping my belt and hauling me onto his lap. I squeal as he does it with ease, scooting his seat back to give me space.

He drops his eyes from mine, taking in the leather pants I quickly changed into before leaving work. "You wore these deliberately, didn't you? To ensnare me in your Collins Mackenzie web."

When he palms the nape of my neck, pulling my forehead down to meet his, I know I'm ready to go further. The truth is, I don't know if I'll make a good girlfriend. All I'm sure of is, I don't want to let Sawyer or Ezra down.

But I'm starting to believe I won't.

"Was I successful?" I whisper. "Are you tangled up in me?"

"Baby Girl," he breathes out, pressing his head against mine, almost like he's trying to merge our minds so I can understand how much he's feeling, "you know I've been enraptured since the day I set eyes on you at Lloyd's. Your web is one I never want to break free from. If you'll let me stay."

This time, I'm the one stealing the kisses, bringing my hands to either side of his face. Sawyer's scruff feels delicious beneath my palms—a sensory bliss I want between my legs as soon as possible.

"I don't want you to break free," I say, voice a little shaky.

I melt further into his body when he releases a long sigh of relief at the words I know he's been desperate to hear for weeks, months, perhaps over a year.

"And what about you, Collins? Can I be sure you won't escape from me, from Ezra?"

This feels like one of the biggest conversations we've had and definitely the most loaded question he's asked me to date. I've never made my need to travel and move around a secret. It's always been a part of who I was and something that made me happy. Staying in one city or even country for a prolonged period of time has a way of making my skin prickle with unease.

But when he just asked me the question, I felt no discomfort at all. The thought of staying in Brooklyn is as easy as sitting opposite Ezra while we devour ice cream and talk motorcycles.

It's as easy as lying in bed with his dad before morning skate and my shift at work.

Truthfully, it's *always* been easy.

I twist my hands into his black henley, and Sawyer rests his finger under my chin.

"Look at me, Collins."

I do as he asks, his handsome face beginning to blur in front of me.

Inhaling a deep breath into my lungs, I know I'll never forget this moment. "I want to give us a go, and I don't want to escape. I like it here, with you and Ezra, just as we are in Brooklyn."

SAWYER'S BEEN DRIVING FOR THE PAST TEN MINUTES WITH ONE hand on the steering wheel, the other in mine. The instant I told him I wanted to give us a shot, he hasn't let go of me. And his smile hasn't left his face either.

I look down at our connection, our hands resting in my lap. "You know if you let go of me, I won't magically disappear."

He squeezes my hand harder. "I know. I'm just making up for all the times I wanted to do this, but didn't get the chance." He pulls up at a Stop sign and turns to face me, eyes crinkling in the corners and beyond the edges of his aviators. "Because you were determined to make me wait and work for it."

I move toward him, my lips finding the shell of his ear. "You know what they say—*good things come to those who wait.* And if you're really lucky, I'll let you put it in my ass later."

I throb at my own filthy mouth.

Sawyer flicks on his blinker, ready to turn right. "Am I right in thinking that would be a first for you? Someone taking your ass?"

"You'd be correct. It's always been a hard line for me. Don't ask why since I love to be tied up and played with in every way possible."

Sawyer releases a pained noise, and my eyes drop to his tenting pants.

He follows my line of sight as we start moving again, and he heads down a street in an unfamiliar part of town.

"Listen, a hard-on isn't exactly inappropriate for where we're going, but it will be painful while I wait to get my chance with you later."

I'm about to ask where the hell we're headed, visuals of a couple's strip joint quickly taking shape, when Sawyer answers my question, pulling into a parking lot for a building named Lustful Luxuries.

"Is this where we're eating lunch?" I muse, one hand on the passenger door handle. I know *exactly* what this place is despite not ever visiting, and my heart rate picks up at the prospect of toy shopping with Sawyer.

"I mean ..." He pulls off his shades and sets them on the dash in front of him. Eyes sparkling, they drop down the length of my body, unadulterated hunger behind them. "I guess this place is loosely connected to eating."

My lips are trembling. I'm not sure who breaks first, but we both fall into fits of laughter. I'm so hysterical that I don't clock when he stops laughing, now sitting in silence and watching me, head pushed back into the rest. I only notice when Sawyer's hand wraps around the back of my head, pulling me into him.

He can't keep his hands off me, and I'm freaking here for it.

"Tell me something, Baby Girl," he murmurs against my mouth. "Is it okay for me to call you my girlfriend now?"

That word.

The label I've spent so long recoiling at falls over my skin like a shot of sunshine on a freezing cold day.

"I guess that's what I am, right?" I reply, still so close to him that I can taste his delicious breath. I want to taste so much more of him.

"Collins, you're so much more to me than just a single word, but, yeah, I want to be sure when I'm asked about us that you're cool with me claiming you. When I think of you as my girl, I want to know you are actually mine to keep."

"You can claim me in any way you want," I tease, so much meaning to my statement.

Keeping his lips against mine, Sawyer reaches behind him and releases his driver's door, ready to get out and head inside the store. "You can't say things like that to me when I'm about to drop a ton of money so I can have you in every way I want."

I palm his dick, and he groans, the guttural noise dampening my panties.

"Baby, you should know by now that I say and do exactly what I want. And I think our first purchase should be our own pair of handcuffs."

THIRTY-ONE

COLLINS

"You realize the chances of someone recognizing you in the store are high, right?" I say to Sawyer just as he's about to pull the door open.

He releases the handle, adjusting my black scarf when he steps closer. "I really don't care. And anyway"—he smiles down at me—"I don't think being recognized is going to be an issue since I called a few days ago and explained we were coming. The owner understood the need for a little discretion, and he's the only one inside. He's closed the store for the next hour."

I don't know whether to laugh, smile, or let my jaw hang open. "An hour? How long do you think it takes to buy a couple of toys?"

Sawyer crowds me further, lips tipping up mischievously. "This isn't only about buying what makes you feel good. This is about me learning what you want, what makes you tick in bed too. I want to spend the next hour discovering all your fantasies and making sure we get a chance to explore them—ASAP."

I go to speak, but he silences me with a kiss before spinning back around and leading me through the entrance.

"Mr. Bryce." The store owner rounds the counter and heads

straight for Sawyer, his arm outstretched. "First, I just want to say I'm a huge Blades fan—have been for years."

Sawyer shakes his hand, almost like they're meeting for a business lunch to discuss the stock market. "Thanks so much." He leans down, planting a kiss on top of my hair. "This is Collins, my girlfriend."

Hold in the squeals, Collins. You're the casual one in this relationship, remember?

"Thanks for offering us the store for an hour. As I'm sure you can appreciate, privacy is really important to us."

The owner—who must be over forty but clearly works out and takes good care of himself—smiles. "It's my pleasure. Now, are you looking for some advice, or would you like to browse alone?"

Sawyer's eyes drop to me. "I'll go with whatever you want to do, Baby Girl."

My attention rests on a display of toys lining the back wall. "Thanks, but I think I have it covered," I reply, already on my way over to the back.

Sawyer follows behind me as he laughs quietly, unsurprised by my confidence.

When we pull up in front of the spanking paddles, his eyes flare wide.

"Have you ever used one before?" I ask.

He selects the brown leather paddle hanging directly in front of us, twisting it around in his hand. "Would you be shocked if I said yes?"

I have no doubt my face tells him I am one hundred percent shocked.

He dips his head to be level with mine, his pupils already blown from lustful thoughts. "Just because your first time with me wasn't as adventurous as you'd have liked doesn't mean I don't have the experience to satisfy you."

I pulsate, so turned on already despite only shopping for less than five minutes. "What are you trying to tell me, Sawyer?"

He smirks, all sexy and oozing a confidence that makes me want to climb him right here and now. "I guess what I'm saying is, I've held back with you. I meant it when I said that I've never had anything like what I have with you. I've had opportunities here and there to explore what really turns me on, but the second you told me what you liked while I drove into you on the hood of my car?" He turns the paddle around in his palm. "I think I fell a little harder." He looks at me, eyes no longer blown but ablaze. "Tell me everything you're into, Collins."

I bite on my bottom lip, needy excitement overtaking me. Maybe I shouldn't be surprised, considering the way he took control at Jack and Kendra's party. "Follow me."

He's still holding the paddle when I interlace our fingers and lead us a couple of rows to the left.

"I think this would be my ultimate fantasy," I say, coming to a stop a few seconds later.

Sawyer releases my hand and reaches up for the spreader bar. "You want me to use this on you?"

"On us both. Edge my pussy until I come. With my legs braced apart, I'll be powerless to stop you, and so will you when I return the favor."

He closes his eyes and swallows, probably walking through the scene in his head. "How would you want to be teased?"

I take the bar from him and check its maximum extension. "Well, that would be telling. I like a power struggle, and this is the perfect piece of equipment."

"What else do you want?" he asks, voice gravelly.

Reaching onto my tiptoes, I speak softly. "Handcuffs and ties. It's not only my legs I want restrained."

"Huh."

"What is it?" I ask.

I begin eating my sandwich as we sit in Sawyer's truck, attempting to satisfy my horny thoughts with calories. We finished up shopping, and rather than fuck in aisle three, like we both wanted, we compromised and headed for Chick-fil-A.

Sawyer reaches over to my food and steals a fry, his eyes fluttering shut as he chews around it.

"When was the last time you had fast food?"

He shrugs a shoulder. "No idea. A long fucking time ago." He grins. "You make me do bad things, Mackenzie."

Swallowing, he shows me his phone—a text from Ezra, asking if he can head home with a friend tonight for dinner and their mom will drop him home later.

My boyfriend is all smiles as he takes his phone back and types out a response. "I also can't remember the last time my son asked to hang out with anyone from school. He's changing, coming out of his shell." He hits Send on the message and looks at me. "So much of that is because of you—you know that, right?"

My heart skips. "What do you mean?"

Sawyer takes another fry, dipping this one in Chick-fil-A sauce. "He was becoming more and more withdrawn, and it was starting to worry me. He'd lost interest in everything other than video games, and he spent huge chunks of his time hidden away in his bedroom." His brows knit together. "He was always so smiley and outgoing, reminding me a lot of his mom. I don't know what changed, but it felt like, overnight, he just stopped finding enjoyment in things he had before, like shooting hoops with his friends on a Sunday." He pauses, and I don't just see the emotion on his face; I feel it on his behalf. "I missed my sunshine boy."

"And then bikes happened?"

He throws me a sweet smile, tucking a lock of hair behind my ear. "And then *you* happened, Collins. To the both of us. You were right that day in the Botanic Garden."

I think back to our date; it wasn't all that long ago, but somehow, it feels like a lifetime. "I said a lot of things that night, most of it being bullshit."

"Like only wanting no-strings sex?" he teases.

I raise a warning brow. "What was I right about?"

Buying himself some time to respond, he picks up his soda and takes a long pull before setting it back down in the cupholder. "You alluded to my happiness and perhaps lack thereof, given it was only Ezra and me."

Jesus, that was an asshole thing to say.

"I didn't mean it like that. I think my defenses went up when you suggested I might not be happy, being alone."

He shakes his head with a look of sincerity. "No, you were right. I hadn't been happy in my life for a long time. I think I was just surviving rather than thriving."

"And now?"

He reaches out, brushing the rough pad of his thumb across my cheek. "Well, to quote you, 'like father, like son.' So much has changed for me too. I feel alive when I'm around you, Baby Girl. I'm not just existing for my son anymore; I'm living for me because I see a future beyond the time when Ezra moves out for college or gets a place of his own." He swallows thickly, rolling his lips together. "If I told you that future was you, would that be too much for you to hear? The last thing I want you to do is run just when I've finally won you over."

"It's okay. I'm not freaked out," I whisper. And it's the truth; I'm not. "I didn't say yes to giving us a shot without having thought through all that it could potentially mean. I know this isn't some kind of fling, Sawyer, and I really don't see it as that. You're the first person who's made me want to stick around to see what happens."

He drags a large pull of air into his lungs. "Okay." He half chuckles, half sighs. "That's really fucking good to know."

I finish the last bite of my sandwich, and Sawyer takes my trash, driving up to a can and throwing it inside.

"Since we have the rest of the day together, what else do you want to do, Baby Girl?"

THIRTY-TWO

SAWYER

Collins answered my question exactly how I'd wanted—she's in my bed, hands tied to my headboard, her pussy inches from my face. There's no other way I would've wanted to spend my afternoon.

"Can you stand them a little wider?" I ask, extending the spreader bar further.

"More," she demands, voice heady and hands straining against the leather strap we bought earlier. "I want to be as wide as possible while you tease me."

I spread her legs further, stopping when her feet are another inch apart.

Completely at my mercy—that's how I like Collins Mackenzie.

I lean back on my haunches, scrubbing a palm over my mouth, words to describe how perfect she looks dying on my tongue. She's naked and ready for me, hair sprawled across my white pillow. Her tattoo is all that covers her flawless, fair skin.

She doesn't say anything either, waiting for me to make a move and do as I please. That's what she wants—for me to take control of her, of us, of this moment right here. Having Collins hand herself to me like this is seismic and likely the hottest experience of my life. After all, it's exactly what I wanted.

Eyes on hers, I drop to my elbows between her legs, fingertips trailing along the side of her left thigh. "How badly do you want me to edge this body?"

She squirms at the sensation, making it clear light touch is exactly what she loves. "Until it hurts and my pussy aches from desperation."

I can see how wet she is already. Dripping. Her release soaking the sheets covering my mattress.

With a gentle finger, I ascend to the top of her thigh, not stopping as it passes through her pussy, the sound of her wet arousal shooting straight to my cock.

I pin my bottom lip between my teeth and swipe my finger through her a second time. "Baby Girl, I've barely touched you, and already, you could take me so easily."

Feet planted firmly on the mattress, she fights against the bar, desperate to close her legs and end the torture.

I push up onto my elbows and climb off the bed, eyes still firmly on hers as she follows me with confusion.

"Where are you going?"

Standing at the foot of my bed, I make her watch as, one by one, I unbutton my Levi's, letting them pool around my ankles in a heap. "Getting myself comfortable. It's going to be a long afternoon, no?"

She bites the inside of her cheek and groans, wrists pulling against the restraints. "Just make me come already, Sawyer."

When Collins was in the bathroom earlier, I took the opportunity to grab something I knew would push her to the brink of her limits.

Ice.

Reaching down under the bed, I pull out a glass filled with a half-dozen cubes. "But where's the fun in giving you what you want right away?"

She scowls at me, and I fucking love it. I round the bed and come to stand by her side, towering over her. When she clocks the ice I set on the nightstand, her tongue peeks out, tantalizing as it runs the length of her bottom lip.

"What are you going to do with that?"

On my hands and knees, I crawl over to her, kneeling just in front of the spreader bar.

I reach over to the glass and grab a single ice cube, showing it to her. "What do you want me to do with this, Collins?"

She wets her lips again.

"Cat got your tongue?" I tease.

She swallows thickly, eyes dropping to the ice as it slowly begins to melt, water trickling down my fingers.

Her focus is pinned solely on me as I take the cube into my mouth, the freezing sensation a stark contrast against the way my tongue burns with the need to be on her.

Lying down on the bed and with my head between her spread legs, I bring the cube between my lips, languidly running it along the inside of her thigh.

The heat of my tongue, combined with her body, melts the cube faster, trickles of water running down her leg and intensifying her pleasure.

"Oh Jesus," she gasps when I reach her apex. "Ice play is my absolute favorite."

A raw sense of pride settles in my chest when I part her open with my fingers and circle her clit slowly with cold lips, being sure not to let the ice cube make direct contact with her pussy.

My mouth is soaking wet with a mixture of her arousal and the ice.

"Fuck!" Her knees shake as her legs desperately try to close around my head, just like they did that time I ate her out in my Lamborghini.

I pull back, lips shining as I shake my head at her reaction.

She wanted me to edge her, so she'll take the torture like a good fucking girl.

My mouth is practically numb from the ice—good and ready to do exactly what I planned.

Moving up her body and braced on my elbows, I hover over my girlfriend and drop my mouth down to hers. Tracing two fingers across her lower lip, I ask for her to open up.

She does as I want, and I drop the cube onto her tongue.

"Can you taste that, Baby? That's the pure perfection that is your pussy."

Her tormented whimper pulls a dark rumble from my chest.

"What was that, Collins?" I turn my ear toward her, knowing full well that she can't speak with the cube in her mouth. "You want me to edge you some more?"

I'm back down her body, my freezing tongue across her clit in seconds, lapping at her with zero intention of letting up. She tastes like fucking heaven, and when she writhes beneath me, I pin her legs to the bed with a firm hand on the spreader bar.

"Patience, pretty girl."

"Sawyer, make me come, please. I'm begging you."

The cube must've melted already. She doesn't sound desperate enough, and I'm enjoying myself way too much to allow that.

I shake my head once. "No."

Reaching over to the nightstand, I grab another cube from the glass, running it across her already-peaked nipple. "You know what might make me take pity on you?"

"What?" she groans, yanking her hands and getting nowhere.

My eyes flick from her nipple to her dilated pupils. "Beg for it."

My dick strains, and I know it's already leaking into my boxers, the torture I'm inflicting on Collins transferring to my balls as my body urges for its release too.

"I'll never beg," she grits out, trying to take back some of the control.

No fucking way. This is my game tonight.

"On your knees, ass in the air."

I know she can twist the leather strap without hurting her wrists. I just need this bar out of the way. Quickly, I unbuckle the cuffs around her ankles, setting the bar on the other side of the bed.

She doesn't move her legs, thighs still parted for me.

"Need some help there?" I say, hands underneath her ass as I roll her over.

"Fuck me, Sawyer," she pleads while rising onto her knees.

"Beg me." I repeat my demand.

She grips hold of the wooden headboard. "I told you, I've never begged, and I don't plan on starting now." Her voice is labored with lust—a sure sign that she's enjoying our tussle.

"You know, the ice wasn't the only thing I grabbed earlier." I drop the half-melted cube back into the glass and reach down beneath the bed, finding the spanking paddle we bought and then a bottle of intimate lube, which I set down beside me.

The first crack to her ass isn't hard. I want to shock her—and I succeed when she squeals and grips the wood harder—but I also want to respect her limitations.

"Harder," she instructs.

My dick leaks again. I'm so fucking close to blowing.

The second smack leaves a red mark, and she moans into the quiet room, pushing her ass back into me.

"More."

I switch to her other ass cheek and hit her harder. "Beg me to make you come, Collins."

"No."

Her defiance is sexy as hell and my goddamn undoing. I lose control of my willpower, pushing my boxers down with one hand and plowing into her tight, hot cunt with one thrust.

"Fuck—fuck—fuck!" she cries out. "Again."

I do the opposite of what she wants, pulling out. Her arousal leaks from her entrance and onto my sheets.

"You can't—can't leave me like this."

"Then beg, Baby Girl. Give me your words, and I'll put my cock back in your pussy, maybe even your ass if you behave well enough."

She falls silent, and I smack her ass again, more redness rising on her perfect skin.

I'm rearing back once more when she stops me.

"Please, Sawyer. I'm begging you." Collins turns her head, ordinarily perfect liner smeared across her face, cheeks flushed crimson. "Fuck me with your dick—in both holes. I want this with you."

I lose it, along with the paddle, throwing it on the floor and driving into her pussy on a guttural groan that fills my bedroom. My finger finds her ass, and I circle it, using her release to tease her opening while I take her pussy with my cock.

She whimpers with delight. This isn't just fucking. This is Collins handing me the reins to drive us.

And I do. The shift in our relationship inflates my chest, tightening my balls as my dick hits so deep that I know she'll be coming in seconds.

"Baby Girl," I pant, "you're so fucking perfect like this—at my mercy, taking my dick and finger like the needy slut you are." I push my finger further into her ass, preparing her for what I really want to do.

"I'm coming, Sawyer."

Her wail acts like a drug, and I want more of it.

"Tell me who fucks you best, Collins." I want the praise; I need the words of this woman before I paint her pussy with my cum.

"You. It's never b-been this good."

I pull out and swipe up the lube, covering two fingers and slowly dipping them into her ass.

Her head lolls forward, arms slack, and her knees practically give out.

I hold her steady with one arm around her waist. "Do you want to take my dick in here?"

"Yes. I want to know what it feels like."

I'm burning with desire and a huge sense of pride that Collins, my girlfriend, wants this with me.

Grabbing the lube, I pop the cap and cover my shaft. The feeling of her release, combined the lube, sends me right to the edge.

I won't last long, and I know it.

I drop the closed bottle and draw in a deep breath, notching myself at her entrance. "Drop your shoulders and relax, Collins. Let me look after you."

She does exactly as I ask, and I feel her body relax in the arm I'm still supporting her with.

"Oh-my-God, it feels so, SO good," Collins breathes when I push my dick into her tight ass.

I squeeze my eyes shut, every part of my body tightening with desire. "You're doing so well. Can you take some more of me?"

She nods once, and I continue to push myself inside her.

"That's right; let that ass eat up what I'm feeding it."

A couple of seconds later, I'm all the way inside. Her breathing is erratic, and I'm so close to coming.

"Move, Sawyer. Move," she pleads.

The first stroke is better than I could've ever imagined.

"I'm not going to last thirty seconds like this, Collins," I say, using my free hand to play with her dripping cunt.

She spreads her legs wider, opening herself for me. "Then don't. The second you come, I know I will too. Shoot it in my ass, Sawyer."

Two more strokes, and my orgasm explodes deep inside my girl. It's all-encompassing, mind-altering, and everything I knew we were capable of.

"Fuuuuck!" It's all I can manage, all I can think to say, as I pull out of her and pump the final jets across her red ass cheeks.

Body satiated and mind spinning out, I gather my cum onto my fingers and push it back inside my girl's pussy, and she whimpers once more.

"Keep this, Collins. Let me sit inside both holes for as long as possible—a reminder of the best sex you've ever had." I chuckle and gather some more. "You can't deny I'm a solid ten out of ten for sure."

THIRTY-THREE

"How many times would you say you've watched this movie?"

Collins shakes her bag of sweet and salty popcorn, twisting her lips to the side as she rests her head on my shoulder. "*The Breakfast Club*? Probably fifty-plus times."

I press my back into the couch, trying to get a better look at her face. "Are you serious?"

"Deadly," she replies.

She holds the bag out to me, and I take a couple of pieces.

"You know I've inhaled my weekly calorie allowance in the span of twelve hours, right?"

She shrugs. "Kendra said the same thing to me recently. She knows about the handcuffs, by the way. It appears we didn't do a great job of covering our tracks and stashed them in the wrong dresser drawer."

"Do you care?" I ask her, snatching another piece of popcorn. *This shit's addictive.*

"Not really. She was definitely impressed that we'd pulled it off though."

My fingertips graze her bare shoulder as I push some of her

hair behind her neck, revealing soft skin I want to caress with my lips. "And were you impressed?"

She lifts her head from my shoulder, twisting around to face me. "You know I was. In fact, I'm trying to decide whether what we just did in there"—she nods toward the stairs leading to my bedroom—"beats it, or if I prefer being suspended with my legs wrapped around your shoulders."

I press my lips to the flawless skin peeking out above the oversize collar of the shirt she's wearing. When we finished up in the bedroom, we showered together, and I handed her one of my original Blades training shirts, desperate to see her in it. She didn't hesitate to throw it on, and now I'm starting to picture what my name across her back would look like.

How much my last name would suit her. Period.

"Can I ask you something?" I murmur against her pebbled skin.

Her body tenses only a fraction, but it's still noticeable, and I hate it—a reminder that despite us officially dating, I know I have a long way to go before her walls crumble entirely.

"Sure, go ahead."

I pick up the TV remote from the couch armrest and pause the movie, plunging my living space into silence.

Without me asking, she turns to look at me, and I interlace my fingers through the hand she has resting on my stomach.

"Come straddle me for a second, Baby Girl."

She sets the popcorn on the coffee table and does as I ask, my dick instantly straining against the athletic shorts I'm wearing.

With a soft touch, her fingernail traces a wave tattoo stamped across my left pec, dropping to the bar pierced through my nipple. She frequently plays with that, and I love how much she enjoys it. It's so sensitive, and it makes me horny as fuck.

I watch her carefully for a second. She isn't wearing makeup since she removed it in the shower—yes, a couple of weeks ago,

I bought a whole bunch of female products, including a Dior cleansing kit and their entire skin care line. You know, just so she didn't have any excuse not to stay over at my place.

"Is the mermaid tattoo significant?" I get the feeling it is since I know Collins well enough to work out that she doesn't do permanence lightly.

Her stunning brown eyes study me, and I feel the heat between her thighs, making me harder.

I set my hands on her hips, a little like I would if she were riding me.

She blows a soft breath through her nose, toying with my piercing. "The tattoo itself isn't really significant. I just liked the design and needed something large and detailed to cover the scars."

I pull back, really not anticipating that answer. "Scars?"

"Yeah, from when I had my motocross accident." She chuckles softly, an edge of cynicism to the sound. "I've had my fair share of incidents, but that was my most serious." She releases my nipple, hands falling to the hem of her shirt as she swipes it clean over her head in one motion.

In a black thong, she's otherwise completely naked and in my lap. In so many ways, this is my dream situation—Collins almost naked on my couch, straddling me in such an intimate position. But the way she's opening up right now fully steals the breath from my lungs.

"What happened?" I ask, tracing my thumb slowly down her side, and I pause when I feel the evidence hidden expertly beneath black ink.

She takes ahold of my hand and moves my thumb lower, and I can feel the bumps left by stitches continuing across the length of her rib cage, stopping just before her hip. Since the scars are old, they're tiny, but it breaks my heart to think of anything hurting Collins.

"That photo album you found? Well, the pictures in there

were taken the day before. I was riding into a hairpin bend, but I didn't lean into the turn correctly, I was too distracted by a girl heading up my inside." She closes her eyes, perhaps reliving the moment. "I lost control of the bike and hit the deck—hard."

She opens her eyes and looks at me, the pain unmistakable. What happened still hurts her far beyond the physical injuries she sustained.

"I was thrown from the bike, and in the unluckiest turn of events, I opened my side up on a jagged rock. I broke multiple ribs and punctured a lung. It was bad—really bad—touch and go at one point, to be honest."

My throat is thick, voice hoarse when I speak again. "Is that why you stopped competing?"

She nods lightly, hand back to my nipple, which is perfectly aligned with hers, only an inch away. "The physical injuries ended my season, but I could've gone back. I just didn't want to. I fell out with the sport that had cost my parents so much in time and money and then almost my life. I ended up resenting it for more reasons than I gave you in the Botanic Garden that night. I guess my passion for bikes didn't die, but my love for the sport and being held to schedules and training and constantly competing to be the best just pissed me off. So, I quit."

I look up at her, thumb still tracing her side. "And do you regret anything?"

She shakes her head immediately. "I try and avoid regrets. It helps nothing since you can't take anything back. I might be a little wild, but I always think things through before making a decision."

The need to kiss Collins moves my hand to the back of her head, and I pull her down to my lips. "I know you do, and that's why I'll never take you or us for granted. I want you to know you have me, and I know Ezra is going to be so fucking happy that we're finally giving us a shot. There's so much more I want to say b—"

"Say it," she jumps in. "Say what's on your mind."

She swallows down my exhale, our lips practically touching.

"I don't know if I'm quite ready to say it all out loud. What we have is so strong but still so fucking fresh. I feel everything for you, Collins. When I look at you, I'm hit with a thousand words I want to scream to the world." I take her hand and place it on the center of my chest. "But it's the beat of my heart that tells the real truth—the way it hammers against my ribs every time I see you, how it feels so fucking full when you sit on my lap like this. Each time you light up my boy, it does something to me that I'll take with me to my grave—it makes me feel like I have a second chance at love."

Eyes shining with unshed tears, she presses her lips against mine, tongue sweeping gently into my mouth.

Earlier, the sex was fast and dirty—something I know Collins is comfortable with. But this time, I want to spill inside her slowly. I raise my hips slightly, and she lifts off, allowing me to pull my shorts beyond my ass and my cock to spring free.

Collins lifts up onto her knees and moves her soaking thong to one side, settling down on me carefully. "You're so fucking huge—you know that?"

A strangled moan rises up my throat, a little like the way her pussy grips my cock. "But you take me so well, Baby Girl."

She rocks over me once and winces.

"Are you sore?" I ask, concerned I went too far when I was pounding into her earlier.

"In the best way possible," she groans, moving her hips again.

I spread my thighs wider, wanting my cock all the way inside her.

"You know how deep I'll shoot inside you when we're like this?" A rogue smile plays on my lips, thoughts of breeding Collins too prominent and sexy to push away. I know she's on birth control, but the fantasy is still there, making me harder.

She instantly grows wetter; I hear and feel her pussy as she sucks me in.

I sink my fingertips into her soft ass. "Does that turn you on?"

She flushes, rosy pink painting her cheeks as she quietly scoffs, "No."

Oh, it absolutely does.

"So, the thought of me claiming your body in more ways than one doesn't make you want my dick on demand?"

Pink travels down her neck, and she whimpers, head falling forward and body shuddering. "I'm coming, Sawyer," she whispers before picking her head back up to look at me. "I'm coming so damn hard."

Satisfied I've unlocked yet another kink of hers, I push my hips into her and take control of her languid body. "Give me another, Collins. Let me fuck you through this one and straight into another."

She releases a laugh, like that's the craziest idea ever.

Until it isn't, and I'm riding her hard, pressing her swollen clit against my pubic bone. "I can feel it, the way your cunt is throttling my cock. You're there, aren't you?"

Collins wraps her arms around my neck and rides with me as we both chase our highs and ultimately fall deeper into each other. The words I held back on a second ago are desperate to spill free. Because I am. I know I'm in love with my girlfriend, and I can tell she's right behind me too. I don't know how long I'll be able to hold out on uttering the words, though I know it will be soon. I can't contain the insane feelings I have.

"Jesus Christ, I am," she gasps. "I'm coming a-fucking-gain!"

Laughter bubbles out of me just as my orgasm hits straight in the base of my spine, pressure shooting into my balls, and I jet into her, warmth surrounding us both.

"Motherfucker," I grit out, unsure if this climax is even

stronger than the last. "That was abso—" I break off the second I hear a car pull up outside.

We look at each other, eyes wide and my blood pumping for an entirely different reason.

Ezra.

THIRTY-FOUR

COLLINS

What is it about us getting caught in the act? Or in this case, almost.

Oh, yes, because we have sex at inappropriate times and in largely inappropriate places.

I guess that's what happens when you can't get enough of each other.

How the hell we gathered ourselves and I made it into Sawyer's bedroom before Ezra walked in the door, I have no idea.

Pulling on my leather pants and a bra, I close my eyes and wince. "Fuck." In my haste to get out of the way, I totally forgot Sawyer's T-shirt.

Dressed in the clothes Sawyer picked me up in after work, I stand at the top of the stairs, which lead directly into his living room. I can hear voices, and one of them is definitely Ezra's.

"Dad, why is your shirt on the floor?" Ezra asks.

I cringe, biting down on my fist in an attempt to rid the embarrassment as it tears through me.

Sawyer clears his throat, obviously just as embarrassed. "I was doing push-ups and overheated. Anyway, how was Nate?"

I assume Nate is the friend he saw tonight.

"He's good." Ezra's reply is brief.

"And what did you talk about?" Sawyer pushes.

Jesus, it's like pulling teeth.

"Mostly the Knicks. He thinks they're the best team right now. They aren't," he adds with confidence.

My phone buzzes in my pocket, and I pull it out.

SAWYER

Come downstairs when you're ready, Baby Girl. I'm making us something to eat.

Nerves swirl in my stomach as I take the first step and head down the stairs.

When I round the corner, Ezra is side-on to me, sitting on the couch, facing the TV above the fireplace, head buried in his phone. *The Breakfast Club* is still on pause where we left it.

A floorboard creaks beneath my foot, and Sawyer pokes his head around the archway leading to the kitchen. He's wearing the T-shirt, a smile, and … glasses?

Ezra's head darts in my direction, his jaw wide open as he tries to process what he's seeing.

I lift my hand in a tentative wave, like some kind of goddamn weirdo. "Hi."

Ezra drops his phone beside him and leaps off the couch, still looking just as confused. "W-what are you doing here?" He looks at me and then at Sawyer, who throws a towel over his shoulder and walks toward me, never taking his eyes from mine.

"Well, I actually invited Collins over for dinner tonight since you were seeing Nate." Sawyer stops just in front of me and turns to Ezra. "We also had something to tell you." He reaches out and takes my hand in his.

Ezra's attention drops from his dad to our joined hands in between us. "Wait, are you two, like, a thing now?" He takes a couple of paces toward us, lips tipping up in the corner. "I knew you were lying when you said you didn't like each other. Friends, my ass."

Sawyer turns toward Ezra, an unimpressed brow raised at his son.

I smirk, rolling my lips together.

"You're right though, Ez," I say, clueless about why I gave him a nickname, but loving how it sounds. "Sawyer and I are more than friends, and I came over tonight because we wanted you to be the first to find out."

The room falls silent, and for a split second, panic shoots through me when I see the glassiness in his eyes.

Shit. Is this not what he wanted after all? I really fucking hope he doesn't think I'm here to replace his mom because I'll never be her. I don't *want* to be her.

My concern is only fleeting though when Ezra makes a beeline for me, wrapping his arms around my waist, and I rest my chin on top of his head when he dips it down, our similar height even more noticeable.

He smells like Sawyer—fresh, clean, and comforting.

Sawyer drops my hand and scrubs a rough palm over his jaw, his green eyes glassy, just like his son's.

"Does this mean you'll definitely come to Alyssa and Dom's after dinner and spend the entire Christmas with us? We don't even have to play board games if you don't want."

I wrap my arms around his waist, my mind hasn't changed since Ezra asked me over pizza. Still, I'm intrigued by the games on offer. "Specifically, what board games are we talking about?"

His face is serious when he pulls back. "I like Jenga and Clue, but I kill it every time with Monopoly. *No one* can beat me, not even Dad. Right?" He turns over his shoulder, and Sawyer shakes his head a little, trying to regroup.

"Alyssa came pretty close last year. You're just lucky with the dice and always get Park Place or Boardwalk."

Ezra releases me, propping his hands on his hips. "Yeah,

well, that's what all the losers say. I've won two years in a row now."

Sawyer folds his arms across his chest, and Ezra spins back around to face me.

"But for real, you guys are actually together?" He points at me. "So, you're my dad's girlfriend?"

I nod once, that label still sparking the tingles I've always felt around the broody hockey captain. "Yep, that's right."

"Have you kissed yet?"

Sawyer immediately bursts into a coughing fit, and I blow out a single laugh.

"I think that's enough questions for now, don't you?" his dad replies, cocking his head toward the stairs. "Don't you have any homework to catch up on since I know you've already had dinner?"

Ezra drops his shoulders, defeated. "Just some math, but it isn't due until the day after tomorrow."

Sawyer motions toward the staircase. "Doesn't mean you should leave it until the final second."

Ignoring his dad, Ezra refocuses back on me. "Does this mean you're moving in with us? You can bring your bikes."

I have zero idea how to respond, but I try my best. "I don't think I'll be moving in anytime soon."

I flick my eyes to Sawyer for a brief second, keen on gauging his response to my statement. He gives nothing away, only shoving his hands into the pockets of his shorts.

"But I may stay over from time to time, if that's okay with you?"

Ezra doesn't hesitate. "Absolutely, it is. It's real boring around here, and Dad knows nothing about bikes." Seemingly satisfied with my answer, he makes for the stairs, taking the first few steps and then stopping, deep in thought. "I'm happy you and my dad are dating. Like I said before, I didn't think he'd find anyone after Mom."

When Ezra disappears out of sight, we stand a few feet apart, staring at each other.

"I didn't know you wore glasses." I break the silence first, walking over and pulling off his silver frames, trying them on for size.

Sawyer scratches his chest as he watches me. "You really think I was going to own up to needing reading glasses? You already think I'm old. Contacts have been my best friend, but now that I have you trapped, I'm about to reveal all my geriatric secrets."

I bite down on my bottom lip, vision blurry since I don't need a prescription. "I'd say keeping this secret has been your loss. They're hot as fuck."

He softly scoffs and steps forward, towering over me. "And you look cute as fuck in them." In what's rapidly becoming one of my favorite things he does, Sawyer tips my chin up to look at him. "Where the hell have you been all these years, Collins? We both needed you so much, and now that you're here, I never want to let you go."

He reaches down, looping his arms under my ass, and I release a high-pitched squeal, wrapping my arms around his neck.

Feeling this free to be myself is liberating, almost like I've been hiding the lighter girl in a cupboard somewhere, scared to let her out and risk being vulnerable.

Being vulnerable around Sawyer is no risk at all—I can feel that deep in my soul.

I lean down, his oversize glasses slipping to the end of my nose.

"And now you look like a naughty teacher, about to ream me out for being a bad boy," Sawyer jests, although I'm ninety-nine percent sure he's going to make me wear them later in bed.

"What were you using these for anyway?"

He spins us around, pressing my back into the side of the staircase, and I loop my legs around his waist.

"I told you, I'm making dinner, and I needed to check a recipe. They always use such small print in those books."

I pull his mouth down to me. "You keep telling yourself that, old man."

Sawyer traces his lips over mine, and already, I'm thinking about the benefits of skipping dinner.

"You know, in a few years, when your eyes need a little assistance, I won't tease you like you do me."

His hands grip my waist tighter. His reference to our future is like an elephant in the room.

I pull his mouth back to mine, eager to show him I'm okay and not freaking out, and we melt into a long kiss before breaking off with our heads pressed together, my fingers teasing the hairs at the nape of his neck.

"I'm not here to replace Ezra's mom, you know," I say, unable to hold the thought that's been turning in my conscience since we told Ezra we were dating.

"I know," Sawyer replies on a long breath, picking his head up to study my face.

He pulls the glasses off and pokes them through the railings, setting them on the stairs behind my head. "Neither me nor Ezra sees you as anything but who you are. I want you to be exactly what you are right now to him—one of his best friends and someone way cooler than his dad." He pauses for a split second. "And I want you to be the woman I've been obsessed with for over a year. Being with me doesn't carry any expectations, Baby Girl. All I want is your time and love and to know you're totally and one hundred percent mine."

He kisses me, sweeping his tongue into my mouth in a show of sincerity as pure and honest as the words he just said. Truthfully, there isn't really anything complicated about being with Sawyer Bryce.

Still, hearing him confirm it out loud melts away any last shred of worry, and with each pass of his tongue against mine, I fall deeper into his world, content to be tangled up with him for as long as possible.

"Knew it!" a small voice calls from above, and we break apart, both looking up the stairs.

Ezra stands with his hands propped on his hips, a smug smile all over his face. "I knew you were kissing. But just for the record, I never want to see it again." He disappears out of sight, bedroom door slamming behind him, closely followed by, "Ewww!"

I turn back to Sawyer to see his lips quivering with laughter.

"Welcome to the world of the preteen, featuring my delightful son, Ezra Sawyer Bryce."

THIRTY-FIVE

SAWYER

Killing it.

I'm killing it against the Pittsburgh Flames. This game is regularly one that goes right to the wire, but not tonight.

As our goalie, Archer has had practically nothing to do all game with Emmett and me cleaning up after the team.

Jack's on fucking fire too. His game was insane at the beginning of this season, but now? Well, this boy is starting to make his stepdad's career look like a mere warm-up to the real Morgan era. Jack runs the show; we're all just featured in it. And the best part? The kid's humble, going about his business like it's just another day at the office.

And when he threads an impossible flip pass to Matt, leaving him with the simplest finish in history, I can't deny the pride that fills my chest. Sure, I consider Jack to be one of my best friends, but there's over ten years between us, and to some extent, I feel like an older brother to him. When he joined the Blades last season, there were so many doubters, and tonight, he's giving the final middle finger to all of them.

He bumps fists with the guys on the bench, and I push forward, making my way to him at center ice.

"Umm, what in the fuckery was that?" I'm referring to the flip pass he just pulled off, and by the cocky look on his face, he knows it was special.

I take it back. *Humble, my ass.*

"Last practice, I bet Archer I could throw it into the game and get an assist," he says, pulling out his mouthguard.

I tip my head over my shoulder, grinning at Archer with a thumbs-up.

He throws his arms out to the sides before propping his hands on his hips, tipping his head toward the ceiling and shaking it slowly.

"Shit," I breathe, "my goalie looks to be in pain. How much was at stake?"

I turn back to Jack, who is wearing a devilish grin.

"Oh, it wasn't money on the line. I told him if I won, then he would be paired up with Lucy at my wedding. I was confident he wouldn't win the bet, and this seemed like a good opportunity to keep him away from my sister in August."

I know August 10 is the date Kendra and Jack—*no, Jon*—has set for their wedding, but the name Lucy is lost on me.

With the game still on pause while the Pittsburgh coach argues with the ref over something, I take advantage and dig a little deeper.

"Who the fuck is Lucy?"

Jack's cocky smirk turns scheming. "Darcy's best friend. Kendra has made good friends with her through my sister and asked her to be a bridesmaid." He leans toward me, hand cupping his mouth like he thinks anyone can hear him over the twenty thousand roaring fans in this arena. "You cannot tell me that when I asked Archer to be the best man alongside you, he didn't think he'd be paired with Darcy, the maid of honor."

I snort and drop my head between my shoulders. "Please tell me that Darcy knows nothing about this?"

He scoffs. "You must be kidding. She'd kick my ass into next week if she knew I was being the protective big brother. She hates that kind of shit."

"But you're going to be exactly that anyway?" I say, one brow quirked.

He nods profusely, subtly motioning to Archer. "I know he thinks she's hot, but would likely never act on it."

Okay, I don't entirely agree with that statement.

"But I'm not about to offer him any half chances to get in her pants." He leans closer to me. "Last season in Colorado, he told me he likes to 'fuck and flee' when it comes to women." He scoffs again, harder this time. "So, yeah, just in case he loses his ever-loving mind and thinks about making a move on Darcy, he can try his luck with Lucy and leave my sister the fuck alone."

I'm gripping the back of my neck and searching for an appropriate response when I'm saved by the ref heading back to center ice.

I motion behind Jack. "Game time. Let's see if we can secure our biggest home win of the season."

HOME WIN RECORD SET, I'M PUSHING INTO THE PLAYERS' BAR, ready to find my girl and son. I'm wearing the dark blue suit that I know drives her wild. I'm also hoping she'll tear it off me tonight, just like she did the first time I took her home.

"Oh Jesus fuck, along with the shepherd," Archer declares from behind me.

Not certain that even makes sense, I spin to face my goalie. "What are you talking about?"

He closes his eyes and pinches the bridge of his nose, releasing a pained noise. "Next to Collins."

I search out my girl in the sea of people and eventually land on pink hair and a petite honey-blonde standing next to her.

"Jesus fuck and the entire flock," I confirm. "Jack didn't say Darcy was going to be here tonight."

Archer massages his nose, eyes still closed. "Don't let me talk to her tonight. Keep me away for my own safety, for the love of God."

I'm keen to get to Collins and Ezra, but Archer hasn't talked about Darcy in a while, and I suspect his outburst in the hotel a while back had something to do with the girl he can't even look at. "Are we going to talk about what the hell is going on with Darcy Thompson or just keep dancing around the issue forever?"

He drops his hand and opens his eyes slowly. "Nothing *is* happening, and I know I need to keep it that way. I've just never wanted a girl I know I can't have before, and it's fucking with my equilibrium."

I clap a hand on his shoulder; it's mainly intended to be a comfort, although it doubles as a warning. "Come talk with me, Collins, and Ezra. Because if you let your dick run the show, I'm one hundred percent sure it's going to get cut off."

"Yeah, yeah, you're right." He exhales slowly, almost like he's giving himself a pep talk. "There are plenty of fish in the sea, right?"

I'm halfway across the bar with Archer on my heels when I wrap a hand around my girl's waist, turning her around to face me.

Breathtaking.

At this point, no one knows we're officially together, not even Jack or Archer, but I'm past caring about announcements. They'll catch up.

"I've always wanted to know something," I say, burying my face into her neck as she giggles at the tickle of my breath.

"Oh, yeah? What's that?"

"How long does it take you to apply that liner so perfectly around your eyes?" I pull back and take her in.

She's mine.

"Maybe thirty seconds per eye?"

I balk. "No way. Surely, it takes multiple attempts to get it that sharp?"

"Actually …" Darcy leans across the bar, her bright smile growing brighter as she takes us in. Archer nowhere to be seen. "When you master the art, it's one of the easiest parts of a makeup routine."

I look at Collins, who shrugs, not arguing.

"So, you guys are"—Darcy motions between us—"officially an item?"

"Yep, they are!" Ezra's voice filters from behind me, and I flip around to face him.

"Where have you been?" I ask.

He pulls out his phone and opens his Pictures app. "Talking to Emmett Richards. He has a Ducati Superleggera and sent me a couple of images. It's awesome!"

Collins scrunches up her nose, practically offended at the sight of it. "Ugh, superbikes are gross."

I wrap my hand around her hip, pulling her into me.

"Talking of gross, I'm going to sit with the team." Ezra shudders and gestures over to a table.

I track to where he's pointing and find Archer sitting at a table toward the back of the room, talking with a brunette and her friend.

"I can't be out late tonight; I have an early start at the garage. The pre-holiday rush is in full swing."

Collins pulls my attention back to her, and I acknowledge her with a kiss right before my attention snags on Darcy.

Taking a sip of her cocktail, she eyes my goalie over the rim of her glass. Her attention on him can't be for more than a second, but I clock it, and so does Collins.

"I wasn't expecting to see you tonight," I say to Darcy.

She flicks her long hair over her shoulder, blue eyes back and focused on us both. "I'll be moving over in the new year and need to find a place. I love Jon and Mum, but there is no way I am living with them. Jon is in full coach-meets-wedding-planner mode, and I've had it up to here already." She rolls her eyes and brings her hand above her head, indicating she can't take it anymore.

"Why don't you just move in with Jenna?" Collins asks. "Oh, or me? We could be roommates!"

I can't help it when my hand tenses around her hip, and Collins looks at me with a raised brow. I stay quiet, knowing now is not the right time to talk about living together. It's not lost on me how much my girlfriend has grown—casually asking a friend to move in with her is a big step and something she wouldn't have done several months ago.

That still doesn't stop me from feeling some kind of way over her living with anyone but me and Ezra. I'm holding off on confessing how wildly in love I am with her. And suggesting she move into my place?

Yeah, remember to pull the pin out of the hand grenade before throwing it in the center of your brand-new relationship, Sawyer.

Darcy looks like she's considering Collins's suggestion for a second, and I hold my breath, praying she declines and feeling like a douche for it too.

"Whatcha talking about?" Jenna sidles up next to Darcy, soda in hand.

Bracing her elbow on the bar, Darcy rests her chin in her palm, looking a touch defeated. "About where the hell I'm going to live when I move here next year. Collins just invited me to live with her, and don't get me wrong"—she reaches out and rubs an appreciative palm down my girlfriend's arm—"I would love to have girls' nights in front of chick flicks. But I just ... I don't know. I kind of want to live on my own. I'm hoping to have a bit of fun dating, and I don't want to get in anyone's way."

"When you say 'dating,' I assume you mean one-night dates?" Collins replies, flicking her eyes to mine as we both recall where it all began for us.

Darcy waggles her brows suggestively, pulling a giggle from Jenna. "I've heard American boys like to dominate, and I can see the benefits in that."

"O-kaaay." Coach approaches Darcy from behind, already turning on his heel with a grimace on his face. "I joined this conversation at the wrong time. I do *not* need to know what my stepdaughter will be doing when she arrives stateside."

"Or in this case, who," I goad, lips trembling with laughter as I pull Collins under my arm.

Jon runs a hand over his mouth, pointing between us. "Collins, right? I've heard Darcy talk about you before."

He smirks, and I internally wince. I'd recognize that face anywhere—he's preparing to get his own payback.

"You must be the girl that rendered my captain useless on the ice for multiple weeks. He was a pining mess; it was kind of gross, to be honest."

Darcy fights to swallow her drink, eventually managing it. "Pining mess?! Jesus, you can talk, Jon. How many months were you chasing Mum for? It was a pathetic display of obsession, and I loved it."

We all descend into laughter just as Felicity approaches the group and Coach swings an arm around her shoulders, planting a kiss on her head.

"Hey, Angel. They're beating me up over here. I need you to rescue me."

She deadpans, and instantly, it's obvious who calls the shots in their marriage. "Are you driving everyone mad with wedding-planning ideas again?"

His eyes light up, and he's about to fly into some kind of ramble when Darcy holds up a hand.

"Yeah, I'm going to stop you there, Jon. We don't need a

recap on seating arrangements *eight months* before the wedding."

"Ugh, I think it's so cute though—Jack and Kendra getting hitched in the same place you two did." Jenna sighs contentedly, staring off into space. "I hope, one day, I can get married in some beautiful English country house with the birds tweeting and bees buzzing."

"What's this about the birds and the bees?" Archer comes barreling toward us, throwing an arm over Jenna's shoulders, attention completely off Darcy.

With a face of pure sunshine that I'm not entirely convinced is real, he looks around the group and doubles back when he passes me and Collins. "Wait, are you two more than just fucking now?"

Collins groans into my side.

"Always the gentleman." Jon shakes his head, chuckling.

Archer extends his hand for me to take. "Congrats, buddy." I shake it, and he moves to Collins, leaning forward and kissing her on the cheek. "Your secret's still safe with me; don't worry."

She flushes, and I quickly tip her chin up, planting a soft kiss across her lips.

"What was that for?" she asks, the crimson on her cheeks spreading further.

I drop my forehead to hers, smiling like a fucking fool. "Fun fact: I'm possessive over my girl—I've waited long enough after all—and from here on out, the last man to kiss you will always be me."

THIRTY-SIX

COLLINS

The rumble of Sawyer's truck as it pulls up along the sidewalk fires off the tingles I've learned to embrace these past couple of months. They no longer represent a warning to back off and protect my space and freedom, but instead, they feel like a promise of excitement and a future I hope to share with my two favorite people.

Since we made us official, I've found myself falling deeper and harder for Sawyer, and the way I care for Ezra feels a lot like a love I never thought possible.

Not for me, anyway.

It's the kind of love where you'd do anything for that person—walk across broken glass or burning embers and lay yourself down in oncoming traffic before anything hurt them. Perhaps one that transcends friendship into something more complicated. The truth is, if Ezra saw me as a motherly figure beyond what he already has with Alyssa, I wouldn't freak out.

It feels like my days of freaking out at any kind of commitment are being left behind in a trail of exhaust fumes while my life accelerates in a way that doesn't feel at all unnatural.

"You already started?" Ezra stands in the entrance to my garage, arms folded across his chest in a huff.

"Well, merry Christmas to you too, Mr. Grinch," I volley back, tossing a microfiber cloth, which he catches. "Anyway, I saved you the best part."

He nods and approaches, offering me a fist bump, which I reciprocate. "Detailing is definitely the best bit," Ezra agrees, quickly kneeling beside my bike and getting to work.

Hands on my hips, I stand, watching him for a few beats before Sawyer appears, wearing a red Santa hat, black jeans, and a gray winter coat.

I burst out laughing and race toward him. We already wished each other a merry Christmas over the phone, but that doesn't stop me from wanting to steal a quick kiss.

I tip my chin up at the ceiling, mistletoe hanging from the roof. "How about a quick—"

Instantly, I'm wrapped in his big bearlike arms, the safety and comfort of them daring me to fall a little harder for my boyfriend.

"Ewww! Okay, okay, can you stop kissing now? You guys are so uncool and gross sometimes," Ezra announces, throwing in a gag to accentuate his point.

I spin around to face him, Sawyer's arms draped over my shoulders. "I guess you won't want your 'uncool and gross' gift then, will you?"

He perks up at that, leaping straight to his feet and setting the microfiber on the wooden dresser at the back of my garage. "No, I definitely want the gift." He smiles wryly. "Did you guys get me a black CVO?"

I scoff and look up at Sawyer. "No, I got you a present myself. And when you see it, I think you might take back what you said about me being uncool."

Sawyer hums in agreement, setting a kiss on top of my head. "I think he definitely will, Baby Girl."

I shrug out from under his arms and head over to the back, pulling a large, flat gift wrapped in blue paper from the top of a storage chest.

Sawyer comes to stand by Ezra. He has zero clue what it is, but clearly has faith in my gift-buying abilities.

I hand it to Ezra, who hesitates for all of half a second before tearing into the tissue paper.

"Oh." He turns the white box around in his hands, still no clue what I got him.

"Open it up then," I urge him, way too excited myself.

"Wait." He pauses when he starts to register what it is. "Is this …"

He slides the sign all the way out and drops the empty box to the floor, frantically pushing back the bubble wrap. "Is this …" he yells.

"It is!" I squeak. "I figured it would look so cool in your bedroom!"

He doesn't say anything, wrapping his free arm around my waist, holding me tight. I swear my heart inflates until it's pressing against my rib cage.

"What does it say?" Sawyer asks, taking the sign from Ezra. "*BikerBryce*." His voice softens to a whisper. "Collins, this is really sweet of you."

"Best gift ever," Ezra confidently confirms, finally releasing his arm and giving me the chance to show him his second gift.

In an attempt to hide it, I deliberately kept my *BikerCollins* sign off when they arrived. And as I flick it on, a replica of the sign I just gave him also lights up, and Ezra looks from me to the illuminated wall.

"You put me on your wall! Like as a partner?"

I nod and tip my head up to look at them, situated perfectly next to each other in neon blue and red. "I did. Bikers for life."

I'M WINNING AT MONOPOLY, AND IT'S REALLY FUCKING awkward.

Alyssa and Dom went bust around an hour ago, and both retreated to the couch to read, which is probably the safest place to be right now because I have two bratty boys sitting opposite me.

"Go to jail! Again?!" Ezra huffs, petulantly throwing his arms out.

I grimace when Sawyer throws a six and lands on Park Place.

"That's …" I calculate how much he owes.

Mirroring his son, he sits back in his chair, grumbling, "It's way more than I can afford, is what it is."

I fight back the urge to laugh. I might be falling hard for this man, but winding him up is still my favorite thing to do. "I do offer competitive mortgage rates, if that's a viable option for you?"

He narrows his eyes and squeezes his lips together. "Don't start, Mackenzie."

"I think she cheated," Ezra speculatively adds.

"Definitely," Sawyer agrees.

"Highlights from your game against Boston are on," Dom shouts across at us.

Sawyer swivels around in his chair as Ezra leaves the table and makes his way over to join Alyssa and Dom on the couch, picking up a Harley-Davidson model kit they bought him. His gifts this year are following a trend.

"Do you want your gift now or later?" Sawyer asks me, packing the board game away. The mischievous smile on his face tells me whatever he got probably isn't suitable to be opened in company.

Funny, because neither is the gift I got him.

"Maybe in a while," I say, resting my elbows on the table and winking.

When he winks back, I feel its effects all the way to my toes. I don't think there will ever be a time when he doesn't make me feel sixteen again.

Sawyer turns to watch the highlights but quickly looks away, wincing.

"What's up?" I ask, my mood shifting from giddy to concerned.

When he closes the lid on the Monopoly box, I see something flash in his eyes that I don't like. I can't decipher it exactly, but it makes me want to climb across the table and pull the feeling out of him.

He motions to the highlights still playing on the TV. "Just that power play in the third. A couple of years ago, I wouldn't have let their winger turn me over the way he did. I felt a length behind and was powerless to catch up." He runs a rough hand through his hair, tattooed forearms flexing.

"You look to be in pretty good shape to me," I jest, desperate to lighten his mood.

He just shrugs—one that, for once, isn't playful or mocking me. "I guess I can't help my mind as it drifts to thoughts of how much longer I have in the game, you know?" His green eyes find me. "Or how much longer I can go before I'm having serious talks with Coach and the GM about where the C should end up."

"You don't want to be captain anymore?"

He sighs, chewing on his bottom lip. "I'm not ready to give it up yet, but I don't want to be that player who retires, still wearing the C. I think I want to play more of a mentor role if I can."

I reach across the table, taking his hand in mine, the roughness of his palm a reminder of how hard this guy works. "You actually aren't that old—you do know that, right?"

He chuckles and brushes his thumb across the top of my hand. "I am, Baby Girl. I'll be thirty-six next year. You bagged yourself a pensioner," he jokes.

"Do you feel ready to hang up your skates?" I feel like I can relate to him way more than the average person. Sure, I retired from motocross for different reasons, but I still had to make the call that was right for me and kiss goodbye to an all-encompassing lifestyle.

He twists his lips to the side, tipping his head over to look at Ezra, who continues to work on his bike model. "Not right now, but time flies. I remember when I was feeding him in the middle of the night, and now he's in middle school and growing up fast. Hockey takes me away from him more than I'd like. More than I should be."

"Y-you know you have me too now though, right?"

He squeezes my hand, so much warmth and meaning in his eyes. "I've waited a long-ass time for you to say that."

"Yeah, well, don't get too comfortable with softer Collins. I have to keep you on your toes."

In my peripheral vision, I see Ezra fighting back a yawn. It's been a long day, like most Christmases are.

I tip my head toward the window behind me. "I think Ezra's dragging."

We both stare at each other for a few beats.

"Come home with me?" he asks—four words I've rejected way more than I ever wanted to.

I run my tongue across my bottom lip, his gift already playing out in my mind. "I don't think I'd want to be anywhere else."

THIRTY-SEVEN

SAWYER

I feel like we've circled back to that night in October.

Back then, I was nervous about sleeping with a woman I knew I wanted more than one night with. She intimidated and fascinated me in equal measure, leaving me desperate for more each time I touched her.

And now? Months later, I'm nervous in her presence for a whole heap of different reasons, the main being about what she has planned for me tonight.

I've had my hands bound to the headboard and the spreader bar fixed to my ankles for the past five minutes as I lie here, waiting for Collins to emerge from the en suite. She's being especially secretive, and the mischievous expression she's worn since Ezra went to bed has me feeling some kind of way right now.

I edged her hard that night with ice play and the paddle. Is that what she has in mind for me? Maybe this is her way of revenge.

"All okay?" I call out to her, a mixture of excitement and trepidation unmistakable in my voice.

No answer.

Despite being exposed and incredibly vulnerable, I'm hard as a fucking rock at the anticipation alone, pre-cum leaking from the tip and slowly beading down my shaft.

I strain against the leather straps, the urge to wrap my fist around the base and draw an orgasm from my already-tightening balls overwhelming, all-consuming.

And as I press my head back into the pillow and try to get ahold of myself, I realize this might be all part of my kinky girl's game—to keep me here, waiting, hoping, and thinking over everything she might do to me.

My cock stiffens again. Jesus, why does the thought of her psychologically edging me drive my arousal to the point of pain?

When I'm ready to rip the headboard clean from the frame, the en suite door handle finally depresses, and a pink-manicured foot emerges first.

Finally.

"Baby Girl, I need you to hurry the fuck up because I …" I trail off, the ability to verbalize vanishing, and in its place is the only image I ever want to see for the rest of my life.

"W-where did you get that outfit?" I stutter the words like I haven't spoken in years, my throat tight and thick.

She's dressed in a black faux leather body suit that dips low at the front, revealing a tantalizing display of cleavage, and my mouth waters at the sight of her. The outside parts of her legs are exposed but secured tightly with a corset-style lace, crisscrossing all the way from her ankles to her hips.

I pull against the restraints around my wrists, desperate to get my hands on her and run my fingers through her soft pink hair as it frames her heart-shaped face perfectly.

"Ordered it online a few days ago," she answers, casually sauntering toward me, nothing but torturous intentions motivating her movements. "What's the matter?" she asks, noticing the way I'm fighting against the leather strap.

"I don't want to play games, Collins. I just want to fuck." I wanted to sound assertive, but the words are more of a plea.

When she kneels on the foot of the bed, I notice her hands are empty, and hope blooms in my chest. Maybe she is just planning to fuck my brains out and give me the quick release I need.

"Where are your props?" I ask, eyeing her empty hands.

Collins drops to her palms as she slowly but very deliberately crawls over my lower body, coming to a stop when her head aligns with my impossibly hard dick.

Eyes on me and never wavering, she swipes one pass of her tongue across the head, circling back around before moving to the slit, teasing the hole with damp warmth.

"I don't need props, Sawyer. Not tonight."

Yeah, I'm fucking done for. RIP me. Farewell, Sawyer Bryce.

"Is that suit crotchless?" I choke out.

"Yep," she confirms, taking my dick into her mouth, but not too far, only enough to tease the head.

She swirls her tongue around me, and my hips buck off the bed.

She doesn't like that, her foot darting out to the side as she holds the bar down.

"Baby, I'm going to blow. For real, I'm right there." And I'm not lying. I really am seconds away from shooting straight down her throat.

Collins pops off me and then blows on the end of my cock. The cool air hits my burning skin, and I wince at the intensity. It's the perfect balance of addictive and unbearable. I want more.

"Suck it," I demand.

Just as I predicted, she shakes her head defiantly. "No." She rises onto her knees and moves further up my body until she's perfectly aligned and hovering over it. "I want it in my cunt."

Instead of lowering down in the conventional way, she simply spreads her knees wider, demonstrating her flexibility as her pussy slowly swallows my dick. Her jaw hangs open, tiny moans filling the space around us.

"Fuck it, Collins. You know that's all you can think about—taking my dick deep inside you, along with my cum."

"No."

I could cry when she lifts back up, leaving her empty and me leaking yet more pre-cum.

That is, until she takes me back into her mouth, swallowing down not just me, but her own release. She gags when I hit the back of her throat, and the involuntary spasm squeezes my cock tighter. I want to blow. I need to come so fucking badly, but, goddamn, she makes it so good that I want to hold out for as long as possible.

She grazes her teeth along my shaft, and I suck in a sharp breath.

"Fuck—fuck—FUCK. I'm going to shoot."

"No," she torments, releasing me and guiding her thumb over the crown, gathering my release on her finger before taking it into her mouth.

She crawls toward me, and every muscle I possess contracts, fingernails biting into my wooden headboard as I grip it with strength I didn't know I had.

Collins has flipped the switch. I knew she was a bad girl; I knew kink was what she liked, but right now, she's a demon—thirsty for my pain and pleasure.

She stops just before our lips touch. "Open your mouth."

I do as she asked.

"Wider," she commands, a determined edge in her tone.

I'm waiting for her fingers or maybe even her lips. Though that's not eventually how I taste us.

The first spit hits my tongue, the flavor of us both combining perfectly, and I swallow it down eagerly, hungry for more.

"Open," she repeats, and again, I'm only too happy to comply.

Reaching between her legs, she swipes her hand through her pussy, taking her glistening arousal into her mouth before releasing it into mine.

Her sweet taste slides down my throat. My favorite treat and flavor that I'll never grow tired of.

"Still hungry?" she inquires.

I nod, reluctant to speak since the taste of her is still on my tongue and I want to savor it.

She shifts her knees up to either side of my head and then falls back over my body, her back flat against my navel and hair tickling my cock. Collins shifts her hips until her pussy rests a centimeter from my mouth, her feet flat against the wooden slats on my headboard.

"Eat."

When I first slept with Collins, she reminded me of a wild animal—unrelenting and unpredictable in the bedroom. Tonight, the tables turn as I devour her pussy and eat her out like I'll never be offered a meal like this again, and if I am, it could never taste as good.

She pushes her cunt into my face, her release soaking me until she's dripping down my chin. "Make me come, and I'll consider returning the privilege."

I need no encouragement. My girlfriend won't last long as I pull her clit into my mouth, sucking and nipping at it.

She moans, the sound shooting straight to the base of my spine, tightening my balls, but I will myself to wait. I want to climax when she gives me permission.

A few more strokes of my tongue, and the crimson flush rises on her cheeks, mouth forming an *O* when her eyelids flutter closed. Her breathing hitches, and a strangled whimper creeps up her throat—all sure signs that she's about to come.

"Soak me, Baby Girl," I murmur against her pussy, willing her to fall over the edge.

When Collins comes, her inhibitions drop, and it's the most beautiful sight in the world—to watch my girl relax and give me full control, even for just a few seconds.

She fists the sheets on either side of my body, and finally, I feel her pussy release into my mouth.

Paralyzed by her high, she holds herself against me while I lick and suck everything she offers, convinced I can pull more from her.

After a few more beats, she pulls away, sensitive and flushed but still holding need in her eyes.

With my hands tied, her release continues to drip down my chin, and I swipe my tongue out, eyes fixated on her while she watches me search for everything I can get.

"Want to come, Sawyer?" Her voice is laced with darkness.

Fuck me, this is the greatest Christmas gift ever.

Like the needy boy I am, I whimper, nodding once in case she somehow couldn't decipher my desperation from the sound alone.

She moves down my body, sitting back on her heels and across my upper thighs. Her soft, warm hand circles my dick, and in one, long languid movement, she strokes me from root to tip, brushing her palm over the head and using fresh pre-cum to lubricate the next pass down my shaft. I've never been jerked like this, not with this degree of intensity.

I'm right there—right *fucking* there.

When she grips the base, I leak more, and she giggles, leaning down and lapping it up.

"I need to come, Collins."

"Beg for it," she whispers against my dick.

The easy way out would be to do just that—plead pathetically until she grants me a reprieve. But that's not what my girl is after. No. She wants my resilience, just like she showed me hers when I had the paddle.

She jerks me again and smirks. "Sorry, I didn't hear that." Her spare hand rises to cup her left ear. "Speak up for me, Baby. I need to hear the word."

"No," I grit out, dying inside a little more.

Oh shit, she isn't. That's my first thought as my girlfriend lowers herself between my thighs, keeping her palm wrapped around my shaft.

She licks and sucks on my balls, pumping me in a rhythm that leaves me in no doubt about how this will end.

"Beg for it, or I'll hold you like this."

The vibrations against my balls draw them tighter still, and I press my head into the pillow, so—fucking—turned—on.

I concede, my willpower completely depleted and head spinning out. "Do it. I'm begging you, Baby Girl."

"Good boy."

Her praise is the final straw, and I snap under ripping pressure that tears down my spine, shooting into my balls.

I squirt, jets of hot cum spraying across my navel, only stopping when Collins wraps her mouth over the end of my dick, drinking down my orgasm.

I'm speechless, motionless, and totally fucking convinced there is and will never be another woman who can do this to me. Not just because she's insanely gifted in bed, but because I'm one thousand percent all in.

"I love you."

For a second, I'm sure I only said the words in my head, still not aware of my ability to form coherent sentences out loud.

But my girl's eyes confirm my suspicions, growing wide.

I regret nothing, repeating once more, "I love you, Collins."

She quickly dives for the ties around my wrists, releasing my arms, and I immediately wrap them around her, pulling her into my chest.

"I don't care if you aren't ready to say it back now, tomorrow, next week, or in a year. I just need you to know that I've fallen so damn hard, and there's no going back for me. You blow my mind every second of the day, and I'm so fucking in love with you. There's not a single part of my heart that doesn't belong to you. If you want me, you have me. Forever."

THIRTY-EIGHT

COLLINS

The hot-as-fuck Blades captain is in love with me.

And I am all the way here for it. In fact, I haven't been able to stop thinking about it since he confessed how deep his feelings were a few days ago.

Was I tempted to tell him I was falling hard? You bet your ass I was. It's kind of absurd to me that I haven't told him how I feel since I'm ten out of ten sure he can tell just by the way I smile at him. My body language speaks a thousand words my brain has always struggled to comprehend.

I don't think there's anything capable of bringing down my mood. I've been dancing around the garage all morning. Some of our regular customers have been throwing me inquisitive looks as they try to work out at what point I had a personality transplant.

The truth is, I haven't. She was always in there—the part of me who longed to open up to the world and show her brighter colors. Fundamentally, I'm still me—black eyeliner, '80s rock T-shirts, and enough sarcasm to power a small city—but I don't feel the need to run any longer. I'm happy to sit in one space with people, and if they start to see all my parts in the process, then I'm okay with that too.

Because Sawyer motherfucking Bryce loves me.

"Collins, do you plan on finishing that bike today? The customer is out front, asking whether he should come back tomorrow and pick her up."

I take it back. There is one person who could dampen my mood—Cameron.

Even though I didn't witness it, I'm certain Sawyer told him where to stick his asshole behavior when he was last in here. After all, Cameron doesn't give out afternoons and days off without good reason—and definitely not to me. Up until today, he's been palatable, which is loosely translated as, I've only wanted to strangle him a half-dozen times each shift. Today though, he's been vile, and I'm at full capacity with his bullshit. If it wasn't for my otherwise good mood, I would one hundred percent be in custody.

Crouched by the exact motorcycle he's referring to, I spin around to face him. "Mr. Booth turned the bike in this morning, complaining of noise. The sprockets on the chain are misaligned and loose." I point to the offending areas. "Right now, it's costing the customer more in maintenance and repairs than it would be to fit a drive belt instead, which would solve all his problems." I stand up and quirk a brow. "I don't know when you last went to check on Mr. Booth, but I spoke with him about five minutes ago and confirmed all this. He's happy to wait it out while I get it done, although I did tell him it would take a few hours."

I thumb at the beautiful vintage bike. "Unless you want to take the lead and fix it yourself?"

Cameron clears his throat, jaw twitching with rage. "You know I don't have the time to carry out a task like that. It's not something management would do."

I consider not responding since my mouth frequently gets me

into trouble at work. Although you will never catch me being silent when I have something to say. "Well, if you don't have time to help me, can I make a request that you kindly leave me the fuck alone so I can do my job?"

Probably shouldn't have thrown in "the fuck."

Cameron looks off to the side, jaw still tense as he stuffs his hands into the pockets of his wrinkle-free black dress pants. "Is this how it's going to go from now on, Collins?"

I throw down the oil-stained cloth I was holding, propping a hand on my hip. "You mean me, on my own in the shop, working all hours to keep on top of the insane new flow of customers we keep getting? Yeah," I scoff. "That's how it's been for months, so I guess that's how it'll be from now on."

Cameron points to the middle of his chest. "You're complaining about the garage being successful? That's how I pay your wages and what keeps us in jobs. It's no coincidence that since I took over the management here, we've seen an influx of new business."

I huff out a sarcastic laugh. "Are you for real right now? Customers are finding us because of my social media. We've had five new inquiries off the back of my Instagram today alone."

He looks doubtful. "Or is it because the world knows you're boning a famous hockey player?"

A knowing smile twists at my lips. *That's what this is about.*

"Go ahead and say what's really bothering you, Cameron."

He folds his arms across his chest. The petulance rolling from him reminds me of Ezra, although this guy isn't twelve years old. *Apparently.*

"I just don't appreciate you bringing your boyfriend to work, especially since he's an asshole who can't respect your boss."

My previously good mood disappears altogether, and pissed-off Collins is kicking back into gear. "The only asshole I see around here is you." I throw my arm out in front of me, motioning around the garage. "You waltz around here like you're

God's gift or something and we should all bow down to your male superiority. And you know all I can think when I see you? How in the hell did the owner of this place give you a promotion since you know nothing about bikes? Literally nothing. That's why you hide away in your office—avoiding being found out that if it isn't a simple service, you have zero idea what you're doing."

Face beet red, he takes a step toward me. "What's the matter, Collins? A little sore I got the job and you didn't?"

The best plan right now would be to walk away and cool off —I know it.

Fuck that.

"No, Cameron. I didn't want the promotion because, believe it or not, I enjoy what I do—bringing bikes back to life and getting my hands dirty."

I feel my phone buzz in the pocket of my overalls, but I ignore it, determined to have it out with this guy once and for all.

"You wouldn't have been offered the job anyway," I hear Cameron breathe quietly.

"I'm sorry. You might want to speak up so I can hear your bullshit," I reply.

He sneers, his anger getting the better of him. "I said, 'You wouldn't have been offered the job anyway,' since the owner knows how unpredictable you are." He takes another step toward me. "That's what I tried to warn your boyfriend about when he was here—that you like to use men and then drop them when you're finished. A little like your life." He scoffs again, only harder this time. "You were fired from your last job, and you're this close to it happening again." He pinches his thumb and forefinger together.

Right now, I have five hundred dollars left from my grandparents and around a hundred in my checking account. Altogether, that's not enough to cover this month's rent, but I've had it.

No one speaks to me like that. No one gets a chance to make me feel anything less than what I am—a fucking good person who's kick-ass at my job.

I pull at the buttons of my overalls, and his eyes drop to my chest.

He's a fucking pervert, even now.

"Let me save you from any further aggravation, *boss*. I quit."

THERE'S ONLY SO MUCH COMFORT SNACKS AND RICHARD GERE can bring. Okay, I don't have a thing for him, but Julia Roberts? A queen.

I wonder what she would do in my position—no money, no job, and putting off a call to her landlord, asking for an extension on the rent. Vivian Ward would probably throw on her big-girl pants and sort her shit out, reminding herself that women don't work for assholes with tiny-dick behavior.

I'm reaching across the couch to grab my phone when a couple of knocks stop me in my tracks, and I stare at my front door, confused as to who it is and how they got past the building entrance.

"Who is it?" I shout, already heading for the door and brushing pieces of popcorn from my Metallica shirt.

Attractive.

"The boyfriend you've been ignoring all day." Sawyer's voice filters in from the other side.

I grimace. I haven't checked my phone since I felt it vibrate mid-Cameron conflict.

"I'm sorry," I say, sliding the bolt across and pulling the door open.

Ugh, he looks glorious—all freshly showered with a backward Blades cap, dressed in gray sweats and a hoodie.

Sawyer immediately steps inside, kicking my door shut as his hands fall to my hips. He checks me over. "I've been going out of my mind. You didn't reply to my texts, and then after practice, I called the garage, and Cameron told me he fired you?" He snarls, "What the fuck did he say to you? And, *please,* for the love of God, tell me that prick didn't try to touch you because I will be in lockup so fucking fast."

I hold up a hand, already feeling better for having my man around me. Even if he is a rambling mess. "Wait, he told you he got rid of me?" I burst out laughing. "He has some balls—I'll give him that."

All at once, Sawyer looks confused and relieved. "I thought he fired you because of me and what I'd said to him." He flushes. "I told him to back the fuck off and stop making you work crazy hours. But you quit?"

I drop my head into his chest, nodding. "Yep. He was a prick to me and then rude about you, and that was the final straw."

I choose not to tell Sawyer about the lecherous looks Cameron gave me; I don't have the money for his bail.

I release a heavy sigh against him, worrying about where I'm going to find another job and lack of money taking hold of me. "I couldn't work there anymore. I couldn't stand to look at him, and he treated me like shit. I only held out as long as I did because I love what I do." I inhale Sawyer's clean scent, which eases some of the stress. "Trouble is, there aren't a whole lot of Harley garages around town, and I'm going to struggle with paying my rent if I don't find something soon."

"Look at me, Collins," Sawyer says softly.

I lift my head but keep my chin resting on his chest.

His soft green eyes take me in, and I relax into his body.

"Neither of those problems are actually problems—you know that, right?"

"They are if I don't make rent in two weeks. I could also do with a fairy godmother to magic me a job if possible."

He tucks a lock of stray hair behind my ear. I'm confident it still has oil in it from work earlier. "How much do you need?"

"I don't want to take your money. I can work this out myself," I reply. "It's my mess to clean up."

He leans down, resting his chin on top of my head.

We're still standing by my front door, having not moved an inch since he wrapped his arms around me.

"No, it isn't. He couldn't get past his bruised ego, even for the best member of his staff. I'm so damn proud of you for walking out and knowing your worth." He lifts his head and hooks a finger under my chin. "It's too soon for you to move into my place, isn't it?"

"Yes," I whisper back. "I don't want to give up my garage and—"

He presses a finger to my lips, smiling. "I know, Baby Girl, and I get it. You like your life and place. So, let me take care of you and pay for the rent."

I'm ready to protest, but he presses his finger a little harder, hushing me.

"I don't want any arguments; this is a non-negotiable for me. Let me take the pressure off and help out while you find another job."

"I-I don't even know what to say."

He cups my head in his huge palms, dropping his lips down to mine. "You don't need to say anything. You're my world, and I'm here to protect you." He blows out a long breath, closing his eyes gently. "Now, show me this bedroom of yours because I've been dying to see what it looks like. Plus, I could use the distraction, so I don't climb back in my truck and beat the shit out of Cuntface Cameron."

THIRTY-NINE

COLLINS

"Remember when Collins was sitting in that very seat, claiming number twenty-nine wasn't her type?" Jenna looks at Kendra as we sit in the family box, watching the Blades crush the Carolina Chiefs.

"I do indeed, Jenna." Kendra taps her chin in thought, mocking me. "I distinctly remember her claiming she'd learned all about Sawyer being a single dad from a magazine interview he had given." She narrows her eyes in my direction. "Do you recall that bullshit tale, Collins?"

I roll my eyes and pop a red jelly bean into my mouth. I do, in fact, recall what I said, and it was, in fact, bullshit. Last season and not all that long after I met Sawyer for the first time, I found myself running a Google search on him, keen to find out more about the Blades captain who had effectively offered me a booty call.

It seems crazy to me to think how long I suppressed my feelings and attraction toward him.

"And now she's wearing his jersey with *Bryce* stamped across her back, and she's likely thinking about how much she loves him," Darcy joins in, giggling with the other two.

I pop another jelly bean into my mouth. "Remind me, when is your flight back to London?"

Darcy snorts softly, releasing a forlorn sigh. "Tomorrow morning. Then it's the final countdown before I'm back and moving into my new apartment!"

Kendra imitates a chef's kiss.

"It's so pretty, and I'm so glad I found something in the end," Darcy continues. "I just want to move in now and leave Oxford behind. I've had enough of boring British weather and crappy exes."

"Is Liam still giving you shit?" I ask, annoyed on Darcy's behalf.

"Yep. Apparently, he's started seeing the girl he cheated on me with, but who knows? Half the time, I think he just says things for effect and to try and make me jealous."

Kendra grumbles, holding out her tray of corn chips for Darcy to take one. "You should tell Jack what he's doing. He has experience dealing with toxic exes."

She isn't lying; Kendra's ex-boyfriend, Tyler, can vouch for that.

"Jack is already way too protective, and I'm going to need him to cool it when I move stateside. I'm a big girl, and I can look after myself," Darcy confirms, eyes drifting out onto the ice. "When he found out about Liam cheating, he DM'd him a dick emoji."

I almost choke on my jelly bean. That boy is fucking hilarious.

Kendra bursts out laughing, shaking her head as she looks down at the red ruby on her left hand. "We have officially entered the year we get married, and August cannot come soon enough," she croons with heart eyes.

Reaching over, her mother-in-law-to-be, Felicity, runs a smooth palm across Kendra's shoulder. "Not that you aren't already, but I cannot wait for you to officially become a Morgan. My son is one very lucky boy."

Thoughts of marriage have my mind drifting back to Sawyer and the name I have across my back.

Could I see myself married to him one day? The thought doesn't scare me. All I feel are the familiar shots of excitement when I think about anything to do with Sawyer and Ezra.

I look down at the red jelly beans strewn across the table next to me. It's the first game in a while where Ezra hasn't tagged along, instead asking if he could stay over at Nate's place again since it's a weekend.

Sawyer was initially hesitant since some of the friends sleeping over are several years older, but I convinced him to go with it. After all, making friends and spreading his wings are what he wanted for Ezra.

It's what I want for him too.

"I think Lee and I might break up."

Jenna's statement tears me from my daydream, and we all dart our heads in her direction. She nods hers in response to our shocked faces. "It feels like the spark has fizzled out. Sure, I get that the longer you date someone, the more excitement gives way to a comforting feeling when you're around each other. I just can't see a future with him, and I get the feeling he feels the same."

She sounds dejected, and my heart breaks for her. I remember last year when their relationship was fresh and exciting, she had high hopes that Lee was *the one*.

"Best to break it off if you aren't feeling it any longer. Trust me, it's all downhill from there!" Darcy confirms.

"Maybe an American boy will steal my girl's heart, eh? Melt away some of the cynical ice," Felicity adds hopefully.

Like that's the most ludicrous notion, Darcy scoffs, waving her off. "You have to be kidding me. A little fun? Absolutely. As I say, I've heard the rumors about American men between the sheets." She winks, and Felicity frowns at the thought. "But like hell am I getting serious with anyone anytime soon. If ever again, to be honest."

When Darcy looks back out onto the ice, the rest of us turn to Jenna.

"She's right though, Babe. Remember what you said to me about Tyler? You deserve better than to be in an unhappy relationship."

She nods weakly, smoothing out her dark hair. "I'm going to give it a couple more weeks and see how it goes. I don't want to make any knee-jerk decisions."

"That's wise," Kendra agrees. "But don't hold onto something if it doesn't feel right."

Jenna leans back in her chair, a smile tracing her lips. "In better news though, my brother just got reselected for Team USA, so he'll be traveling home more for games, et cetera."

I pick up my Diet Coke, bringing the straw to my mouth. "Now, rugby thighs? That's a concept I can get on board with. Let me know when your brother is back home, and I'll be sure to go support a game."

Kendra swats me on the thigh. "Disgraceful behavior. You're a taken woman now."

I shrug, smiling around my straw. "Just because I have a man in my bed doesn't mean I don't have eyes. And best believe those babies will be firmly planted on tight rugby asses. Nothing compares, trust me."

"Mmhmm," Darcy agrees. "Take it from a British girl who has been surrounded by them for years at college. Those thighs are unique, and I just want to feel them." She reaches out to nothing, smoothing her palm down in front of her.

"Oh, hell yes, Jack!" Felicity punches the air. "That's my boy! I knew he'd be amazing. I knew he would kill it in this league." She steps behind Darcy and rests her hands on her shoulders, squeezing them gently in her palms while her daughter watches Jack fist-bump the guys on the bench. "I'm proud of you both, and I can't wait to have you back with me. It's been too long, Honey."

Darcy tips her head over her shoulder, covering one of her mom's hands with hers. It's a sweet moment that has me thinking about my own mom and how I wish she were still around. Living life from a young age without her was tough, and sometimes, I catch myself wondering how different it would've looked if that truck driver had been more interested in the road and not his playlist. Still, wishing for things to be different doesn't change anything. I can only control my future.

I watch as Sawyer knocks helmets with Jack. That goal just sent them four up in the third, making a home win within touching distance.

"Jon has worked wonders with this team." Kendra looks over at the Jumbotron as Coach Morgan, dressed in a black suit and high-fiving his players, lights up the screen. "The team dynamics are perfect. They're unrecognizable from previous seasons."

The camera pans to Sawyer as he continues talking with Jack. At Christmas, when Sawyer talked about stepping down as captain, I knew he only had one person on his mind as his successor. Part of me thinks he's holding on to the C to buy Jack a little more time in the league.

"Any luck with the job hunt, Collins?" Felicity turns to me as the game restarts, only a minute left on the countdown.

I shake my head. Nearly a week of searching, and nothing suitable has turned up. "Ed offered me some hours in Rise Up, and I'm thinking of taking that for a while. I'll probably have to concede and get a job at a regular garage that doesn't specialize in Harleys."

Kendra's brows knit together. "But they're your passion and expertise. There has to be something around."

I offer her a defeated shrug. "Trust me when I say, I've been scouring the internet for opportunities. I even called a couple of garages to ask if they'd be interested in taking on a Harley specialist. They weren't."

"Well, they're just plain stupid then," Jenna grumbles. "They don't know what they're missing."

"They're missing a badly behaved employee who can't hold down a job to save her life." I snort. "No one wants the wild child, and most garages take one look at a woman and think she's clueless."

"Nope." Kendra speaks up. "That award goes to Cameron."

"Hell yes, it does." I reach across and high-five her, just as my cell starts vibrating in my jeans pocket.

The buzzer goes off, and the home crowd explodes into cheers, celebrating a big win against a strong team, but I can't hear anything as I put the phone to my ear.

"Hello? Ezra?"

"Collins, I-I need your help."

I can't be sure that's what he says as I push past our chairs and out into a quiet hallway, my heart thumping behind my ribs, hand gripping my phone tightly.

"What's the matter?" I ask, voice shaking.

I can hear voices in the background and outside noise and then, to my horror, a siren.

"Please don't tell Dad." His small voice sounds wobblier than mine, and my heart breaks.

"Tell me you are okay. What happened?" I ask, just as Kendra pushes through the door to the hallway, concern etched across her face.

Ezra doesn't respond, and other than background noise, the only voices I can hear are those in my head, telling me something is very wrong.

"Hello? Is this Ezra's mom?" an unfamiliar female voice says.

"Yes." I look over at Kendra, eyes wide at my own response.

Did I just say that out loud?

"I'm one of the EMTs called to the scene. Your son has been involved in a traffic accident involving a motorcycle and a car. Everyone is okay since it wasn't at a high speed, but we will be transferring him to the hospital for a checkup. Only light injuries were sustained."

"I-injuries?" I repeat, blood draining from my face.

Kendra rushes over, keeping me steady as I fight to stay upright.

"Yes, ma'am. As I said, everyone is okay, but we do need to make sure what we are seeing is only superficial and there isn't anything more serious internally."

My palms sweat, and my heart rate is at an all-time high. I begin to tremble from the adrenaline as it pumps through every part of my body.

"His dad just finished a hockey game, but give me the name of the hospital, and we will be there immediately."

As the EMT reads out the details, I open my Notes app and type in the name, pulling it back off loudspeaker. She says something else, but I don't hear it. I'm spinning out, sinking panic taking ahold of the very depths of my gut.

This is my fault.

I knew he had ridden on that motorcycle, and this is on me. He wouldn't be in danger, and he wouldn't be heading to the ER right now if I hadn't fueled his passion and convinced Sawyer when he raised his initial doubts about the safety of bikes.

"Collins?" Kendra speaks as I disconnect the call and stare blindly at the Blades logo stamped on the wall in front of me. "What happened to Ezra?"

I feel the first tear as it hits my cheek, initially warm but turning cold as it runs a track toward my chin. "We have to find Sawyer. Now."

FORTY

SAWYER

Life has this funny way of creeping up when you least expect it, blowing your cozy, safe bubble apart in a matter of seconds.

One second, I was swooning over Jack's incredible slap shot and congratulating Archer on yet another shutout, and the next, I've got Coach Morgan standing in front of me. All the blood has drained from his face as he hands me his phone.

His mouth is moving, and I can tell he's forming words, but I hear nothing. Only the murmur of background noise as my conscience screams that whatever has happened cannot be good.

I take the phone from him, staring down at *Felicity* written across the screen. That's his wife. What's she doing, calling me directly after a game?

Jack wraps his arm around my shoulders, saying something to his stepdad, which, again, I can't process.

"Hello?" I say, my greeting an auto response.

"Sawyer, it's Felicity, Jon's wife. I'm at the hospital with Collins."

At the sound of her panicked voice, I come to, adrenaline switching from fight to flight.

Shit, it's happening again, isn't it?

I've fallen in love with a woman, and she's being ripped from me in the cruelest way possible.

Sophie's face as she lay in the morgue flashes in front of me, and instantly, I'm leaning into my center, relying on his steady arm to keep me from collapsing.

"Is she ..." I trail off, my numb brain unable, or perhaps unwilling, to finish what I'm saying. I don't know how to complete my sentence since I don't really want an answer.

"It's not Collins," Felicity clarifies, voice still frantic. She blows out a long breath, trying to center herself, likely for her own benefit as much as mine. "It's Ezra. He got brought into the ER a few minutes ago. We're only a five-minute drive from the arena." She pauses for a second, taking another steadying breath. "He got into a motorcycle accident with a friend. Everyone looks to be okay, but he does have some cuts and bruises."

All I hear is "motorcycle accident" as I look up at my coach, a wave of nausea that hasn't hit me in many years tearing through my stomach. I swallow down the urge to empty the contents all over his shoes.

"Pads and skates off now, and let's get to the hospital, stat," Archer booms from beside me, already sitting me on the bench as Jack works on my laces.

Jon takes the phone from my hand since I've lost all ability to speak. "He's going to be fine," he says, trying to soothe me as best he can.

"Sawyer." Jack's voice is commanding.

He snaps his fingers in my face, breaking my panic-induced trance, and I blink a couple of times. He snaps them again, and I'm back in the room.

"Sawyer, can you hear me? You'll be in Brooklyn Central ER in the next few minutes."

I jump to my feet, practically knocking Jack out in the process as he crouches beside me. "Fuck the next few minutes. I need to be there now," I roar, ripping at my jersey and pads. "Get me there—now."

THANKS TO POSTGAME TRAFFIC, IT TOOK TEN MINUTES TOO LONG to reach the ER room.

I barrel down the hallway toward where Ezra's being treated.

"Collins is with him right now. He's fine, Sawyer. The nurse just said he's fine." Archer pulls me to a stop, his hand wrapped around my upper arm in a firm grip.

Other than in the hotel room, I can't recall a time when he's looked so serious, like he's demanding my attention, and calm. He has the former from me, but not the latter.

"Look, you cannot barge into his room like this, all guns blazing. The kid has just been in an accident, and he's likely already scared shitless." His eyes soften, and he brings a palm to my other shoulder, squeezing it gently. "I get it, man. Of all people, I get why you would have such a visceral reaction—you know what it's like to lose the person you love and in the worst and most dramatic of ways."

He tips his head in the direction of Ezra's room. "Behind that door, you're going to find a son likely petrified of what's happening around him, still in shock and probably shitting himself that his dad is going to ream him out for riding a bike when he knows he shouldn't have. You're also going to find your girlfriend in a mess. My best guess would be that she's blaming and convincing herself that he wouldn't be here right now if it wasn't for her and their shared love of riding. She's wrong, obviously, but neither of them needs anything other than the controlled Sawyer I know is in there."

He moves his hand from my upper arm to the center of my

chest, and I draw in a deep breath and exhale, relaxing my shoulders.

Archer smiles in response. "That's good, man. That's what they need right now." He looks to the room they're both in. "Are you ready to go and be the cool, calm, and collected captain I've witnessed on the ice for years?"

"Yeah," I reply, emotion turning my voice hoarse.

He taps my shoulder and turns to walk away.

I grab him by the upper arm this time, stopping him in his tracks. "Hey."

His eyes wear a foreign gloss to them. "Yeah."

"Thank you," I say, never anticipating I'd share a moment like this with my crazy-ass goalie.

Apparently, this guy has more layers than I gave him credit for. Or perhaps that's how he likes to portray himself. Either way, I'm grateful because I needed the check-in. Someone needed to ground me before I burst into Ezra's room, doing exactly what Archer told me I couldn't.

"You're welcome," he replies, the sheen across his blue eyes growing more obvious. He blinks rapidly, attempting to push down his emotion. "Now, go see your family."

"Sawyer!" Collins leaps to her feet the moment I push through the door to Ezra's private treatment room.

She rounds Ezra's bed and throws her arms around my neck, and I immediately feel the tremble in her body.

I pull her close, desperate to let her know it's okay and if she is blaming herself in any way, she absolutely shouldn't.

"Hey, Baby Girl." My voice is calm and quiet, exactly how I want it to be right now.

Her face is free of makeup, and when she unwraps her arms from around my neck, I see the black staining the cuff of the jersey I gave her to wear tonight. She's been wiping at her eyes, and my heart breaks because I know she's been crying without me to comfort her.

She cocks her head toward Ezra's bed. "He's sleeping. They gave him some pain relief for the stitches on his left knee."

Despite my best efforts, the adrenaline kicks up, and I push a shaking hand through my unwashed hair. "He needed stitches?"

A tear falls from her right eye, and I reach up and swipe at her cheek.

"Not many, and it wasn't serious. The doctor wanted to be sure any risk of infection was reduced, and this way, the healing process will be faster. They're dissolvable too. I offered to hold his hand, but he said that wasn't cool. Once it was over, he wanted me to take a picture for him to show his friends at school. He said it will *up his status* on campus." She chuckles, but I can tell it's more out of awe for Ezra's bravery than it is humor.

I laugh quietly, finding a sense of relief in her words. "What else did the doctors say? How did it happen?"

I stop myself from asking why he was on the bike in the first place. This isn't her fault. Last time he rode a bike with a friend, she had made the dangers one hundred percent clear to him.

She drops her head to the floor, guilt flowing from her in waves.

"No, don't do that. Look at me, Baby Girl." I tip her chin up and demand her attention.

I'm not allowing her brain to go there.

No fucking way.

Collins swallows thickly, eyes flicking to my son as he sleeps peacefully and then back to mine. "He told me that he, Nate, and some other boys finished up on a Fortnite battle when one of them got a text from a kid named Brett, who is several years older than Ezra but they know each other through playing video games. He asked if they wanted to meet them at the arcade. Allegedly, they all snuck out of the house when Nate's mom, Imogen, wasn't looking."

"Jesus, she must've been going out of her mind when she couldn't find them."

Collins shakes her head. "That's the thing. They'd had dinner, and she assumed they were all hunkered down for the night in Nate's room, gaming. That's where she last saw them. She didn't realize what had happened until Nate called her at the same time Ezra phoned me."

She bites down on her bottom lip, stressed and overwhelmed.

I lean in and kiss her, brushing my lips softly over hers. Sometimes, words aren't enough, and this is one of the moments—she needs to feel that none of this is on her.

Pulling back, she starts talking again. "Anyway, when they got to the arcade, Carter—who I told you about the last time …"

She trails off, and I nod in understanding.

"He was there and offered to give Ezra another ride on his bike. When he was admitted, he was wearing a leather jacket and gloves. Both were too big for him since they belonged to one of Carter's friends. Supposedly, Ezra refused to ride unless he lent them to him, along with his helmet. He said his 'stepmom is an expert biker, and that's the only way to ride.'" Something like pride fills her face, color flushing her previously pale complexion.

Another tear slips down her cheek, and this time, she pushes it away.

"Unfortunately, jeans don't provide the same level of protection, and that's why he needed stitches. The doctors said without the jacket and helmet, it could've been much worse."

I scrub a hand over my jaw, all my senses stinging as Collins blurs in front of me. "How did he fall?"

Between us, she takes my hands into hers. The warmth of her soft palms is exactly what I'm craving.

"They took a ride around the parking lot. Carter is inexperienced and consequently doesn't expect drivers who aren't anticipating bikes. A woman was backing out of a space and didn't see them. She clipped his back end and knocked them off-balance.

Ezra put his hand out first, and the glove did its job, but then his knee hit the asphalt, followed by his head."

I know the arcade they were at since that's where a lot of the high school kids hang out. I take Ezra there sometimes, and we play air hockey and shoot a few hoops.

The accident is vivid as I imagine it in my head, but mainly, all I can see is the look on Ezra's face, along with the terror he must've felt.

"He called me just as the ambulance was arriving. He knew you were still on the ice." She releases one of my hands, cupping my face as her eyes search mine. "At this point, he's more worried about how much trouble he's going to be in. He thinks you're going to yell at him."

Collins swallows again, though it's more of a gulp. "I know I'm not his mom, and I have no right to tell you what to do. Hell, he likely wouldn't have been on that bike if it wasn't for me being in his life. But *please* don't give him a hard time. Yes, it was the wrong decision to accept the ride; however, insisting on protective gear likely means he'll be leaving here tomorrow with clear scans and not undergoing some kind of surgery or even being treated for a head injury. I think he's learned enough lessons today."

Her tears are flowing freely now, and it breaks my goddamn heart to see her this way.

I bring our joined hands to my lips, kissing across her knuckles. "I never want to hear you utter those words again. You are not to blame for Ezra getting on that bike. Kids sometimes make silly mistakes. Without you, he would've been wearing only the jeans and hoodie he'd left the house in earlier. My boy hangs on your every word—he always has. He listened to your warning and made the right call when it really mattered. *Because of you.*"

My mouth moves from her knuckles to her lips. "He loves you. I love you, and I'm so damn lucky to call you mine. From the second I laid eyes on you at Lloyd's, I knew you were something special. I could see it beneath the layers you wore. And I was right to trust my gut and pursue you, even when you kept pushing me away. I never want to live another year of my life without you by my side, beside Ezra's too."

I press my lips against hers, speaking into her mouth in the hopes that she'll digest my sincerity. "And I know if Sophie were here right now, she would thank you for being precisely the woman you are."

A salty sensation trickles into my mouth. Even her tears taste incredible, although I never want to experience them again.

I'll make it my life's mission to protect Collins Mackenzie at all costs—at least until I change her name to Bryce, and then I'll be her keeper for life. And after I'm no longer on this earth, my protective arms will still be around her.

"Don't cry, Baby Girl," I plead. "It's all okay, I promise."

She shakes her head softly, another tear passing between us. "I don't think these are tears of sadness, Sawyer. More of realization and relief." She pauses, swallowing once more. "Because I love him. I love Ezra with my whole heart. I think I have for a while, but I didn't know how to say it, or maybe I didn't even recognize that feeling."

Nothing in her declaration surprises me—I knew she loved my son. I worked it out right about the time my own heart fell for her.

"And the other side of my heart? The one that beats at the same rhythm, but for so many different reasons? That belongs to you. To my boyfriend and the only man I want. I'm as deep with you as you are with me; I know I am—I can feel it. The difference is, I don't want to deny or hide it anymore. I'm in love with you, and it feels so fucking good."

There's nothing but the soft sounds of my boy's breathing as we stand in front of each other, our bodies glued together.

"Just one last thing though, okay?" she whispers.

"Anything," I say. And I mean it. I will do anything for her at this point. There are no limits when it comes to my love for this girl.

"You asked me not to be upset, but I'm not the one crying anymore, Sawyer. The last tear was yours." She swipes at my cheek and smiles, a promise of forever clear in her deep eyes. "So, no more tears, all right? They aren't needed because we made it. You achieved exactly what you'd set out to do—you caught the girl you'd wanted and made her yours."

FORTY-ONE

COLLINS

Update: I hate chopped cheese sandwiches.

I never want to look at them again. Never want to make, serve, smell, or taste another one for as long as I live.

"Collins, why don't you take an early lunch?" A red-faced Ed checks his watch as I balance a tray of empty dishes over to the kitchen. "Brunch was way busier than I'd anticipated, and you've barely had time to catch your breath."

I set the tray down by the sink and walk back over to the counter. Rise Up was packed a half hour ago, but is now almost empty with no one waiting to be served.

"No busier than my usual shift," I reply, picking up my strawberry shake and taking a sip.

Everything hurts—and not because Sawyer was inside me all night, testing every position possible. The past week has been a baptism of fire. I thought I'd worked hard at Smooth Running. It was nothing compared to the workload Ed gets through in the café.

Despite my aching muscles, I enjoy it. It's not working with Harleys, but it is nice to have a boss who treats me right.

Customers are generally kind, and in the past few days, I've developed an appreciation for British baked goods—something Jack likes to torment my American ass with each time he pops in. Which is basically daily.

How he gets his scone habit past his nutritionist, I have zero idea. I have threatened to rat him out though if he starts telling everyone I prefer a cherry scone to a brownie.

"Nah, you're good," Ed says as I begin unlooping my apron. "Take the full hour, but don't worry if you're a little late back. I don't expect it to be a heavy afternoon since it's not payday."

Ed finishes his sentence just as the bell above the door chimes, and I spin around to serve one last customer for him.

"Hey. How can I …" I trail off when I find Sawyer standing in front of me, a bunch of pink roses wrapped in black paper in one hand.

Ugh, he looks better than the cakes in this place. Black jeans and a matching winter coat, his dark gray beanie pulled low. He hasn't shaved since I saw him this morning either, the scruff along his jawline making him handsomer than usual.

He keeps his sparkling eyes on me when he speaks to Ed. "If it's okay with you, sir, I'd like to borrow my girlfriend for a while. Though it might be for longer than an hour."

From my peripheral vision—since my attention is locked on Sawyer—I see Ed wave a hand in front of him.

"Ah, what the hell? Take the rest of the day. I'll pay you in full since you're my hardest worker."

"Thank you. Much appreciated," Sawyer replies as I side hug Ed on the way over to my boyfriend.

"I know I said it already this morning"—Sawyer's eyes flick over to Ed as he heads into the kitchen—"but happy birthday, Baby Girl."

He sets a kiss on my lips and hands me the roses. "Can you take a drive with me somewhere?"

I inhale the floral scent and smile when I see the black gems set in the center of each rose. "I have the rest of the day, so if you want to make another stop at Lustful Luxuries, I won't complain."

Sawyer chuckles and takes my hand, leading me out into the freezing January air after I grab my coat and scarf from the stand by the door.

"Don't be disappointed," he says, opening the passenger door on his Lamborghini. "But we aren't heading back there today." He shuts the door when I get in and rounds the hood quickly.

I'll never look at this car in the same way. Memories of that night in the parking lot live rent-free in my brain.

Sawyer pulls his driver's door open and climbs inside, immediately starting the engine. "Where we are heading is way more exciting."

I narrow my eyes at him. "Be specific, Bryce."

He shakes his head, delighted his secret has me bothered. "Nope. It's only a ten-minute drive." I clip in my belt, and he does the same. "And only a couple of blocks from your place, soooo … once we're done, I can take you back home and spend an hour or two making you scream before Ezra finishes school."

As he pulls away from the sidewalk and drives toward my part of town, my thoughts drift from wherever he's taking me to the accident. Jesus, he was so lucky that day. Lucky the lady backing out of that space hit the brakes when she did. Sure, she still clipped Carter's bike, but any faster, and they would've been thrown rather than knocked off.

On the doctor's advice, Ezra took the week off school and has been driving Dom and Alyssa crazy with his new model-making addiction. I internally chuckle at the message I got from Alyssa last night, telling me she's calling the shots on her grandson's next gift since each time we do, he develops an addiction. Although this time, I'm sure she's relieved it doesn't result in Ezra being glued to the TV every chance he gets.

"Penny for your thoughts?" Sawyer reaches across the center section, taking my hand in his.

I smile and shrug—old habits die hard. "I think it would be a good idea if I started taking Ezra out for rides with me a little more often."

Sawyer throws me an inquisitive side-eye, waiting for me to continue.

"Some of the best and most experienced riders start out their journeys as pillion passengers. They spend a lot of time studying the road and observing how best to deal with situations. My dad used to take me out on his bike a lot, and that's how I learned best practices. Plus, if he's out with me, he'll be less tempted to seek rides with other people."

Sawyer squeezes my hand. "You never mentioned your dad was a rider."

Rolling my lips together, I allow some of the memories to come back. Rides with my dad were some of the best. I was a similar age to Ezra too.

"He did, but I never appreciated them enough. Sometimes, you don't know what you have until it's gone. We have to make the most of the time we have with those we love while they're still here with us."

He smiles knowingly and takes a left, then an immediate right before we're back in my part of town. But when he takes another left at the end of Fuller Street, my curiosity is piqued. There isn't much down here other than a few previously abandoned buildings that were being restored back to …

"Wait," I say, spinning to face him fully as Sawyer pulls up outside a large brick building with a red roller door—a bigger and flashier version of my own garage.

My boyfriend's face is all smug and sunshine. "Yes, Baby Girl?"

He reaches into his jeans pocket and pulls out a black fob. When he hits the left button once, the door begins to retract.

"Oh, holy hellllll," I drawl, a trembling hand flying to my mouth as I reach for the door handle.

Sawyer's hand darts out to stop me from getting out. "Let me drive you in. There's plenty of space inside."

"You didn't," I say, voice as shaky as my hand.

He chuckles and edges the car closer to the entrance before driving over the small ramp and into the most beautiful garage I've ever seen. "You bet your ass I did."

I jump out of the car before he even stops it, spinning around in the vast white space. It has everything, even a huge replica *BikerCollins* sign across the back wall.

"Oh my God!" I squeal, pulling a drawer open on of the many state-of-the-art Hilka heavy-duty combination chests. They're all red, and they line the side walls of the garage.

In the center of the black-and-white checkered floor are four separate scissor lifts—something Smooth Running only had one of, which often meant I was breaking my back to work.

"Sawyer," I croon, trying to take in the white space surrounding me. "It's perfect."

I set my eyes on him as he moves across to a single side door that I didn't notice until now.

"But what will I do with my current garage?" I ask.

He changes direction and walks over to me, taking my hands in his. "Keep it—for storage, for personal use, for whatever you want. I got it, Baby Girl. Whatever you want."

I raise a brow. "Personal use?"

He loops his arms under my ass and lifts me up, and I wrap my legs around his waist, hands clutching the back of his neck.

Jesus, I'm so happy.

"That's right—for personal use. Just like it's always been. This place will be transferred into your name, and I bought it so you could do what you do best—work with Harleys."

I audibly gasp. Oh *Jesus*, he didn't just buy this garage; he bought me a business.

"I … don't even know what to say." I flail my hands around the space, pointing to nothing and everything all at once. "This is a dream. *You* are a dream."

"One last thing," he says, carrying me over to the door he was about to open earlier.

My heart races faster from so much excitement. "Oh Lord, what else?"

Sawyer holds me in one strong arm, reaching out and depressing the handle. When the door opens to a large closet, overhead lights come on.

The room is pristine white with the same flooring as the main garage area. But that's not really what I'm looking at. Because I can't look at anything else.

There, sitting in the center of the room, is a brand-new, all-black Harley-Davidson CVO Road Glide ST. She's beautiful, stunning, perfection.

I turn to Sawyer, jaw agape.

He chuckles and kisses the underside of my chin before dropping me down to my feet. "She's all yours, your dream bike—and if I remember correctly, my son's too."

My heart grows bigger, filling the space in my chest. "You're right; it is our dream bike."

Sawyer smiles knowingly. "Alyssa told me this model was all Ezra could talk about at a hockey game. Plus, you both spoke about a CVO when we came over to your garage at Christmas."

I run a hand over the pristine black seat, overwhelmed by this man and his heart. "I think I want to name her."

He scrubs a hand over his jaw. I can tell he's recalling our conversation outside Rise Up that time—the one where I told him I didn't name my bikes. "Yeah? What were you thinking?"

Nodding a couple of times, I continue inspecting the beauty. "There's only one name I'd give her, one that would give your son a little piece of his mom when the wind's in his hair. Something permanent. Sophie."

I hear his breath as it catches in his throat, and I see the tears as they fill his eyes.

"Do you have any leathers and helmets here?" I ask.

"Yes." His voice cracks. "Every size I could think to order."

I walk across to him, looping my arms around his waist. "Then let's take a ride, Sawyer. Just you and me."

FORTY-TWO

SAWYER

Which is sexier—Collins in leathers, straddling a Harley while we head toward Brighton Beach, or Collins in a faux leather body suit while she straddles me? It's difficult to say, though both have me hard as fuck.

This woman isn't just the hottest woman I've ever met; she's got a heart of gold to match.

She rides the road like she owns it, just like she does me.

I tighten my grip on her waist as she moves into the next lane and kicks the speed up. She's incredible, her hair blowing over her shoulders, amber scent somehow finding its way to me despite the helmet I'm wearing.

"How are you doing back there, old man?" She chuckles through the headset I had fitted into every helmet I bought for her garage.

When she quit Smooth Running, I was initially pissed on her behalf—she had put so much work into that place and didn't deserve to be treated like she was. Then, after a few hours of digesting the news, I got to thinking the situation wasn't so bad after all. I could help her for as long as required, and maybe the final straw with Cameron turned out to be the break she needed to go it alone. She has the potential client base, thanks to her growing social media presence.

Trouble is, establishing a business for fixing up and servicing Harleys isn't cheap, and I knew even if she'd previously considered opening her own garage, it would be a long-ass time before she could make that happen.

All it took was a phone call to get the ball rolling on securing the place that was half finished. A previous sale had gone south at the final second, and the owner was willing to sell fast for someone who could pay the full asking price up front.

Making my girl's dreams a reality is a no-brainer. And buying the Harley she'd always wanted made me so fucking happy, especially knowing she'd get to see both on her birthday.

"What's the matter? Cat got your tongue?"

"Just taking it all in, Baby Girl."

When we reach the entrance to the boardwalk, she pulls along the sidewalk and sets down the kickstand, swiveling around to look at me. Her cheeks are rosy, face illuminated with happiness as she pulls off her helmet.

"I think this place might be my favorite part of Brooklyn."

"You like the ocean?" I ask, pulling my helmet off too.

The breeze rolling off the waves spins hair around her face, pink strands catching on her full lips, and I reach up and pull them away.

Collins edges closer, turning her body one-eighty degrees so she's straddling the bike while facing me. The traffic is reasonably light for a weekday—not that I'd notice anyone but the girl sitting in front of me.

"I love the water. I've always been a sensory girl, and there's something so soothing about the lap of the waves. I think, one day, I'd like to live by the beach."

I slip down the seat and lift her knees so her legs wrap over mine. "Tell me something, Collins."

"Anything."

My gloved hand palms the back of her head, pulling her heart-shaped face closer to mine. "Do you think there will ever be a day when you don't surprise me or I don't learn something new about you?"

She twists her lips to the side, considering her response. "I think there's a fair chance I'll keep you on your toes."

Taking her helmet, I set both down on the ground beside us. "Come here, Baby Girl." The first kiss I give her is soft and longing—a promise of forever. "You always keep me guessing, and that's one of the main things I love about you."

When I break from her lips, she rolls them together, loving the taste of us both. "What else do you love about me, Sawyer?" She asks a question I could never have imagined hearing from the Collins I first met at Lloyd's.

"Hmm, let's see." I set a third kiss across her mouth, this time sweeping my tongue against hers.

She whimpers, the sound barely audible above the ocean and traffic noise, but it's there, and I hang on to its beauty. I drew that from her. *Me.*

"I love the way you made me work for you. You didn't care that I was a rich and famous hockey player. Hell,"—I laugh—"you practically told me as much when you threw that ride home back in my face."

She scuffs the ground lightly with her boot. "I was really gutted when you denied knowing me to the media. I think, honestly, that was the first moment I realized that you'd really gotten under my skin. That my attraction to you was more than superficial."

I bring her back in for a fourth kiss. She teases me, running her tongue across my bottom lip until I'm the one whimpering, trying desperately to suppress the hard-on as it fights against my leathers.

"Thank you for making today so perfect. I still can't believe you essentially bought me a business." There's a flash of uncertainty in her eyes. "I hope I can make a good go of it."

I scoff. "Are you kidding me? You had new customers coming out of your ears at Smooth Running. There's no way they won't follow you wherever you go." I twist a lock of pink hair around my finger, unable to keep my hands off her. "You've earned this, Collins. You know everything there is to know about Harleys and have an online following who hang on your every word. This is your time to take a front seat and shine, and I'm all the way here for it."

I go in for a fifth kiss. "Soon, I'll be the retired hockey player with a famous influencer girlfriend heading up her own Harley empire."

"You really think so?" She cocks her head to the side, studying me.

"I do. Because good things happen to amazing people. You only have to look around yourself to see how loved you are." I run my nose against hers, smiling like an idiot. "Although don't look too far. I'm not the best at sharing, especially when it comes to my favorite things."

Silence falls between us as we sit comfortably in each other's presence, foreheads resting together. I'm aware we only have a couple more hours before Ezra gets home from school, and I'm determined to make the most of them.

"Collins," I say, picking my head up to look at her.

"Yeah?"

"I want you so bad; it's killing me."

Her breathing picks up, chest rising and falling quicker than before. "But we're out in the open, and you know how I feel about public sex. The deserted parking lot was the exception."

Tucking a lock of hair behind her ear, I lean toward the shell, my lips barely touching her skin. "That's cool, Baby Girl. Like I said, I'm not a fan of sharing, and that includes anyone's eyes on what's only meant for mine."

"So, what do you have in mind?" she asks, her voice still breathy.

Since I had them installed, it's all I've been able to think of.

I lean closer to her ear, a wry smile pulling at my lips. "How about we christen one of your new scissor lifts?"

Collins

On his knees for me—that's how I like Sawyer Bryce.

I'm sprawled out across the scissor lift, my entire lower half exposed as I wrap my toes around the edge, so turned on.

Sawyer plunges his fingers inside me, curling them toward my front wall, while his other hand fists my gray Metallica T-shirt—something he insisted I leave on when we pulled back into my new garage and he stripped every other item of my clothing away.

My boyfriend's sex drive is off the charts, and to think, my first impression of him was vanilla.

He sucks my clit into his mouth, teasing the growing bud between his teeth, and I moan, long and loud, not caring if anyone can hear us.

"Give me your cock," I implore. "I need it inside me right now."

Sawyer rises to his feet, hovering over me with delight while he sucks on his dripping fingers. "Is my bratty, back-talking girl finally breaking?"

My toes curl again. He isn't touching me, but my pussy pulsates from the desperation for him to do exactly that.

"I just want to be fucked. Hard."

Dressed in a fitted white shirt, he's still wearing his leather pants from the ride. That, combined with the tattoos that paint his thick forearms, easily makes him the hottest man I've ever seen. Especially when he wears a sexy kind of confidence that tells me that here, in this moment, he—and he alone—is in charge of my fate and precisely when I get to scream his name.

Popping the top button on his pants, he slowly pulls the zipper down, holding me captive with his dark green eyes and torturing me with the protracted way he's undressing.

His hand dips into the waistband of his boxers, pushing them down, along with his pants, until they fall just below a hockey butt I want to sink my teeth into.

When he fists his cock, his eyes still locked on me, I expect him to replicate the fast and brutal way he entered me on his hood.

He doesn't. Instead, he keeps fisting himself, dragging his hand from the base to the tip before smoothing his palm over the head, using his pre-cum to lubricate the next stroke.

Oh, holy *hell*. He's masturbating in front of me.

He dips his chin at me, tongue peeking out and swiping across his bottom lip. "You want this cock, Collins? Well, you'll have to wait. First, I want you to play with that pretty pussy. Show me how you come when I'm not around. I want to know if the way I've fantasized about you playing with yourself is true to reality."

Sawyer tightens his grip around the shaft and groans, throwing his head toward the ceiling. In the vast, open garage, his noises sound more like primal growls that settle right between my thighs, and I grow wetter, compelled and eager to find my high, along with the relief I crave.

He's been edging me for at least a half hour, and I *need* this.

"That's it, Baby Girl," he praises, his bottom lip pinned between his teeth, watching me push a finger deep inside myself. "Are you picturing that you're taking my dick?"

"Yes," I breathe.

Sawyer strokes himself faster, a flush rising up his neck, tousled hair falling over his eyes when his head lops forward.

I can tell he's close, and I seize my opportunity to be the one to take him all the way. "Look at me, Baby."

He picks his head up, pupils fully dilated.

"You want to fuck this cunt, don't you? It's all you can think about when you pleasure yourself." I pull out my finger and spread my legs wide, wishing I had the spreader bar to hold them in place. "So, give it to me. Decorate my insides with your cum and show me all the ways you own this pussy."

"Oh—fuck—YES!" He lurches forward and slams into me, and I cry out, certain the whole of Brooklyn can hear us at this point.

Thrust.

"You like to be owned, don't you, Collins?"

Thrust.

"You like it when I play rough and pound into you so you can feel it for weeks." His hand wraps around my throat, and he smirks down at me, licking his lips with feral need. "What about like this? With my hand around your throat? I know you aren't big on jewelry, but this hand necklace was made for you, wouldn't you say?"

Thrust.

Somehow, I spread my legs wider, the sound of being fucked echoing around the walls.

I will never forget this. Yes, this is raw, unadulterated fucking, but it's also so much more than that. This is Sawyer letting go and revealing exactly how much he's wanted me for months. This is him taking what he can now be sure belongs to him and not holding back.

"Take everything," I gasp, lying back on the scissor lift. "Do what you want to my body."

This time, there's no mistaking the growl as it reverberates off the walls. Wrapping his hands around my calves, he picks my legs up, suspending them in a V shape as he pistons into me, harder than ever before.

The faster he goes, the better his aim becomes, hitting every delicious spot deep inside me, drawing more arousal from my pussy as it coats us both.

"Good boy, Sawyer." I applaud, admiring the way he fucks me so well. "You've wanted to do this for so long, haven't you?"

His jaw tics, green eyes burning to more of an amber. "I've been desperate to show you the man I can be, Collins. All of me," he grits out, his voice as strained as the muscles in his body.

On the next thrust, I feel the way his dick hardens again. He's ready to blow.

"Where do you want to come, Baby? Inside me or somewhere else?"

He lets go of my legs, but I keep them in place as he pulls out and quickly climbs onto the lift, resting on his knees between my parted thighs. "Tilt your hips up for me, Collins. I want to see your pussy and ass."

I do as he asks, and he sucks a finger into his mouth. Covered in his spit, he swipes it through my pussy and then moves further down, pausing when his attention snags on me.

"I want to play with your ass and come so deep in this tight pussy that I won't need to push any of myself back inside. Take every drop, Baby Girl. Keep it."

"Do it," I bite as he pushes back inside my pussy and circles my tight hole with his finger, teasing it carefully.

The pleasure is so intense that I shudder, and he licks his lips, bringing his finger back into his mouth before lowering it to my ass.

He pushes inside a little more, and I groan, "Give me more."

"Relax, Baby Girl. Let go," he encourages, working his dick inside me so well.

I drop my shoulders on an exhale, and he pushes his finger halfway in. *Fuck*, it feels so damn good.

On his next stroke inside my pussy, he moves his finger deeper, and I hold my breath.

"I won't last another second like this," I push out.

Still fingering my ass and fucking my pussy, Sawyer leans over my body, finding my lips with his. "Then don't, Collins. I'm not seeking your pleas this time. I'm chasing your high."

Impaled in multiple ways, I orgasm harder and louder than ever before.

He roars, and I cry. It's the best experience of my life. Being with Sawyer Bryce is the single best experience I could have ever hoped for.

Often, the greatest gifts are the ones we were never seeking out. And I was never looking for him or the family I'm now a part of and love with my entire heart.

Nothing has changed about who I am. Only now, I have love —a permanent fixture in my life that brings me the kind of happiness I was sure I already had, but in reality, I could never have imagined how complete it would make me. Make us.

"I love you," I whisper, the words feeling natural as they fall from my lips.

Sawyer empties everything he has inside me, collapsing onto his elbows and covering my mouth with his.

He pushes a few strands of hair from my face, kissing me with earnestness. "Say you'll come home with me to live, Collins. Forever."

It's the easiest answer I'll ever give, not even a little hint of conflict within me.

"Yes."

EPILOGUE
SAWYER

August

"Where exactly are you planning to put it?"

I look across at Collins as she smirks back. "We don't need to find a new place for it. It's already built and ready to go," I say, answering my center's question.

Jack sits back in his chair, his platinum wedding ring shining beneath the restaurant lighting. It's the best kind of surreal to see him happily hitched. And never in the history of ever have I witnessed a wedding like it. Jack sure wasn't kidding when he claimed his stepdad was a wedding planner enthusiast. We made the playoffs this season—which was an incredible achievement —but if Coach Morgan's career in ice hockey doesn't work out in the future, he sure as shit has a backup option.

"So, you're taking over an existing business?" Jack asks Collins, who's sitting beside him.

She nods, crunching down on a breadstick. "And you'll never guess which one."

From her other side, Kendra gasps, snapping Archer from his daydream—one I don't think he's left since we were seated at the table at least twenty minutes ago. "Wait. Oh. OH. No, you did not do what I think you did?!"

Collins points the remainder of the breadstick at her friend, winking. "You bet your damn fine soccer ass I did."

Jack holds up a hand. "Can we please stop talking in code? Because I'm confused as fuck." He winces and looks at Ezra, who's tucking into a plate of wings because he couldn't wait for everyone else to get their entrée, like a regular person.

"It's fine," he says with a mouthful. "Everyone at school swears constantly anyway."

I choose not to hear that and focus back on my center and recently confirmed assistant captain. "Smooth Running, Jack. Collins just bought the business as part of her expansion plans."

Folding his arms across his chest, he looks at her. "For real? Wow, that's impressive. Only seven months running your own business and already branching out."

My girlfriend flushes. Taking compliments has never been her strong point, but over the past ten months, she's gotten used to it. She's perfection, and my mouth can't help but spill everything I'm thinking.

When she left Smooth Running, their business plummeted. Which was unsurprising, given that the quality of work went downhill and so did their customer base. Her followers switched to The Gear Change—the name Collins eventually settled on for her garage. True to her word, she's keeping all current employees as part of the takeover. Apart from Cameron since he was shown the door the second the former owner found out exactly what he couldn't do. Which was everything.

"Well, I, for one, am so damn proud of you." Jenna reaches across and takes Collins's hand in hers. "Really and genuinely, you are living the dream." She looks around the table. "I guess we all are. Turning our passions into careers. And me? I'm newly free and single."

She smiles, but it doesn't quite reach her eyes. I can tell she's still torn up that things didn't work out with Lee.

Ezra raises his soda. "I'll drink to that."

We all stare at each other before falling into hysterical laughter and clinking glasses one at a time. The only person not joining in? My goalie.

"Hey, earth to Archer." Jack thuds his foot on the floor, trying to gain our goalie's attention, his head currently buried in his phone.

Archer flicks his eyes to Collins. There's a genuine warmth in them, though it isn't the only emotion I can detect.

"It's honestly really great, Collins. You deserve it."

I keep my attention on Archer as he goes back to his phone while the rest of the table falls into conversation. I would ask him what's up, but I get the feeling if I did, he wouldn't tell me. Not right now anyway.

"Dad?" Ezra leans into me as I take a sip of beer.

"Yes, son?" I ask, stealing a wing from his plate.

He narrows his eyes at me, although I know it's not in response to me swiping his food.

"When are you planning to do it? Because I'm nervous."

I bite into the wing, already regretting it since my appetite has been off all day.

He isn't the only one feeling anxious.

"When do you think would be best?" I ask.

He casts his eyes around the table, just as Darcy dives in through the door. Hair windswept and looking like she just ran a few blocks, she mouths an apology at me and pulls out the remaining chair—directly next to Archer.

Looking across at Collins, wearing a trademark all-black dress, I realize there will never be a better time to ask this girl to be my wife. I've agonized over it for months, wondering how many years would be appropriate to wait before I popped the question.

I don't want to wait though, and I get the feeling she doesn't either. The past seven months of living with her have been, hands down, the best of my life.

My son has bloomed into a twelve-year-old with the world at his feet and a clear idea of what he wants to be when he's older —"just like Collins."

He idolizes the woman sitting opposite me, and honestly, so do I.

Everyone around the table is expecting me to ask at any second, and I can feel the ring as it burns a hole in the pocket of my jeans.

"Now," Ezra whispers to me. "I think you should ask her right now."

I can feel my heartbeat in my ears as I rise to my feet and round the table. Archer sets his phone down and casts a quick glance at Darcy.

The table falls silent, other than Collins, who continues to talk to Kendra about her plans for Smooth Running.

Let's make some more plans together, Baby Girl.

Maybe she thought I was heading for the restroom—I don't know. All I can be sure of is, she has zero idea I'm standing behind her right now, holding a black box open in my shaky palm, a black opal sitting in the center, waiting for me to slide it onto her ring finger.

If she'll have me.

Collins continues talking when Kendra places a palm over the top of her hand, and she stops in her tracks, slowly turning in her seat to face me.

"Oh, holy Jesus, shit." Her hands fly to her mouth, and the table collapses into more laughter, me included.

I take a seat at the empty table behind us since I booked out the entire restaurant to give us added privacy. "Come sit," I say, tapping my thigh invitingly.

All our friends are here, watching, but all she can do is keep her eyes fixed on mine, and it's everything I ever hoped for—to eventually have the full attention of the girl who, a while back, would barely give me a second glance.

She does as I asked, seating herself across my lap and wrapping her arms around my neck. Her amber perfume is a symbol of home.

She stares down at the ring, her hand reaching up to touch it.

"Uh-uh. I have this huge speech for you first," I say.

Her eyes search mine, big pools of brown that will forever ground and excite me, all at the same time. "What if I told you that I've already made my decision?"

I cup her face with my free hand, pulling her ear down to my mouth. "Then I'd say this proposal is on-brand for the woman I'm desperate to be my wife. Spend a life with me, Baby Girl. Since our friends are here to bear witness—and so you can't run away"—I chuckle softly—"give me your forever, and I promise you I'll never stop chasing. Because I won't, Collins. You're the kind of woman who deserves to feel the deepest kind of love, just like you show me and Ezra. And I promise you I'll forever give you that feeling—with my eyes, mouth, hands, heart and ..." I trail off and laugh softly, Collins doing the same.

I lean to the side and drop my hand from her face, flipping it at Ezra and asking him to join us.

The kid's in front of us in two seconds flat, eyes wide and full of hope. Sure, I could've asked Collins in private and away from everyone, but the truth is, I wouldn't even be here, with the woman of my dreams, if it wasn't for my boy or the people watching on.

"So, what do you say, Miss Mackenzie? Will you let me give you our name and call you my wife?"

She takes Ezra's hand in hers, squeezing it gently, and the tears begin to flow. "Goddamn." She sniffs. "I wish I'd worn waterproof liner. Yes, Sawyer. I've said no to you way too many times, and this time, it's a hundred percent—not even a hesita-tion—yes."

She looks between us as I pull the ring from the box and slip the opal onto her left finger. "I guess you could say my life has pivoted in the best way possible. I love you both—forever."

THE HOUSE IS QUIET WHEN I CREEP DOWNSTAIRS, BEING CAREFUL not to wake Collins or Ezra as I make my way to the kitchen and pull open the fridge door for a bottle of water.

Just like our home at past midnight, my life feels calm—a far cry from where it was twelve months ago. That said, I can't sleep, and I've chalked it up to excitement. I just got engaged to my girl, and now, all I can think about is how I want to arrange the wedding day.

If Coach thinks he's getting his hands on the plans, he can think again. This day is one I want to remember—from the second we set the date all the way through to exchanging vows.

Unscrewing the cap on my water, I take a pull and set the bottle down. Reaching into the pocket of my shorts, I pull out my phone, the screen the only source of light in an otherwise dark room.

It's been a long while since I scrolled through photos of Sophie. Not because I want to forget her or will ever not think about her, but mainly because I don't need to so much—I see her in Ezra. In his smile and addictive laughter.

The irony is, in finding Collins, I also got a piece of my wife back. She lives on in my son and his sunny personality—which he once had but somehow lost along the way. Collins brought that back, and even though I've told her a thousand times, it'll never be enough. I'm not even sure if I'll ever find the right words to properly convey how much she means to me and how deep my love runs for her.

I swipe to another photo just as it disappears, only to be replaced with an incoming call.

Archer.

Knowing it's unusual for him to be calling so late, I press Accept, and I'm immediately hit with blaring music and a million voices.

"I can't hear you," I whisper-hiss. It'd be pointless to yell since the only people who would hear me are the ones peacefully sleeping upstairs.

"It's Arch ..."

It's all I can decipher as his voice booms down the phone, the background noise slowly getting quieter.

"I know it's you, genius. You're saved in my Contacts and, funnily enough, under your name. Get to somewhere quiet and tell me what's going on," I say, bracing an elbow on the counter.

The raucousness completely fades, and I wait for him to speak.

"Archer, what the fuck is going on?" I repeat.

I *knew* he wasn't right earlier tonight.

He blows out a steady breath. "You have to promise you won't go nuclear on my ass."

I close my eyes and will this to be a dream. *Not a-fucking-gain.*

"I promise," I reply, although I'm not convinced I won't.

There are a few more beats of silence, and then I can't stand the tension any longer.

"Archer!" I announce.

"Oh fuck, man. I think ..." He blows out one last deep breath. "I think I fucked up again. Only this time, it was over Darcy."

THE END

ALSO BY RUTH STILLING

Seattle Scorpions

Boarded Hearts

Frozen Over

Dead Rinker

Ruled Out

The Blade Kings

Perfect Deke

Total Shutdown

Shots Fired

Full Tilt

Within Range

The Rules of Rink

Fair Game

Code Violation

Break in Play

Close Quarters

ACKNOWLEDGMENTS

My Husband: Tattooed and loyal to a fault. I wonder who inspired Sawyer's character? I love you forever. Thank you for being my real-life book boyfriend.

My Dad: I know I've said it countless times before but you truly are my cheerleader and an inspiration behind everything I do. Sawyer tells Collins it's okay to "pivot" in life and, honestly, I know I've learned that from you. I wouldn't be here, doing what I'm doing today without your outlook on life.

My little boy: One day I hope I'll be able to ride with you on a bike and watch the breeze as it blows through your hair. You are forever in my heart when I write these stories.

Sariah: Because I know you love to be edged, I wrote you Sawyer and Collins. Thank you for just being you.

Tina: I think we both know chapter twenty-five is for you. Or for me. Who knows at this point. LOL. Thank you, as always, for your help and support.

Nay: So I thought I'd peaked when Jessie and Jack made it into your bio. Then along came Sawyer Bryce. Not that I can blame you, the man is incredible, as is your friendship.

Lauren: I feel so fortunate to have met you through our shared love of books and your wonderful support of my stories and characters. The irony is I'll never be able to explain how much you and your constant shouting about my work means to me, but know that it does. And the fact that Sawyer may have snatched the top spot from JJ? Well, that's just the icing on the cake!

To Autumn and all at Wordsmith Publicity: Our sixth book together and certainly not our last. Sometimes life is all about finding your people, and I feel so lucky to have you in my corner. Autumn, on a personal note, I want to thank you for every second you spend working with and guiding me. You are a shining light in this industry with a heart of gold.

To the Bookstagram community: Okay, I know we joke about me edging, bit seriously, it had to be done. I also had to take a cold shower after chapter thirty-seven! Thank you to each and every one of you for all the love shown. I can't wait to bring you more in a series which has stolen my heart.

To all my readers: A book would never be complete without its readers, and neither would my life as an author. I hope Sawyer and Collins's story is exactly what you hoped for and I can't wait to bring you the next installment with Archer and his girl! Thank you for picking up my books and loving them so ferociously. You have made my dreams a reality.

ABOUT THE AUTHOR

Ruth Stilling is an avid romance reader turned writer. Having spent many years reading about and dreaming of her ideal book boyfriend, she finally decided to create her own and to share them with the rest of the world.

Living in a small town in Derbyshire, England, Ruth is an introvert by nature and spends much of her time talking with her equally book-crazy friends from across the globe.

When she isn't writing your next book boyfriend, Ruth enjoys watching all kinds of sports and is an Aston Villa and Derby County fan. The outdoors is a real favorite, and if the British weather were kinder, she would spend all her time writing outside.

Ruth is a wife to her best friend and number one cheerleader, whom she married in 2015, and a mom to her beautiful son, who has shown her a new perspective on life—enjoy and celebrate who you are as a person and cherish those who are there for you through rain and shine.

Ruth is incredibly excited to share Perfect Deke, the first installment in her second generation series, The Blade Kings!

You can follow Ruth and keep up to date with what's coming next via Instagram and TikTok by searching @authorruthstilling